SACRIFICE

—·—

ISEKAI FANTASY ADVENTURE

PATRICK UNDERWOOD

D1522514

COPYRIGHT

CONTENTS

PROLOGUE

"Crap," I said as I scraped what I hoped was dog excrement off my black shoes. "This day just gets better and better, doesn't it?"

The sarcasm was almost dripping off me.

That should have been a clue right there that the world was about to end. I had just invited whoever controls the universe to show me that, yeah, it gets much better, just you wait, asshole.

With most of the ick removed from my shoe—the overnight snow had partially frozen the foul substance, making the task easier—I continued to walk my beat in the Beacon Hill area of Boston. The shops and streets had changed little over the years.

Glass fronts on each store, plus the cobblestone streets were a nice beat for a cop like me most of the time. The day I got assigned to it was one of the best in my law enforcement career. Though, right now, it smelled of spoiled booze mixed with tons of regret from the night before.

"Good day, ma'am," I said as I passed by a woman pushing her stroller up the street, her baby making cooing noises in the covered stroller.

"Officer," she said, her head and hair wrapped in a scarf and cap so tight I could only really tell she was a light-skinned woman with dark hair.

The days of me enjoying my beat were over, however, as I soldiered on down the road, my attention strained to see most of the activity that occurred around me. Luckily, this morning was quiet. The evidence for this was clear as I stepped over several discarded '2133' emblazoned celebration hats and the other discarded detritus common after any New Year's Eve celebrations.

I walked into a corner store to get out of the cold. The little bell on the door rang merrily in sharp contrast to my mood.

"Derk," the clerk said. "You workin' New Year's Day, too?"

I nodded to the old man, his gray hair and shaven but wrinkly face familiar to me after three years on this beat. "Charles, I am surprised you're open today."

"Meh, I go to bed at the same time, regardless. Too old to party anymore. Figure I would open up for the one or two people that didn't celebrate the new year...or the transit, who might actually need something."

My mood darkened at the mention of the transit. This must have been noticeable on my face to Charles.

"You alright, son? You don't seem so happy about the colony ship leaving."

I shook my head. I was about to say it was nothing but changed my mind as I dropped my face down toward the floor. "You remember Jessica?"

"That pretty young thing that you showed around once? Yeah, I remember, a real looker. Thought you guys were getting married?"

I nodded. "We were. She, uh...got selected for the Sally Ride last year...I didn't." A spike of emotional pain threatened to wail up inside me. I suppressed it down back into place as best as I could.

Charles' facial expression changed from happy to one of sorrow. "Oh, I am so sorry, son. I didn't know. So, she went through yesterday and left you behind? I thought married couples got to stay together?"

"We missed the cutoff to get married in time, and I...they assured me I was going to be selected...but something changed, and it didn't happen. We were both shocked. The captain of the ship even called me personally, said he fought it, but it was out of his hands...and he was sorry. Going to try for the next one, but that is...what? Ten years from now?"

"Oh, Derk, I am so sorry to hear that. If there is anything I can do, let me know."

"I'll be okay. Survived six years in the marines and a shoot-out in space. I can wait for her."

Charles rolled his eyes at me. "I don't care how heartbroken you are. I don't need another story about how you saved an officer from certain death again."

I couldn't help but laugh a bit. "Said that one too many times, huh?"

"Once or twice that I can remember at least, and I am old and forgetful. It's okay, though." He smiled as he said it.

I held up my hands in defeat. "It's fine. Thinking I might go out to California and visit my kid, steal him from his mom, take him to Disney, or something to clear my head. I need to try to be a better father, anyway. Thanks, though. Just going to go get some coffee before I head back out."

Charles nodded and went behind the register as I walked to the back.

An old flat-screen television was on. Its volume was low, but I could hear it from where I now stood. I poured myself the straight black coffee that I personally thought was the best in the world, and I listened to what the broadcaster said.

"—you, Marie, for that global weather report," the news anchor said on the screen. "We now turn our attention back to the top stories of the hour."

The woman paused as she smiled. Her black hair was done up, her smile was damn near perfect, and her brown eyes shone on the ultra-high-definition screen.

"In the latest news, worldwide celebrations continue as the first three colony ships and their six escorts crossed the event horizon of the planetary gate bridge connecting our solar system to the New Terran system just twenty-four hours ago. All nine ships reported a safe arrival and were making their way into parking orbit above the planet."

They showed a video of the Sally Ride as she crossed the event horizon. The great ship, which looked like a beer can with a nose cone strapped on its front, seemed to dematerialize bit by bit as it passed into the event horizon of the wormhole on its way to the New Terran system.

A tear fell, streaming down my face at the image of the ship leaving me behind. I reached up and wiped it away with the side of my uniform sleeve. I tuned the news anchor out for a second as I remembered Jessica's last words to me before she left.

"Don't worry, Derk. This is not the end. Even...even if we never see each other again, I will always love you. This is just...too important to pass up."

"I know, Jess. I don't want you to wait for me. I just wish we had more time. It doesn't seem fair—"

My thoughts were upended when I heard the alarm in the newscaster's voice.

"—ing news that the planetary bridge connecting the Sol system to New Terra has collapsed. There is no sign of the phenomenon on any live cameras at unity station orbiting nearby."

The camera cut from the reporter and switched to archived footage.

"As you can see from this footage, taken only moments ago, the wormhole seemed relatively stable before it just collapsed in on itself. No radio, electromagnetic signatures, or spikes were reported at the time of the collapse. It just simply ceased activity. For more on this, we go to—"

My stomach dropped. "No..." I said aloud. My hands were suddenly numb. I turned and stumbled back to the front of the store, my heart aching. "Please, don't let it be true..."

"What is it, D—" the sound of air raid sirens interrupted Charles, the forgotten system leftover from the Pacific War years ago. I looked outside and saw the young mother from before staring into the sky. I ran out to see what the trouble was, my coffee forgotten on the counter.

I grabbed my sidearm, pulling it from my holster as I went through the door, looking up to see what the woman was staring at. Above me, a giant black cube was hovering over the city. Easily blotting out a quarter of the sky, its shadow now falling over Boston.

"Wha...what is that?' the woman asked, her hands gripped tightly to the stroller's handlebar.

"I...really have no idea," I said.

The center of the cube began to glow with a purple ball of energy forming at its center.

"Oh shit, run! Get indoors now!" I yelled at the woman as my atrophied combat instincts screamed at me to take control. She startled, then turned her stroller toward the store I had just exited a moment before. Everything slowed down just a bit as my adrenaline kicked in.

A beam of purple energy, at least a mile wide, fired down toward the city's center, then slowly raked up the streets right toward us. I holstered my pistol in a flash, knowing it would not be of help.

I heard screams in the distance as others panicked, but I could do nothing to help them, focusing on what was in front of me.

"Move! Now! Leave the cart," I said as I came up behind the woman to help.

The woman reached over to grab her baby while moving toward the storefront. However, like in every movie I have ever seen, she tripped on the curb, falling forward then rolling sideways to protect her baby.

I came up to her fast, but as I reached down, I gazed back to where the beam was coming from, now only half a mile away as it swept up the city streets. I froze momentarily as the few people in the street running from it instantly disappeared as it engulfed them. The wide purplish swath of energy spread over the cityscape towards me, and panic welled up into my chest.

Knowing it was too late, I threw myself over the woman and her child in a futile attempt to save them from the approaching death ray.

Darkness consumed me.

"Controller, I have urgent news for you," Vex said after he materialized into the Chief Archivist office. The Controller himself was sitting at his shadow wood desk.

"What is it, Vex?"

"The games have expanded to the human habitat area on Timeria. I do not know who is leading our people that have entered that part of the construct, but they have moved much faster than expected. The last of the human matriarchs will soon fall... Her army is walking into a trap as we speak."

The Controller sighed, closing his eyes for a moment. "I was afraid of this. I have pushed back against the council for as long as I could, but they said two hundred and fifty years was long enough for the human test subjects to establish themselves. They believed we could no longer keep the mob from their entertainment before... problems from the lower cast arose. They forbade me from telling anyone with a Compact of Secrecy. I could not warn you, and for that I am sorry, Vex."

Vex startled. "Do they suspect?"

"Possibly, some of them at least, but they have nothing they can use against me yet. We have taken what steps we could, and now we must implement them. Are you ready?"

"Yes Controller, I have set aside a few humans that may accomplish the task we need. One in particular stands out to me, but he will need to be handled... carefully."

"Good, start with one for now, and we will be more aggressive as needed later. We do not want to bring notice to our activities. Best if we avoid doing too much too quickly for now, it might sway those in the council who are still neutral against us."

"Can you tell me the name of who leads our kind on Timeria?" Vex asked.

"Seir... He was the one who volunteered to risk his immortality as a human."

"Seir? I thought only the lower cast could enter?"

The Controller paused a moment before answering, considering his words. "I do not know why he volunteered. I think someone on the council offered him... considerations. Timeria... I mean, habitat four-five-two will turn into a living hell for the beings living there if he wins the games."

"Agreed. We must stop his machinations, whatever they may be. At the very least, he would ruin all chances for our research to continue there. Do you have any further questions for me?" Vex asked.

"Does this human of yours have a name?"

"Derrick Schultz, he calls himself Derk."

"Part of the group you took an interest in?" He paused, looking to Vex for confirmation and getting a nod. "Good."

"I noticed him when I picked the others, that is correct. Not as intelligent as the one I chose to lead the expedition through the planetary bridge, but his emotional imperatives should have him follow the path I seek."

"Proceed. I may have something that could give him a slight advantage over our kind. I will insert it into the code when I can. Now go."

Vex dissipated in a whirl of light without responding. The controller considered his friend and the task before them. Not sure if they would succeed but knowing if they did not stop the rest of his kind on this world, countless more would fall to the same existence.

His hatred for what his own species had become increased and his resolve to stop them intensified.

He brought up his interface, examining the code of Timeria and thought how best to give them an advantage without the council's notice.

Then he smiled to himself when he figured it out.

Chapter 1

Rude Awakenings

Oh God, the pain.

Those were my first thoughts as I came to from... I couldn't remember what. I struggled through the pain to remember what was going on. Something about an attack... but the details were just out of reach.

My eyes opened to a woodland setting, and I was laying with my back on the ground, looking up at a tree canopy of flora that did not seem right to me. I took a deep breath, but my nose filled with the smell of something coppery which mixed with the earthy smell of the woods I was in.

It was warm but not hot. Nor was it overly humid either, so at least it was not a jungle. I hated jungles... even if I could not remember why I hated them.

With the pain making any movement excruciating, I just gazed upon the leaves of the trees above. They reminded me of... the word willow tree entered my mind with the way the branches hung down. But there was something wrong with the leaves. As I focused on them, their pattern seemed familiar.

"M... Maple?" I asked.

My voice sounded odd, higher pitch than what felt right to me. I tried moving my head, as the pain seemed to be lessening bit by bit. First, to my right, seeing bushes of various shapes and sizes, some familiar, some not.

"Blackberries?" My voice was a little stronger that time, though still much higher in pitch than what seemed right.

Turning my head, the other way, I saw more bushes on that side, another mix of the blackberries and even a couple other fruits that I did not recognize at all.

Finally getting the confidence in my ability to move, I shifted my arms to make sure they functioned. It felt odd, like moving someone else's arms and not my own. Bringing them in front of my face, it surprised me to see that they were skinny, the arms of a youth, or a young man.

Why is this surprising to me?

A memory flooded in my head. Of me at a... gym? Yes, a gym, pushing weights with a bunch of other men with closely shaven hair standing at the various stations. They wore shirts that had a 'Boston Police' on the front, and I distinctly remembered my arms being much bigger than what I was seeing now.

The mix of half memories was too confusing, so I dropped my arms back to my sides with a loud thump. Closing my eyes while the memories continued their assault on my mind.

The attack!

I felt it all click into place. The attack, the mother, the image of the wormhole disappearing... Jessica. Suddenly I knew who I was again, though that did not help explain where I was at. I should be dead, but maybe there really was a god, and this was the afterlife?

If so, then why does it suck so badly?

I opened my eyes again, put my not-right-arms underneath me and pushed off the ground, just enough to look down my front. First, looking at my chest and the shirt I was wearing, which was torn as though bitten by a wild beast. I could see wounds underneath and the blood that had soaked the shirt.

I should have felt shocked at the amount of blood, not to mention the wounds, but something kept me from the panic that I would think would set in for any normal or sane person. Almost as if my emotions were being pushed into a box, which was likely not a good sign for being as sane as I had hoped I was. However, the panic was there, along with fear and anger and a full range of other things running up and down me. It was just as if they were not important right now, along with another thing that told me not to touch the wound while it healed.

Healed?

The wounds were closing in front of my eyes. Knitting themselves back together at a rate that was impossible, even with the most modern medicine back home. I stared at it while it finished closing, then scab, and finally even that flaked off into scars in but a moment. Like watching a time-lapse movie on a holo-screen before even those scars started shrinking and closing to nothingness.

I studied my clothing for a second, still amazed by the healing, but trying to move my brain onto topics I could understand. The shirt itself was a greenish homespun material, coarse in nature, that I could not fully identify. Certainly not the modern cloth I knew. The pants were brown but made of the same material. My feet were wrapped in leather, which was sewn up and wrapped around my feet with a leather string right where laces would be on shoes back home. Like someone made a pouch you could just slip your feet in rather than tie up. More of a wrap than the type of shoe as I was familiar with.

When my wounds seemed about gone, the dam broke; my emotions came flooding back into me. Almost overwhelming me back into the blackness I woke up from. I fought against the tide and breathed in and out slowly, using all the meditation techniques I learned over the years to deal with stress. I focused on each emotion one by one, acknowledged them, and then put them into a box of my own making for later study. I was not sure how long I sat there while I got control again.

I heard a crack in the forest beyond, my senses coming alive with the strange sound.

"Shit," I whispered to myself.

I had forgotten that the wound looked like a bite mark. Fresh too, from the blood still wet on my clothing. That means whatever caused it was still nearby.

I opened my eyes and studied my surroundings. About six feet away was a bag on the ground and a small bed roll tied with a leather twine. Next to it lay a plate with some berries on it along with a small knife about five inches long, as though someone was having a meal of mixed fruit and the knife was the eating utensil. Then it occurred to me it belonged to whoever had this body previously. Provided I was not crazy and this really was my body.

I pushed myself up off the ground, my legs unsteady, and got into a crouch, trying to keep as much of the woodland setting in my peripherals as I could. Listening to all the sounds around me as I slowly made my way over to the knife.

It was then that I noticed that the forest was silent, and I could hear no birds or other animals in it. Just a light rustle of the trees as the wind passed through them. While I was unfamiliar with this wood, I could not imagine it having none of the same noise making animals as the ones back home. I reached for the knife and picked it up. Testing the weight in my hand as I moved my arm back in front of me.

The knife was cheap but serviceable. Adjusting my grip, I moved it in several directions. Trying to combine what was muscle memory in my mind with movements from the current set I had never actually used before. This was going to put me at a significant disadvantage to anything that could pop out of these woods.

Play the hand they dealt you, Derk, don't whine about what you can't change.

I moved in a crouch over to the nearest tree trunk, wanting to have a barrier at my back while I figured out the best course of action. As I neared the Oak-willow-maple tree thing, I heard a growl come from the bushes on the other side of the small clearing.

I faced the threat, the knife angled in my hand for a quick stab, with my other arm reaching out in front of me to block whatever it was that came out from the bushes. The blackberry bushes acted as a kind of fence to keep the animal at bay, as I could see a shadow moving just beyond the green barrier.

My senses all came alive. More than I have ever felt before. My hearing jacked up to eleven on the scale, hearing things I did not notice before. The sound of limbs scraping against the trees from the light wind. The sounds of the... whatever it was, stepping and cracking the organic debris on the ground.

My smell heightened, almost overwhelming me with that coppery tang from before. Now I knew it was the blood that soaked into the clothes I wore, overwhelming the other smells in the area.

My vision sharpened. The dark shadows cast by the trees and other vegetation suddenly brightened. It didn't quite eliminate the darkness in the shadows, but made it fade so that I could make out the details that they previously hid from me.

I watched as the creature approached the opening in the bushes. The enclosed area could make you feel somewhat safe, and that was probably why whoever this body belonged to choose it.

I banished that thought and prepared myself for what was to come.

The snout of what appeared to be a big ugly dog moved its head around the last blackberry bush, its eyes glowing a dull mix of orange and red, like embers in a fire that had just burned out but had not yet cooled.

The body followed a moment later as it prowled around the corner of the thick vegetation, keeping its head down and sniffing the ground. When it saw me, a low growl came from its throat.

Sweat ran down my forehead, but I ignored it, never taking my eyes off this strange beast. My ears tuned in to the rest of the world in case it was not the only threat.

We studied each other for a moment, each of us unsure about the other. I recognized that the black and brown fur was matted with blood stains around its mouth, probably my own if I were to guess. This settled my suspicion that it was what led to the demise of the previous owner of this body.

The wolf tensed as I readied myself as best I could for the blow I knew was coming.

It did a jumping leap and pounced, moving so fast I knew I could not stop it from breaking past my meager defenses.

Then the world seemed to slow.

Everything went into what seemed like a slow-motion video. The wolf was still moving towards me in a bounding lope, but slowly enough that I could consider my actions before I was forced to move. Not looking a gift horse in the mouth, I waited until it made its final leap towards me before I acted.

When it leapt into the air to use its body weight to pounce on me for the kill, I somersaulted forward, underneath the large beast. My shoulder tucked underneath into the roll as I had trained to do so long ago.

Even with all the techniques I had, the roll hurt much more than it should have , like I hit a wall at thirty miles an hour. I tumbled over and back on my feet while the wolf was still in the air, surprising both myself and the animal as it tried to turn its head to follow me. Causing it to go into a roll of its own when it hit the ground.

I gritted through pain and stood up, not sure what was happening to me, I lunged toward the beast as fast as I could and stabbed my knife down towards its head. Missing my target by only a few inches, I ended up stabbing the place where its neck and its shoulder met, hopefully all the way to the heart or lungs. A mortal wound, to be sure... but not the instantaneous death I was really hoping for.

The speed and heightened senses I had been enjoying abruptly cut off from me and I felt an exhaustion settle over my body. I stumbled back, and the wolf spasmed its body into me, knocking me back several feet. My head bounced off the ground after the impact.

The wolf got up and stumbled towards me, the look in its eyes made me think it was intent on taking me with it. But just as it reached me, it collapsed. Hopefully dead or close to it. My feeling of relief was short-lived, however, as unconsciousness consumed me a few seconds later.

This really was just not my day.

CHAPTER 2

— • —

LET'S... TRY THIS AGAIN

I woke up more slowly this time, not in as much pain as I was before. Though the smell... something really stunk.

The beast!

I startled awake and got to my feet. Looking down at the body of the mutant wolf before me. It laid unmoving on its side, the knife still sticking out of its back.

Just for good measure, I kicked it. Hard.

"That's right, motherfucker!"

I almost kicked myself next, metaphorically at least, sure that the loud noise I created would attract another of its ilk. I bent down and extracted the knife. The smell that rose from the wound was even worse. Imagine a week-old trash can filled with meat in the middle of a hot Georgia day in July. Well, that was like cinnamon and spice in comparison. So I backed away and focused on not gagging.

"Man, I need to get out of here," I whispered. I still was not used to the sounds of this unfamiliar voice coming from me.

"Should just keep talking to myself till I get used to it. Someone might think I am crazy, but... they might be right, too."

I grabbed the bag on the ground along with the fruits that the 'not me' was eating before I arrived. I piled everything into it for later, noticing some more clothing in the bottom, before tying it up with the leather cord.

"New... Well, less bloody clothes would be nice. Better get this blood off me first, though." I snagged the bedroll and made my way out of the clearing.

With the small clearing of stinky death behind, I could now breathe easier in both a literal and figurative sense. I even felt better than I had since before I woke up. Of course, after taking stock of my surroundings, I realized I did not know which way to go.

"Fuck me."

The forest was thick, but not so thick that I could not see an outcropping of rocks sticking above the tree line to the... South? I was not one hundred percent sure, but I think the sun was setting on me to my left. So, I was going to go with south until I could figure out how things worked here. Because at this point, I was not sure that I was on Earth anymore.

"South it is."

I carefully made my way towards the outcropping. Judging it to be about a mile away, I reached behind my head and felt pain when I touched the occipital bone. A bruise had formed, and it was going to be a good one.

"Guess that healing shit wore off before it fixed this, must have been out for a bit too."

The woods were full of those willow-maple-oak trees, but it also had some other varieties that were more familiar. I saw pine trees here and there, not as abundant, but trying to break their way through in the old growth woods. Since on earth we found pines in cooler climates, I should prepare for chillier nights around here at some point.

"It's warm enough though, we are probably in summer, if this place even has seasons."

As I neared the outcropping, I came to a small brook. The water was rushing, but it was narrow. I could easily jump it if needed.

I sat the pack down and got the change of clothes out of the back. I disrobed... Damn, at least I have one thing going for me in this new body.

Believe me, I was not ashamed of what I had on Earth, but whoever this kid was would have had a shot in the porn industry. "Change my name to John Holmes or something," I said, chuckling to myself.

I shook my head and chastised myself for the not at all helpful thinking, instead going back to the task at hand. I washed myself in the cold water — that helped tamper some of the enthusiasm with my newfound appendage — and I got as much of the blood and filth off me as possible, too.

I jumped up and down and air dried before putting the change of clothes on. Then cleaned off the old clothing in the fast-moving water, finding a small bar of soap in the bag. It was useless as clothes now, but could be helpful as bandages or something, so I wanted to keep it on hand. After wringing out as much water as I could, I laid the wet clothing on the rocks to dry while I walked around the area looking for anything else that might help.

"Score," I said a few minutes later, as I picked up a stick about my height. It was a sapling that had gotten knocked over and was just a little thicker than I could wrap my hand around it. One end tapered off slightly so that it was only about three quarters as thick as the base.

"This should buy me some time if I run into another death wolf or whatever that was. I might even have some twine that I can tie the knife to the end and give myself a longer reach with it... Not to mention its other uses."

I made my way back to the now only damp clothing, and I gave it one more squeeze to check. Not perfect, but I did not want to stay here any longer. I hung the clothing over the ends of the stick and put it over my back like a yoke and continued to the rock outcropping.

Just before I jumped over the water, though, I glanced at the reflection below me, having avoided doing so before.

My hair was brown and unkempt, hanging off my head in a mop that almost touched my shoulders. It looked like it was at one point groomed regularly, but recently allowed to grow uncontrolled. My face was that of a kid in his early twenties, just old enough to drink in my old world. Pale skin that had seen too much sun in recent days and not built up a resistance, with a fair complexion and grayish green eyes. Like the stormy seas off Ireland in all those pictures I saw as a kid.

My shoulders still had the square shape of my old self, but lacked the bulk I preferred. I was going to have to do something about that, eventually, if I survived that long.

Hopping over the flowing water, I continued on my way.

The rocks of the outcropping were not that bad to climb. There was a dirt game trail up the back of the hill that got most of the way up. From there it was a solid gray stone that was only cracked in a few places, which supplied good holds for the hands and feet. I left the stick, my pack, and the drying clothes at the first rock and made my way up to the top. Just my dagger on me now.

Fifteen minutes later, give or take, I was up at the top. The skinny body I was in did not prove a hindrance and allowed me to climb without being winded. Small victories.

I observed the lands below, easily seeing for miles as the forest ended only a few hundred yards off in the south. In the distance, I could see a road going from my left to my right on the grassy plains beyond. No villages or towns were in evidence, but a road ought to lead me to something that could help me.

To my far left the forest pushed out into the plains a couple more miles than the rest, so I could not see where the road went in that direction. To my right, it seemed to go off towards some grassy hills.

Which path do I take?

Then I heard a sound that did not match the forest.

A scream in the distance called out to me. A woman's scream, if I was to guess. The hairs on the back of my head stood up, the protective impulses inside me started demanding that I do something now.

"Calm down. Rushing in will help no one and get you killed."

I forced back the urge to do something and cupped my ears to hear better. Closing my eyes and standing as still as a statue, I struggled to pick up anything more.

In the distance, I could hear some men laughing while they tramped through the foliage. Not the woman's scream, but it was enough for me to come up with a reason to act.

I turned and slid down the rocks as fast as I could get away with. Moving much faster than my trip up the slope, I dropped my bag where I landed, pulling my knife out of the sheath that I had found in the bag and had attached to the leather cord that acted as a belt.

I hesitated, looking over to where I had started my climb. "Should I grab the stick?"

I shook my head and left it behind. I might need stealth here, and I did not want to lose more time going back for it.

I moved at a quick shuffle, a combination of speed and silence I had learned years ago, finally getting used to this body that was not originally mine.

The sound of someone running through the bushes reached my ears, and I hid behind a thicket of plants, my back to the rocky outcroppings' base as I gazed at another small clearing, hoping the shadow of the bush hid me from any prying eyes.

I crouched as low as possible, just able to see inside the small clearing, the sounds of running bodies telling me it was right in their path.

So, I sat still and waited for whatever it was to come to me.

CHAPTER 3

SAVING TYLA

I was motionless as I waited. Years of training came back to me, but the body I was in protested the crouched position, letting me know its discomfort through minor pains. I did not have enough time to shroud myself in shrubbery and mud to break up my outline, so I relied on lack of motion and the bushes to keep prying eyes from noticing me.

A crash, followed by a flash of motion appeared to the right side of me, as a woman ran into the clearing, tripping halfway through and landing on her side away from me. All I saw was a low-cut white shirt with a leather corset. The shirt was torn and tattered, and her long brown hair disheveled and filled with scraps of the forest. Her clothing looked more like undergarments than what one would normally wear in a forest.

She was crying... sobbing, really combined with the heavy breathing of running from something, obviously moving for a while now, and looking like she was on her last legs.

I resisted the urge to go to her, thinking of the sounds of men's laughter from earlier. I could not help her if I did not understand the threat, so I waited.

She tried to get up to run again, but her legs failed her. She instead started crawling along to my left. My heart almost broke from sitting there doing nothing. My will power to stay still, pressed to the breaking point.

I didn't wait long, soon four men entered into the clearing behind her.

They did not look like the most competent foes, thankfully. Each was slightly overweight, dressed even more shabby than me, and had a club or baton on them. All breathing heavy from the chase.

"Oy girl, you ain't got nowhere to run now, do you? Thought you could get away?" the asshole on the far right said. He had several missing teeth and a bald head. Along with the club in his left hand, he had a collar in his right.

The girl glanced behind her with a small squeak, then got on her feet, moving with a stumbling forward lope, one last attempt to flee. The guy in the middle pulled out a bolo and swung it over his head in a circle. After a few good swings, he launched it at her. It wrapped around her legs, sending her back to the ground.

She whimpered when she landed, and I almost lost control again. I just needed them to move forward a few more paces, and I could come in from behind.

"We are gonna have a little fun with ya before we turn you in for that reward, girlie. Make you pay for all that." Bolo said with heavy breaths.

"Oy, don't touch her till we get the collar on, Nate." Asshole said before bolo... or Nate I guessed, reached her.

The other two big ogre looking guys just stood there and leered, a small chuckle escaping their lips at their companion's byplay. They looked like bodybuilders, and I couldn't tell if they were twins or just brothers. They might be a legitimate threat, given their size.

"Well hurry then and get it on her then, Og." Nate said.

The stupidly named Og moved up to her, reached down to put the collar around her neck. "Don't you do nuthin' stupid girl."

Just as he reached her neck with the collar, she came alive, reaching up and grabbed the man around the face. "Die!" she yelled. Her face streaked with tears, and her eyes opened in rage.

"Arrghghhhhhhh," Og screamed when she touched him.

I used the distraction to move around to an opening in the clearing.

Just as I rounded the bushes, Nate came up to the girl and hit her in the head with the club. "Stupid Bitch!"

Og fell backwards on the ground after she let go.

My emotions spiked and rage filled me. Time did that thing where it slowed down to a crawl. Rather than question it, I came in behind the largest of the ogre twins with my knife drawn as fast as I could.

I leaped on to the man's back, the knife in my hand piercing the vertebrae in his neck, and I rode his body down as it crashed. All the while, I felt as if moving in slow motion. I pulled at the knife, but it had wedged in his neck and was not coming free, even with all my strength behind the pull.

I quickly let go of it and rolled to where he had dropped his club, right towards his ugly twin. The man was just registering that his brother had hit the ground and was turning towards me, his own club coming up.

"What the hell did you do to Blotter?" he said. His voice was distorted through whatever was causing my senses to move so fast. I finished my roll and popped up to my feet, the club of my enemy now in my hand. I ran straight at ogre number two as fast as I could manage and ducked under the slow blow of his sideways swing.

I nailed him in the balls with the club as I passed, causing him to drop his club and bend over. A high pitch scream, even through the distortion, slowly bled out of his lips.

Before he could finish cupping his family jewels, I turned and jumped on to his back like I did for his brother. This time bringing my arm underneath his throat.

This was a mistake on my part, looking at it in hindsight. Since I did not have the mass that I had in my earlier life, the chances of me being able to pull off a move like this was low, especially with two other men in the clearing. A tactically unsound move, to say the least, and something old colonel Trino would have kicked my ass for if he saw me do it.

But I was angry.

They hurt this girl right in front of me, and my sole purpose in life right now was to make them die.

So, I finished reaching under the guy's jaw, dropping the club like a complete idiot while I did so. I used my other arm for leverage around the top of his head and used the motion of my whole body to twist and break his neck. Given the size disparity, and my lack of muscle, it should never have worked.

But his neck cracked, and his head almost went backwards. He died instantly, and I was truly shocked when we came down to the ground together.

I stood while I let him slump to the ground. Confidence in my newfound abilities flowed through me like water.

I faced the last man standing, the one who kicked the girl. He was looking at me with shock on his face at what I had just done to two of his crew. I smiled at him, letting him revel in the fact that I was going to kill him next.

Then the flow of power, or whatever you want to call it, stopped. I suddenly felt weak and exhausted, dropping to one knee, barely holding myself upright as the sweat poured out of me from all the effort.

Nate got his confidence back when he saw me drop to the ground. "Imma gonna kill you for that fucker!" He raised his club and started towards me.

I pushed up, back to my feet and held my hands up in a defensive posture, no longer riding the high of superpower anymore. That did not, however, make me defenseless against this guy.

He moved forward and swung the baton wide. I backed up just enough for it to miss my nose and rushed in with a right hook in its wake, connecting my fist to the man's jaw. He grunted in response to the hit.

I shifted the hand that punched him around his neck and moved to his side like I was giving him a hug. I put my right leg behind his and used my arm to leverage him over and down onto the ground with a thump.

He cried out when he landed, his breath going out of him. I followed that up with an elbow to his nose, breaking it instantly. I stood up and picked up his dropped club and hit him one more time in the head, hearing a deep and meaty crack as it landed.

A killing blow.

I kept the club in my hand this time as I moved over to Og to finish him. I would not have a survivor hunting me down later. Especially since I already killed three of these clowns.

When I approached, he looked sick. Discoloration, pustules, and sores marked his face. He was breathing rapidly, and his eyes were open in pain.

"P..please don't kill me," he whispered, his voice hoarse and pain coming through.

"Why were you chasing the girl?

"Bo... bounty." He coughed and continued. "She is worth a lot of money being a witch and all." His voice was already improving. Maybe he will recover after all.

"Witch?"

"She's the daughter of the matriarch of Blackrun, worth a bloody fortune. We were lucky to catch up to her. I'll split it with you, and we can live like kings."

I paused, as if considering his offer. "What was the collar for?"

He looked at me as if confused. "It's a control collar, you ain't never heard of one of them before? It's the only way to take away a witch's power. The only way we can ever be on equal footing with those controlling bitches."

"I am new here," was my only reply.

"Help me up and we can collar her and take her to Seir for a reward."

"Seir?"

"He is the new overlord... Demigod, actually. You ain't heard of him neither? Where did you come from? Uh... He is the one who can take the power of the Chosen women who treat us like shit. Just like what happened with the other races on Timeria."

His health was returning, the sores on his face disappearing much too quickly now, and I did not want to risk fighting someone until I recovered a bit.

I leaned forward like I was going to give him my hand, giving him a slight nod and what I hoped was a friendly smile. Just as he reached up to take it, he put his head in a perfect position.

I took one step to the side and swung like I was going for a one-handed home run. The blood splattered throughout the forest.

"I'm not a slaver, you fat fucking pig." I sat down on the ground with my head bowed. Utter exhaustion taking over.

"Hopefully, I can get more information when she wakes up," I said to myself as I took several deep breaths.

A noise came from behind me.

Before I could turn around, I had two hands grab each side of the head, a tingling sensation going through my body.

"Make one move and I will poison you." A young woman's voice came from behind me.

Ah, fuck.

Chapter 4

First Impressions

"Look Miss... I don't know what's going on. I have no idea what you mean by that, but I promise you I am not here to hurt you... I was only trying to help."

"Oh... thank the gods." She said and collapsed back on the ground.

I turned to face her, slowly getting up, the pains and bruises I had somehow given myself protesting in the absolute strongest means. I stood over her as I stretched them out, trying to keep them from getting worse.

She had passed out, eyes closed, in a fetal position where she landed. Now that I could see her calmly, I noticed she was quite beautiful. Her messy brown hair faded into a lighter color as the hair approached the tips, obviously well-kept before her current predicament. Her face and shoulders were tanned and flawless in their complexion. I did not see a single birth mark or blemish at all, which was kind of weird to me.

Her eyes were closed, but her nose was rounded and pert with lips that stuck out. Her neckline was regal and long. She could definitely be a model back home...

Let's not think about home right now. Focus on the problems at hand and all that.

I adjusted her position, as lightly as I could, to not disturb her sleep. I figured I would give her a few minutes to recover before I moved her.

I proceeded to each of the men in turn, checking them for anything of use. Besides the clubs, they each had a dagger and a coin pouch. Opening each pouch, they had a few copper coins with a picture of a woman on them with a name of whoever she was underneath.

As I looked at the writing of one of the larger copper coins, I decided it was a language I had not seen before. The letters looked like one of the ancient scripts I had seen in history books about ancient Greece. I shrugged and moved on.

Moving on to the last body, Og had one small silver one in addition, and I put them all in the best-looking leather pouch of the bunch and tied it to my belt.

"Who are you?" The woman said from behind me.

I turned and saw she had lifted her head a bit but still laid on the ground. Her brown eyes were lovely now that I could see them.

"Derrick, but my friends call me Derk."

"May I call you Derk then?" She asked.

I nodded. "Sure, I have water up the rocks with my gear. Not sure I would trust the pouches these guys have on them until we clean them out. Let me finish going through their stuff, and we can head up there."

"That would be... acceptable."

She seemed a little proper. Well, if she was one of these matriarchs, that meant she came from a ruling class or something. So, it made sense.

"What's your name?" I asked.

"Tyla-Rose... Russel. Daughter of the Matriarch of Blackrun, Patricia Gerund. You may call me Tyla."

"Ok Tyla. It is a pleasure to meet you. I am going to finish up here."

I finished going through each of the four men, then dragged their bodies over to the bushes while she sat up and watched me. Not a proper burial or hiding spot, but I didn't much care either way about these guys either.

"Have you killed men before?" She asked.

"Once. While saving a life."

"How noble for one so young."

I stopped and gazed at her, confused for a second. "Young?"

"Um, yes... you could not be much older than me, if at all."

Right, I'm a kid again.

"Oh, yeah, sorry about that. I feel older sometimes," I lied... horribly, I might add.

If she sensed something, she did not say it and instead asked, "What are you doing in these woods?"

"Funny, I was going to ask you the same question, but I'll go first," I said, making up a story on the spot. "I wanted to get away from people and live off the land for a while. Been out here for a bit too, so I don't know what is going on out in the world."

I hoped that might explain my lack of knowledge and earlier remarks, at least enough to get by.

She nodded. "I would rather not say any more about where I am from. I think that Og character said more than enough already." She pointed to the body.

"You heard that?"

She nodded. "That was why I had to be sure of your intentions."

"No offense lady, how can you tell my intentions by grabbing my head?"

"I am Chosen and have a water affinity." She said, as though that explained everything.

I debated on what questions to ask, do I risk sounding like an outsider or not? "Not familiar with whatever that is. I was a nobody from a backwards place before I came here. So you will have to explain what that means, as I am ignorant of the world."

She looked at me oddly, a single eyebrow raised. It was then that I finished with the last of the bodies and stopped to study her again.

The clothes she was wearing were not something I would think of as proper attire. The blouse was a mesh material that allowed for airflow but was a little revealing. Then the leather corset went over the shirt at her midsection, giving her ample breasts support. But it honestly looked like it was supposed to be part of something else, like half her outfit was missing. She also wore leather shorts that cut off below her hips, and leather boots that went up to her knees. They looked of high quality at least.

As much as I tried to keep my thoughts in check, the hormones of the twenty something I now inhabited took over. My eyes drifted to her chest and hips. Both were what most men say they desire in life. Her breasts were not overly large, but they were of significant size and perky. It would attract my attention in any bar setting in Boston. Her wide hips emphasized her narrow waist, which was helped by the leather corset she wore. She was absolutely stunning in that girl next door sort of way.

I quickly averted my eyes back to our surrounding area. She had not spoken at all during my observations. Her eyes locked to the ground as she continued to sit up with her legs crossed over each other. Kind of like we did in kindergarten back on Earth.

"My mother is... was... the Matriarch of Blackrun," she said, as several tears leaked from her eyes. "Though I had siblings, I was her only Chosen daughter and was the one that would have succeeded her in time. My water affinity allows me some control over the fluids in your body. I can do minor healing and cause the opposite, if only temporarily. I can feel your emotions when we touch, so I knew you felt you were telling me the truth when you said it. Given the circumstances, that was good enough for me."

"Hey, I don't know your past any more than you know mine, but I meant that. I... kind of have a soft spot for women in distress. If you want to run on without me, I won't stop you, but I... don't really have anywhere else to go right now. So, if you want me to help you get away, I can do that too. I'll let you make the call."

Tears started streaming down her face in full force now. "Th... thank you. I will accept your generous offer of aid."

"Alright," I said, moving on. "These guys had almost nothing on them. They were traveling too light to be in these woods."

"They..." She sniffed and wiped the tears away. "Chased me on horseback on the road. I ran into the forest to get away from them. They left their horses behind."

"Hmm, I might be able to use that. Let's go get my stuff and get you cleaned up. Then we will check on these horses."

She nodded. I reached over and held out my hand to help her up. She took it and stood. I felt a tingling sensation again in my arm.

"Did you just use your water magic on me?" I said since it was the second time, I felt that sensation now.

She pulled her arm and looked at me in shock. "You felt that?"

"Uh, I did. Why?"

"You should not be able to feel that kind of magic. Only the Chosen should be able to pick it up at all. But Chosen are all women. Except... for what I have heard of Seir, of course."

"I am not sure what you are talking about. I only felt a tingling up my arm, and I don't have any magic that I know about. Here, test me with... whatever it is."

The tingling resumed after she grabbed my hand, but went throughout my body this time. I stared straight into her eyes and repeated myself word for word.

"You believe what you are saying," she said, but still unsure in her voice. "But they say that the Demigods can fool even a matriarch of the elves."

"There are elves too? Wait, don't answer that. Okay, I do not know what else to say to make you believe me. If you want to run off by yourself rather than take the risk, I understand. I will walk—"

"No," she interrupted. "I... believe you. I'll take the risk. I just need... help." Her shoulders drooped, and she sobbed again. The stress seemed to be getting to her.

Without thinking, I grabbed her in a hug. "Shhh, I know it sucks right now, but we will make it alright... somehow."

She gripped me tight, her head coming just to my jawline, now crying uncontrollably into my shoulder. The floodgates had opened, and I could feel the wetness soaking through my shirt as she cried.

I put my hand on the back of her head, stroking the back of her hair, taking a few twigs out with my repeated motions.

We stood like that for several minutes, just standing there as she came to grips with her situation. My emotions were mixed, the feelings of lost love and this girl to protect mixing in and making my own emotions swirl inside me. A tear dropped down my own cheek as I consoled this lovely young woman in front of me. I pushed back against my pain to keep from breaking the dam that I had built to keep back all the trauma.

There would be time for that later.

CHAPTER 5

— • —

A NICE JOG

We ended the hug and made our way around the rocks to where I had placed my supplies. Taking the coins and the water pouches with us. I also tied a baton to my back with twine and the daggers with their sheaths to my belt. Even if it weighed me down, they could all come in handy later.

"Here, take this," I said, handing her two of the three empty water bladders, their contents dumped onto the ground. I knew I should get used to the lack of sanitary conditions in this medieval, at best, looking world, but I would not swap spit with those guys.

She looked at me in surprise for a moment, but relented. "Umm... Yes, sure."

I wondered what that was about, but said nothing. "Let's get to my stuff, get you some clean water and we can make a move for those horses."

She nodded and followed me around the rock formation. A few minutes later, I gave her my water bladder. She drained it dry in a minute.

"We can get more at the brook over there, clean out these three, and fill up. You know how to use a dagger or staff?"

"I have had basic training in dueling swords, but the men do all the fighting."

"Wait, you're like a noble, right? Don't they expect you to fight?"

"We have men for the fighting, while the Chosen lead, and use our power for the benefit of womankind. Occasionally we may duel each other for a grievance but no, we do not fight directly."

"Huh," I said and left it at that, putting the dagger I was going to give her in the bag. Going to have to train her later, but let that be a battle for when we were out of immediate danger.

We stopped by the brook, and I rinsed and filled the water bladders, giving her two to carry. Again, I got a look like I was breaking some kind of rule, but I let it slide.

"You want to do a quick wash? I'll go stand over there," I said, pointing back towards the rock outcropping.

"Don't leave. Just... turn around," she said with a blush.

I nodded and went up the embankment, turning away from her and keeping a lookout. I resisted the hormones inside me, telling me to turn and watch as I heard her undress. I may have caught her naked form in my peripheral vision once or twice, but if someone called me on it, I would deny it until the day I died.

Stupid hormones.

"Do you have anything I can dry myself with?"

"Ugh, hold on a second." I checked my bag, the only thing that I had was the semi-clean and torn clothes I had from earlier. That would not do.

"I am sorry, I don't."

"That's fine, I will make do. Can you hand me my clothes?"

I backed towards her until I passed her clothes on the ground. Picking up the clothes, I handed them back to her without turning around.

"Thank you."

I moved back to where I was standing and resumed my post, hearing her get her clothes back on.

"Finished," she said.

I turned around the same as she did after securing her corset.

"I'm sorry," I said, immediately avoiding my eyes on her body.

I felt a flush flow through me. I could see her breasts right through the now wet material, her nipples clearly outlined.

She covered herself. "It's... it's fine, no avoiding it until I get more clothes."

Her face was also blushing when I turned back to her.

"What uh... happened to your clothes, anyway?"

"I was in a battle with my mother. In armor towards the rear. We thought we were ambushing my cousin, but it turned out to be the other way around. When it was certain all was lost, my mother sent me with a few bodyguards. They died so that I could get away. I threw off all the armor I was wearing so that I could run faster." Her face was downcast again.

"Hey," I said, reaching out and hugging her again. "I don't know what you're going through right now, but I will do my best to make sure you stay safe. We will figure it out."

She nodded in my shoulder again. This time, the tears were only a few and not the waterfall from earlier. She moved away from me, took a deep breath, and put her noble face back on.

"Thank you. We should be off, though."

I nodded. "Ok, follow me, stay silent, keep your ears open, and try to step where I step. If we hear anyone out there, we run back into the woods. Got it?"

She made a face like she was about to argue, but then stopped herself. "Yes, I approve."

Something about the way she said that sounded odd. I debated whether it was worth calling her on it. Eying her for a second, I decided it was not worth it yet. Have to observe it more still and see if my suspicions were right, "Alright, let's move."

I put my hand up in a stopping sign. Tyla still almost walked right into me, completely ignoring it. Guess I was going to work on signals with her later.

"Why did—"

I put my hand over her mouth. "Shhh"

She nodded, and I let go. I pointed to my ears and then pointed to where we were going. I heard voices, but they were too indistinct to make out.

Her face took up one of panic when she heard the noise, too.

The shouts of men.

I leaned into her, "we are going to make a run back up into the mountains and get away. Do you know if they have dogs?" I whispered.

"I have not seen them use any, but I know they can track people. Several of my mother's men had hounds for hunting man and beast," she said, her voice much softer now.

"Ok." I thought for a second. If dogs were a thing, then I should take that into account then, just in case. "We are going to do a lot of running in a short amount of time. Can you keep up?"

She nodded. "I will do what I must."

I turned and grabbed her hand, keeping her right behind me as we ran low to the ground, back to the brook. After a few minutes, we came to it, and I helped her jump over it and followed.

Stopping briefly, I listened for the sounds of pursuit.

"Ok, I don't hear anyone, that gives us a chance. I am going to go to a clearing up ahead with a real foul smell that will hopefully distract the dogs... if they have them, then we will head up into the mountains and hide out for a bit. Step where I step as best you can."

"I agree and approve."

I realized this must indeed be a power thing. In this world, it would be someone like her that makes or approves of all the decisions. I needed to get in front of this.

"Tyla, I am going to be right up front with you now. I do not care that you are royalty or whatever. If you are with me, I will call the shots for now. That does not mean I will not listen to your opinion, or even defer to you if the situation calls for it. But you do not need to give me your permission, because frankly I am not asking. You had the chance to go off on your own, you wanted to stay. Is that going to be acceptable with you?"

She deflated and looked... relieved? "That is... fine with me. I kind of hate being in charge anyway, but that is what they always expect of me so—"

"It's fine," I said, cutting her off. "We do not have time to get into it right now. I am not some asshole that will treat you like property, but I also do not plan on being anyone else's property either. Right now, though, we need to run. So, let's go."

She nodded as I grabbed her hand and ran back to the clearing I started in. I could smell it, a good way off. The stink of that beast was nasty and even worse now.

"Ugh, stop, I smell a dire-wolf," Tyla said in disgust and fear.

"Is that what they call them? It was disgusting before I killed it, then it smelled even worse in death."

"You killed one?"

"Yeah, when I showed... when I woke up this morning. Got the jump on me."

We continued around the clearing. Hopefully, the smell would throw off our scent, then we headed straight for the mountains.

"Killing one is next to impossible without a group of men or a Chosen with you. How did you do such a thing?"

"Luck. I avoided its jump, then knifed it in the back through the heart."

She just looked at me in shock but said nothing. We picked up our pace and began jogging up the incline. Running on fallen logs as they became available, or other things that would remove footprints and make tracking more difficult. After a mile or two, we slowed down. Tyla was huffing something fierce, and I feared she could not take anymore.

We approached a nearby creek, bigger than the brook from earlier, and drank our fill and refilled all the bladders.

"Let's walk up the creek bed for a while. Do not step in the mud, only on the rocks. It will help us lose any trackers if they are out there. Understand?" I asked.

"Yes, I will follow."

I took my shoes off and grabbed the boots she was wearing and put them in my bag. Hiking up my pants, we walked up the shallow creek for a few hundred yards before going back onto dry land again.

"How much daylight do we have left?"

"Umm." She looked into the sky. "A couple more hours?"

"Okay, we walk up this incline here till it gets dark, then we find a place to sleep for the night."

She nodded, and we continued on our way.

As the sky turned red, I finally found what I was looking for.

"There," I said and pointed to one of the willow-maple-oaks. "See how those leaves are hanging over? We will sleep there. No fire tonight though, sorry."

"That will... I understand." She caught herself before she gave me permission. I smiled at her, and she returned the gesture.

"What are these trees called, by the way?"

"You live in these woods and do not know? Hmm. The elves have a name for them, but I forget what it was. Humans call them traveler's trees. I do not know where the name came from."

"Interesting. My guess is that they make good shelters, but who knows. This will do, though."

I cleared out the detritus from under the tree and rolled out the bedroll from my bag.

"Here, you can sleep here tonight, I will sit up against the tree. We should have someone on watch, but I think we are both too tired to expect that to happen tonight."

I handed her some of the fruit I had placed in my bag earlier. There was a jar of jerky in it as well and I handed some to each of us. We ate in silence for a few minutes.

"Umm, you can... sleep with me in the bed roll... it can get cold in the mountains at night, and you are still wet, we can face away from each other," she said, adding the last part in quickly. I saw her face redden even through the gloom and shadow from the tree and the approaching darkness.

"If you're fine with that," I said, simply. Part of me hated the idea, thinking of Jess — no, not going there. The other part of me thought it was a fantastic idea. I crushed both thoughts and shoved them back into the box to deal with it later.

She just nodded.

We each did a few basic preparations before bed. I had to escort her into the woods so she could relieve herself since she refused to go anywhere without me nearby. Soon we slipped into the bedroll. I had removed my shoes, and she removed her leather corset and boots to make sleeping easier. We settled into the sleeping bag as best we could in the tight space with our backs together, otherwise fully clothed.

She was asleep instantly, while I struggled with the memories and emotions that struggled to break out of their cage. Eventually I fell asleep, exhaustion finally overcoming the thoughts about my previous life and what I was going to do in this one.

But the nightmares soon came to me after I lost consciousness.

Chapter 6

Bad Dreams

I was floating in the void when a view screen of some sort appeared in front of me, a picture of a blonde woman appeared in front of me, and my heart was suddenly in my throat.

"Hey Derk," the blond woman said. She had a small smile when she said this, but her eyes were red rimmed, like she had been crying. "I don't know if you will ever see this, but... Captain Smith gave us all permission to send a transmission back to Earth to say goodbye. We don't know if it will make it, and even if it does, you will probably have died hundreds of years before it arrives."

She wiped away another tear that had leaked out of her eye.

"So, they woke us up early from cryosleep. We must throw away the original plan and do a mass landing. Turns out the wormhole collapsed right after we came through, but you probably saw that from your side."

She giggled and hiccupped. "That is not the worst part of it all, though. Apparently, this was all arranged by some super powerful aliens to put us in a kind of nature preserve, according to what the captain said, anyway. They are going to take away all our tech and put us on a planet where we can live naturally or some bullshit. God fu—" She ended that last part with a scream before she stopped the video.

The screen paused for a second, and her position changed when she resumed. Her eyes were redder than they were before, and she was wiping them with a tissue.

"So, we are doing an emergency landing in a predetermined location tomorrow and they say all our tech is going to fail within six months, I don't know how or why it will, but things are already breaking more than they should, so I believe it.

"I am so, so sorry I left things with you the way I did. Now that I know I will never see you again... along with all the other stuff, it is hitting me hard, and I want nothing more than to be with you one more time. I just... wanted you to know that I still love you."

I could feel the hot tears running down my face.

"I hope you move on and find someone that will make you happy... I... you deserved so much more than I gave you. That is what I regret the most, I think. You will always hold a special place in my heart, but please, live your life and be happy. One of us deserves it at least."

She looked into the camera one last time. "Goodbye, Derrick."

The screen cut off, and I sobbed. I learned long ago that crying did not make you less of a man, it just meant you were human. Sometimes, no matter how much you try to prevent it, the dam just needs to break and release some.

I floated in the darkness, letting those feelings leak out.

"Goodbye Jessica."

"Derrick! Derrick! Please wake up!"

"Huh?" I said as I came too. I could see dawn light peeking into the overhand of leaves we called home for the night. The dream was so vivid it felt real. So much so that even now, the dream was not fading from my mind. I could recall it like I could recall a conversation from yesterday.

"Oh, thank the gods!" Tyla hugged me. "I was so worried."

"What? Why were you worried?"

"I, um... kind of felt your sadness while you were sleeping. It woke me up and just kept increasing. I worried about y — it. You wouldn't wake up when I tried, for several minutes at least."

It was then I noticed she had wrapped her arms around me, and we were still laying in the bedroll together. I was on my back with her on my side cuddled next to me.

Normally this would be a very... intimate pose, but I was still feeling the effects of the dream, so I just laid my head on the torn shirt I was using for a pillow and put my arm around her to return the embrace.

"I was having a... not a nightmare, but a dream of something that is painful to me. A painful memory and I am still getting used to it."

Tyla gazed into my eyes briefly before looking away, still not letting go of me. "I can feel it, even now. What was her name?"

"Jessica, she's... she's gone now... forever. I don't know whether that dream was real or not, but I know I will never see her again."

"I understand... I never knew someone so young could have loved so deeply. I have always wanted a love like that."

I just nodded. It was not time to tell her about my past, I had to know more about her first.

"Just give me a minute," I said. "Let me get through this, then we will start moving. We have some decisions and plans to make today."

She nodded and moved away. I stopped her, not sure why, other than us holding each other felt good. She did not fight it and pushed back into me. I guess we both needed a human's touch with all that has happened to us.

We just laid like that for a few minutes.

It felt good.

The sun rose, and so did we, both taking care of our morning absolutions deeper into the woods.

Finishing the last of the fruit and more of the jerky, then polishing it off with water.

"I would give anything for coffee right about now," I said while massaging the sore muscles in my body.

I had pushed myself the day before, much harder than the kid who I now inhabited probably ever did in his life, and I was feeling it.

"Coffee? You have had coffee?"

"Yeah, it's a thing here too?" I asked hopefully without thinking, then regretted my word choice.

"You are strange, what do you mean here too? You say it like you are not from this world at all."

"Sorry, poor choice of words, I don't... talk to people much anymore, forgive my odd phrases occasionally."

She eyed me for a second, but moved on. "Yes, coffee is a delicacy from the south in the Casting Harbor, usually only the Chosen or burgesses can afford it. I was just surprised you knew what it tasted like. Are you from the south?"

"Let's just say further than that. I may tell you my full story someday, but I ask for your patience as we get to know each other." I needed to get a lay of the land without looking too suspicious right now. These slips were going to get me in trouble.

"Of course, but trust is a two-way street, Derrick. If you wish me to tell you my stories, I will need some in return."

I nodded, not able to argue the point.

I changed the subject. "So here is the plan. I am going to turn my walking stick into a spear before we leave. As soon as we see another stick suitable, I want to equip you with the same and teach you to use it. They are the simplest weapons a person can be effective with."

I stopped to rub my arm again.

"But I..." she stopped herself from whatever she was going to say. "That sounds wise. Are your muscles in pain?"

"Yeah, sore from yesterday. I'll live."

"Here, let me," she said and scooted over behind where I sat. She put her hands on my shoulders, moving them over my shoulders, reaching into my shirt. The tingling sensation returned, and then the pain started receding. I breathed out a sigh of relief.

"Thank you. That power of yours must come in handy."

"It is both a blessing and a curse. Others decided my path because of it. This... this is the first time I can remember deciding for myself without someone's input. Well, mostly." She finished, giving me a sheepish grin as she said it.

"You still make your own decisions. I just... make the calls for what we are doing right now in the woods. Unless you are some kind of secret wood woman and just playing dumb on me?" I asked, my eyebrow raised in question.

She giggled. "No, only if I were, I might not be in this predicament. It could be worse, though."

She finished her magic massage and scooted to sit next to me. "I also healed the minor wounds you suffered. If anything else bothers you later, just let me know."

I nodded. "Thank you, Tyla," I said, as I finished using the leather cord to wrap a dagger around the end of the stick I found. Tightening it as best I could, it was not perfect, but it should do against anything short of a bear.

"Do you mind explaining how your powers work?"

"It is... complicated, and not something I am supposed to share with those that are not other Chosen or more importantly in my family's service. Secrets that are kept guarded from our competitors."

"So, you learn how to use it through your family?"

"Not exactly. We have... had an academy in our city. Anyone who was with power could go and learn if they swore themselves to my mother's service in return. I had just started there myself six months ago... then the civil war broke out...."

She looked down, her face conflicted with emotion and pain.

"Want to talk about it?"

She wiped her eyes and sniffled. "Not yet, but thank you, Derrick. Maybe in time."

I put my hand on her shoulder and squeezed. "Fair enough, let me know when that changes and I will listen if you want me too."

She put her hand on mine and returned the squeeze, smiling softly.

"In the meantime," I said, pulling another dagger. "Keep this on your belt at all times. We will train with it tonight, but pulling it and stabbing something is fairly straightforward. Just keep stabbing till whatever it is dies. Understand?"

"Yes, thank you Derrick."

I finally picked up on the name she used. "I thought you were going to call me Derk?"

"It seems so crude of a name. You are anything but crude. Maybe a little uncouth, but not like any of the other men I have met. Sweet, yet barbaric in your way, especially compared to those in mother's army. You are different... in a good way. Thank you again for being there when I needed someone. For killing those men."

"I don't tolerate anyone who says they are going to rape a woman. Ever... and I kind of lost control for a minute. I do not regret my actions in the slightest... and you're welcome," I said and smiled at her, staring straight into her eyes.

She blushed and turned back to packing up our meager belongings.

"Ok, we should get moving. We don't know if they are actually tracking us, but staying here is going to be a bad idea. I want you to grab that tree branch over there and rake the ground behind us as we walk, break up our footprints on the game trails. I'll take point, I mean the lead, with you behind. That's good with you?"

"Yes, I think I can handle that."

"Good, let's get moving."

We traded smiles.

CHAPTER 7

— · —

DAY IN THE WOODS

We had been walking for a couple of hours now, just entering the higher elevations following a game trail that mirrored a creek we had crossed several times to throw off pursuit.

There were several paths leading up into the mountains, which resembled jagged teeth more than any mountain range I had ever seen on Earth. I picked one at random... well, I think it was at random, though I did feel very strongly about it more than others if I was being truthful to myself.

Up until now, I had been intentionally ignoring all the things I could not explain that seemed to be happening to me, given how rapidly things had evolved, but I was going to have to confront them before too much longer.

"So, mind if I ask you a few questions that might seem... off?" I asked.

"Um, sure."

"This might seem weird to you, but just realize I have truly little knowledge of this part of the world. I was hoping to know a little about the history and other... races?"

She gave me that puzzled look, like I was a Rubik's cube that she wanted to figure out. "You are odd. I know you say you are not from here, but I just find it hard to believe you do not know this. I am sure you have an interesting story, whatever the truth is."

I smiled and nodded. "Fair, I have secrets, so do you. If you don't want—"

"No," she said, interrupting me. "Someone should probably extend the branch of trust, and I will do it, after all it's common knowledge, for what you ask."

"Thank you."

"Humans came to this world two hundred and fifty years ago, or thereabouts, the exact date is unknown to us now. The story is that the gods transported us from a doomed home world. I put little stock in this growing up, but then..." She shook her head. "I will get to that later."

"You okay?"

She nodded. "Yes, the Demigods have changed my outlook on the world we live in. It is still very... emotional for me right now."

"I understand, we can wait if you want."

"No, I am still just in shock over the recent events, but I will continue. According to our histories, the gods created this continent so that humans would have a place to call home. Protected for a time from the other races while we established ourselves."

"How long?"

"It was never said, none of the other races ever invaded our lands, so we assumed it still applied until Seir showed up."

"I have heard that name before."

"He is a Demigod. I will discuss him as well. First, you should know that our race is but one among the five known races. The gods gave humans the continent of Neuerde and parts east. The elves are a secretive race, but the rumor is they arrived in southern Griyvania. They were the first race to be put here by the gods and have since expanded to most of the western continent. They make their homes in the vast forests."

"Real elves? They were a fantasy where I came from. I didn't think they really existed."

"They do. I met a delegation of them when I was a little girl. They have the most beautiful silver hair, the entire species does. Or at least the ones that humans encountered. Rumor is that some have pink hair, but they are extremely rare. They are also long lived. Some say as long as four hundred years."

"Not immortal?"

"Only the gods and Demi's are immortal. Everything else dies," she said, sadness entering her voice and her facial features.

"Um... Then there are the orcs," she continued. "A vile species, though I have never met one. They are nomadic and inhabit the great plains of western Griyvania. They attack and pillage both themselves and others. The descriptions I have heard said their skin is greenish and they have tusks that come out of their mouths. They have not ventured to human lands, but our trade delegations have been attacked multiple times near their lands."

"Heard of them too, sounds spot on with our mythology, though that's all they ever were in our stories."

"The names we call them differ from what they call themselves. The world magic translates everything for us, so we never know what they truly call themselves."

"World magic?"

"You do not know the world magic? That should be impossible even if you are from an unfamiliar land all together. You have not studied the words coming out of my mouth carefully, have you?"

"What?" I asked, bewildered.

She smiled. "Do you not notice that the words you hear do not match the movement of the lips on my face, for I have surely noticed yours do not match what I would expect. Several of your words are... strange looking."

"Holy shit." I was watching her lips closely, now that she said that I could not unsee it. What should have been an 'O' sound on the word 'do' looked more like she was saying 'un' with her lips right behind her teeth. "I have never heard of it before, uh—"

"It's fine, I expect that from you now. You are odd, but it is nice. Makes me forget about my own troubles."

She genuinely smiled at me, and her brown eyes sparkled.

"Thank you," I said, returning the smile as we walked side by side. Not a proper walking formation, but it was good to get to know her. "You said five, that leaves two more."

"Oh, um...," she said, distracted by whatever thoughts had invaded her head for a moment. "The dwarves are next, another species I have met often as a girl. They live in the mountain ranges of northern Griyvania."

"Let me guess, short with beards?"

"Short yes, beards on the men, much wider than humans. Stronger on average, too. Their matriarchs are powerful in the earth's magic. We actually hosted several of their refugees."

"Refugees?"

"Oh, that's right, I keep forgetting how little you know. The Demigods have corrupted all the other races that we know of. We have heard the elves still fight, but we have not heard from them in over a decade. That was when I met them as a girl."

"How?"

"The world, before the Demi's, lived under the rule of the matriarchs of each of the various species. Only women can be a Chosen and given command of an element. This increases our strength and speed, along with the elemental power, giving us a significant advantage over others and our own men. When we first arrived here, a war occurred between the men who coveted our power and the women who had it. They tried to control us and use us, but eventually we broke away from our yokes of enslavement and ruled the human lands. That was about two hundred years ago according to the records that survived from that time."

I nodded. "Makes sense, my land was patriarchal for most of its history, but women did not have any special powers, putting them at a disadvantage throughout our history."

"Yes, the new laws after the war for freedom said that men could not hold power, though they enjoyed many more freedoms than they ever gave us. The Chosen rule alone now... or did. The Demigods came to our world about fifty years ago. It was said they were gods that were cast out of heaven and forced to live as mortals for their sins. But they have the power to enslave the Chosen. They can take your free will and force you to love and serve them. All the Demigods have been men so far that we know of."

"Force you to love them?"

"We are unsure. Fallen Matriarchs who were loyal to their sisters before capture are later fighting for their captors. There have been many stories from rape to torture, but they all end up the same. The Chosen that have succumbed to the Demigods will do anything they command. They also share their powers somehow with them. The dwarves said that the first of Demigods they encountered were strong but not unbeatable. However, the Demigods soon captured some of their dwarven kin and took their powers, able to command the elements at a level never seen before. They become difficult to fight, especially when you are also fighting someone you called sister only a few weeks before. It is how they have taken so much, so quickly."

"It's hard to fight family," I agreed. "Why have you not tried to take them back?"

"We humans have only been fighting Seir and his minions for a year. Actually, we did not even know we were fighting a Demigod till a few months ago. We just thought my aunt Josephina had gone mad and was fighting to take over the whole of the Matriarchy instead of just her half. But the dwarves tell us that the few Demigods they killed also... led to the death of ones they had turned. We do not know what magic causes this, but it has made it extremely hard to fight when you know your mother, daughter, or sister will die if you win."

"That's horrible."

She nodded. "That is why the world has fallen. Our own empathy is our doom."

I had a thought to ask about her mother but could not bring myself to ask about such a sensitive topic.

If they captured her mother, that could mean...

Burn that bridge when we get to it.

"That's four races. What about the last?"

"Oh, the Mer people. I have never met one, but the elves told me about them. They live in the Sentar isles south of Griyvania. They do not interact with outsiders from what I was told."

I nodded. "Thank you for that information."

"The world is falling apart. I sometimes wonder if it's worth living in anymore."

"Hey," I said as I put my arm around her. "None of that. We have issues, both of us. But we can get past them and make something of this mess. We just have to figure out how."

She leaned into me. "I hope you are right."

CHAPTER 8

— • —

DINNER IN THE WOODS

We found another traveler's tree to sleep under that night. Its leaves supplying an adequate shelter to keep us moderately hidden.

"I am going to take a gamble tonight and start a fire when it gets dark, cook some food, then snuff it out... well, after I find us some food, anyway. We still have jerky and some berries you picked on the trail, but we need more calories than that, with as much as we have been burning."

"What is a... Sorry, the magic did not translate that word correctly, which usually means I do not have an equivalent."

"Oh, sorry, something from my w... land. We figured humans burn energy at a specific rate of measurement and can calculate what must go into what we use daily to make sure we eat enough. Think of it as a log on the fire. Some logs are better than others, but if you burn two logs, you get about an hour's worth of fire. The longer you need to burn the fire, the more logs you need. Does that help?"

"Cal-o-ree, I think I understand."

"That world magic thing is still crazy to me. How about writing? Does it do that for you, too?"

"No, not writing, hence the reason we still teach reading and writing."

"I have so much to learn," I said with a sigh before I could stop myself. Luckily, she let it go with just a knowing smile.

"So," I said, changing the subject. "You set up camp, and I am going to scout the area, see if I can get some food."

"Wait... umm, please do not leave me here alone," she said, her face turned red, and her head bowed down.

"What's wrong? I will hear if you yell and not be gone long."

"I uh... have always had someone with me growing up, then I was alone and running for my life. I really... I just do not wish to be alone right now. I am sorry."

I reached out and stroked her hair. "Shhh, it's okay. I understand, I didn't think about it that way. It's understandable. Let's set up camp, scout around, and then go down to that creek and see if we can get some fish or something for dinner. Before we come back to eat, train, and sleep. Deal?"

She nodded, grabbing my hand from the side of her head and moving it to her face.

"Thank you," she whispered.

We set up the camp by laying out the bedroll and grabbing the dried sticks that littered the area and put them in a pile. There was a fire starter in the bag, so that shouldn't be an issue to get going later with all the kindling available.

"Alright, keep the spear I made for you, the water bladders, and we will leave everything else behind. Just in case we see something in the woods to hunt, keep as quiet as possible."

"Umm, I can do that," she said, her expression still a little nervous.

"It's okay, nothing to be stressed about. There may be nothing out there, but we need to get into the habit now."

We made our way down through the brush in a circular pattern outward from our camping spot. Nothing jumped out at us, and the area seemed calm. The birds flew away from our approach, but no large animals seemed to be in the area. Tracking was never my strong point and limited to humans, and that was more about evasion than tracking, but I knew enough to look for animal scat on the ground near game paths. I could occasionally even see animal tracks now that I was looking for it.

With nothing of note jumping out at me, we made our way down the creek. My hopes of finding a rabbit or other small mammal dashed.

"Alight, I have never done this before, so I am not sure how successful I am going to be, but I am going to try to spear some fish."

"You—"

"I know, I live in the woods and do not know how to fish, it's odd." I rolled my eyes at the comment I knew was coming.

She didn't answer, just crossed her arms and sat on a nearby stump, a wily smile on her face.

That was a little bit of an odd reaction. I expected a laugh, or something at least. Something to ponder later.

I let it go and focused on the task in front of me. Taking off my shoes and hiking up my pants, I would have removed them, but undergarments were not a thing I had in my bag, and I was not ready to go there with her staring at me buck naked just yet.

I waded out in the water and stood motionless, my makeshift spear above my head. The fish darted to the other side of the creek from where I entered.

I waited, eventually, as they slowly swam back to the side of the creek I stood on. I tried to get that time dilation thing to work, but I could not seem to grasp how to use it when I was calm. It only ever worked when I was in a fight so far.

Whether it was natural to my new body, or something that was given to me, I couldn't tell. But whatever it was, I would have to spend more time figuring it out. Part of me wanted to ask Tyla about it, but I did not want to say the wrong thing and spook her, ruining the progress we had made in our trust with each other.

A fish slowly came into range. It looked just like a trout, and a big one too, much larger than what should have been in a creek this size from my time fishing in the mountains of California. I guess these waters were not overfished much, allowing them to get bigger. That was good for our survival chances. I really did not want to figure out what bugs were edible. Memories of marine survival and evasion school caused me to shiver momentarily.

I timed my shot, studied its motion, waiting for the perfect time to strike. The seconds ticked by... almost there. I struck with the spear, confident in my shot.

Of course, that meant I completely missed it when I drove it down.

The spear changed directions as soon as it hit the water, sending me a little off balance when it struck the sandy bottom instead. The fish darted off, and I tried to pull the spear out to try again rapidly, moving off emotion rather than letting my brain keep control. As I yanked the spear out of the ground and repositioned, I slipped on an unstable rock and fell right onto my ass in the water, soaking myself up to my chest.

Stifled laughter came from behind me.

I cast my view at the offending noise and gave her my best marine glare. "Not helpful," I growled.

She gave up all pretense of holding the laugh in and let it go with a deep belly laugh, falling forward off her log.

I got up, shook the water off me as best I could, and waded back to shore. "Done yet?"

She laughed even harder. I glared at her for a few minutes when the shock of the moment and the bite of the icy water finally let go. "Yeah, probably right. Funny, from the sidelines. It's good to see you laugh at least, though."

She finally got control of herself enough to speak. "Thank you, I needed that. Come here and I will dry you off."

"Dry me off?" I said with a raised eyebrow.

"Water is my power. I am not strong yet, or skilled at the externals for that matter, but I should be able to coax the water to leave your clothes... mostly."

I walked up to her and stood still. She placed her hands over me and then rubbed down the outside of my clothes. Water dripped off me much faster as she moved her hands up and down my body.

Before I knew it, she had crested her hand over my manhood, and it stirred at the woman's touch. As much as I tried to stop it, it had a mind of its own. She jumped when she realized what she had done, her face flushing red while I pretended not to notice, then she continued with the rest of my clothes.

"There, all dry, I have never been good at physical magic, my strength lies in healing and sensing, but I can do a few things."

"So, couldn't you have done this to your clothes yesterday?" I said it before I could stop myself.

She flushed again. "Oh... um, yes, I supposed I could have. Must have slipped my mind."

She was lying. I could tell by the change in her body movements. She suddenly started wringing her hands, her face flushed even more than when she touched me before. The change in behavior was at odds with her normal mannerisms. Instead of saying anything, I filed that bit of information for later. It's good to know people's tells.

She was probably trying to seduce me into helping her, so I better let it go.

"Anyway," she continued. "Do you want me to see if I can get the water to push a fish or two near the shore where you can grab it? I might have the strength for it."

"Wait, you can do that? Why didn't you say so before?"

She glared at me, raising an eyebrow. "Because you interrupted me when I tried."

"Oh... sorry about that."

She smirked. "Next time maybe you will wait to hear what I have to say then?"

It was good to see her get some confidence back. "Deal, though I am a man, and we have been known to be idiots around women most of the time. Please allow me some grace."

"Acceptable, let's try to get some fish, shall we?"

I laughed. "Sure, I am hungry and need more than just fruit and jerky."

The fire snapped and crackled as it died down enough to put the two fish we had over the fire. I had cleaned and gutted them at the creek bed before we returned, putting the guts back in the water for the other fish to eat.

"Ok, this will only take a couple of minutes," I said, my mouth watering for cooked food. The smell of the... I think they were trout... smelled good, and I was starving.

"What did you do to them?"

"Little thing I picked up years ago. We don't really have any cooking utensils, so by getting these green branches and splitting them in two at the ends, add a couple more sticks through the fish itself, we can create a modified grill basket to cook them evenly."

I placed each fish over the flames, holding the sticks just a few inches over the coals that had formed as the flames died down, watching them cook. My thoughts drifted to my past and then back to the present.

"A copper for your thoughts," Tyla said.

I smiled at that. "Where did you hear that saying?"

"Something my grandmother used to say, said it came from her grandmother."

"Was she a matriarch too?"

"Grandma Russel? No, she was on my father's side, but her grandmother was a great matriarch according to the stories, though. It's why my father was picked for my mother's second husband."

"Picked?"

"Yes, it's… complicated. My father, his name is Micheal, is the second husband. Jason is her first husband."

"So, wait, multiple husbands at the same time?"

"Yes… I keep forgetting your lack of knowledge. We do not fully understand how women are Chosen for their powers. It can completely skip generations. We think, at least according to what I learned in school, that having a father with Chosen in the blood and a Chosen mother increases the odds. So, it is normal for women of power to have multiple husbands and children with them. I have a brother and sister from my father, and two half-sisters on my other father's side, none of the other girls had power. Though Titiana, my full sister, is too young to know yet."

"Interesting. We called that polygamy in my, uh, land. Wait, was that when a man does it? Maybe polyandry? It was becoming a thing where I came from, and the words get mixed up in my head."

She nodded. "Yes, well, that is where my last name comes from, my father. Even though my father took my mother's name when they married. I would have eventually taken the Blackrun name from my mother when I graduated from school and became an adept. Without power, I would have just kept my father's name."

"Kind of confusing, but I think I understand. Here, take this but let it cool. Have you eaten fish before?"

"Yes, it's a staple in my mother's estate," she said, taking one stick from my hand and blowing on the fish.

"Wild caught with bones on it?"

"Umm, no…"

"Wanted to make sure before I explained it to you this time," I said, a smile on my face, which she returned with a giggle. "Alright, you can pick the fins off like this, and then pull the meat away from the bones, or pull the skin off and the bones should come with it. Sorry, I don't have any seasoning, so it's as basic as you are going to get."

I displayed what I had explained on my fish, pulling off a fin and throwing it in the coals, followed by pulling some of the skin and bone, leaving only white meat, which I blew on and popped into my mouth. "Mmm, even without it, it's not bad."

She mimicked my motions, though not as skillfully. I could tell she wasn't used to getting her hands dirty from the squinting of her face.

It was cute, though.

She finally popped some fish in her mouth. "Oh gods, I did not realize how hungry I was."

"Well, we only have two, but the berries you picked ought to help fill the meal out. Let's save the jerky, though, if we can."

We sat in silence while we ate. The distraction of finding more about this world wore off, and I went back to my inner thoughts. I finished the food and placed the stick down, deciding to trust Tyla a little more. "I said her name was Jessica, she and I were... in love."

Tyla nodded, not saying anything, but looked a little pensive.

"We were together for a few years, planning on getting married someday. Just kept putting it off for one reason or another. Then this... grand expedition came, and we both decided to go. I was told at the last minute that I was not going, but Jessica still was, and it tore us apart. She's gone, and I... am still processing it inside."

Tyla scooted next to me, not saying anything, just laying her head on my shoulder. I wasn't sure how we had grown this close so fast. But damned if it did not feel good to have someone just listen.

"In the dream... again, it felt so real, but I do not know how it could be, she said the expedition was trapped and not able to return. She said she still loved me but wanted me to be happy and move on."

Tyla placed a single hand on top of mine and squeezed. No tingling sensation, no magic, just the power of human touch.

It helped.

"Then my land was overrun by... I don't know what they were, but I thought I was going to die... I could swear that I died, but I woke up in the forest just before I met you. No memory of how I got there."

There, the easiest to understand version of my story was out. Minus a few key details I promised myself to tell her if we got closer and knew she would not think of me as a complete madman.

Rather than judge me or my story, she told her own.

"My mother is... was the Matriarch of Blackrun, part of the Matriarchy of Nitre, named after a great city to the west. We have allied our families for generations and our twin cities ruled the lands down the middle. The Matriarch of Nitre was nominally our liege lady, but her and my mother were friends since they were little girls and even lovers for a time. I called her my aunt for my entire life."

I pulled my hand from underneath hers and wrapped my arm around her. She left her hand on my lap.

"About a year ago, she and my mother had a falling out. My mother never said the details, but suddenly, and as a surprise to all in the Matriarchy, we declared our independence from Aunt Josephina. My mother raised her banners, and all her ladies and mistresses were called to war. The following spring, about six months ago, there were several battles."

She took a deep, steadying breath before continuing.

"Josephina's armies drove us back. It was not until a few months ago we found she declared herself a lover and disciple of Seir, the Demigod. My mother begged for help from the Matriarchs of Riven Hold and Casting harbor, using a Demigod in human lands as the reasoning. Only Riven Hold sent an army, but it was enough to double my mother's forces. My mother pulled me out of my classes to help with healing and we marched to engage his forces. We thought we had the numbers... but it was a trap. Our armies were superior, but Seir was so powerful, he and his harem moved into the battlefield and destroyed our Chosen and our warriors alike. I don't think my mother had seen such power before. I..."

Tears now streamed out of her eyes. I picked her up and put her in my lap and held her as she cried and buried her face into my neck.

"She...." Tyla sniffled as she tried to talk, raising her face to mine. "She sent me away at that point with my bodyguards. Her and Miranda of Riven Hold were going to engage and try to stop them... but I don't think she had much hope. The look in her eyes when I saw her last was of resignation, not hope. So they all probably died, and I am all that's left." She started crying uncontrollably at this point.

I did not say the obvious, that they could have captured her. If what she said earlier was true, then she might also have been corrupted, but I really hope I was wrong, for Tyla's sake.

I let her cry on my shoulder for a while, all plans of training were now in ruins as it was now too dark to do anything. Before I knew it, the crying stopped, and I could hear sounds of snoring from my new companion. I struggled to rise, then got her in the bedroll before covering her up and putting the ripped clothing we used as a pillow under her head.

I smiled at her, hoping that we were developing in a positive manner that was healthy, and not coming together out of fear and loss. I would have to be mindful of that, not let our passions consume us until we knew more. The lower brain of this twenty-year-old body disagreed with me. Luckily, that part of... me, I guess now, did not get a vote in the deliberation.

I snuffed out the last of the fire, grabbed a flat rock I planned to use as a whetstone and got to work sharpening the cheap daggers. Trying to search my brain for the pieces of knowledge that could let me figure out how to make a bow or some other type of range weapons to add to our arsenal as I kept watch through the night.

CHAPTER 9

CLOSE PROXIMITY

"Thrust, twist, and then rotate it around with a downward slash. This is one of the most basic dagger fighting movements, and it's where we will start for now. You did good with the spear, but this is if it gets knocked out of your hand and you need to go to a backup."

"Like this?" Tyla asked as she duplicated my movements.

She pushed out with the dagger at the sapling tree, twisting it just like I showed her, then she pulled and slashed in a cross motion down the simulated chest of her assailant.

"Yes, but don't make contact with the tree right now, I just want you to feel the movement of the knife. We don't want to dull the blade any more than we have to just yet. I will find a stick or something later you can feel the impact on. Just do that about twenty times on each arm, then we can get moving again."

She nodded.

We had stopped for a midday break and another of the many creeks that littered this area, heading up a wide pass in between the mountains. We decided to do training during each of the breaks in smaller increments rather than at the end of the day, while we moved.

"What is our goal, Derrick?" she said as she switched arms.

"What do you mean?"

"Well, umm. My original goal was to seek shelter in Riven Hold... and they found me before I could get there. Then you showed up and we kind of just ran into the mountains, but... I am not sure what our goal is. Are they still chasing us? Will we just hide in the mountains for the rest of our lives? I do not know what to do now."

"That is a... valid point. I am honestly not sure myself yet, things have been happening so fast lately. All I can tell you is I have a powerful feeling about going up this mountain. Why? I am not sure. I just feel drawn to something. But a plan? Nothing yet, I'm sorry."

Tyla finished and stretched out her arms from the workout, eventually walking over in front of me. She smiled up at me and I returned it. "I am fine with following this feeling of yours, and I know this sounds weird but a part of me feels freer than I have in a long time, even with the pain of my mother's loss."

Our eyes met, and I could feel the pull towards this young woman, our faces started inching closer. Human attraction doing what it does best. I almost gave into the sensation when at the last minute I reined the desire back in, seizing her shoulders and moving my face to the side.

"I'm sorry, Tyla, I... really want to kiss you right now but I don't want us to do something we will regret later. We have only known each other for a couple days and things are still... fresh for me with the memories."

"I... understand," she said, shaking her head and huffing. "If you do not want me in that way—"

"No!" I said, cutting that off. "I just don't want us to move so quickly that we have regrets we can't reconcile later. Everything is just so raw for both of us, let's give it a little time before we decide whether it's something we really want, or just a survival instinct telling us it is what we should do. I... really hope that makes sense."

"I think so, my mother's mistresses talked often of battlefield flings that did not work out later. Though I never thought it would be this... overwhelming inside me."

We hugged for a minute, and she pressed right up against me. I suddenly felt the blood flowing away from my thinking head and to the feeling one. As it hardened right into her stomach. Rather than push away, Tyla pushed tighter.

"Uh, Tyla, that is kind of the opposite of what I need right now."

"Sorry," she said as she shifted away from me, her cheeks flushed, and she was panting this time.

I took a few deep calming breaths, closing my eyes. "It's fine, even with the brief time I find I... care for you, Tyla. I don't want us to ruin it by moving too fast. Let's make sure this attraction, or whatever it is, is real."

She nodded. "I... think I can do that, though that looks painful."

I opened my eyes to her staring at my groin. My little buddy was arguing in the strongest possible terms my decision to wait, standing at full attention in my pants. "I'll be fine, just need to start walking and things will ease on their own. I hope."

She smirked at me and glanced away, suddenly realizing she was staring at my crotch, her face burned even redder than before.

"Alright, let's get moving, see that outcropping up there?" I pointed up to the side of the pass, trying my best to focus on the rocks and not her body, as her hardened nipples pushed through the thin fabric of her shirt.

"I do."

"That looks like it has a good vantage point down the mountains. I want to head up there and see if I can spot anyone following us. Then we will use the game trail going up from there to head up higher. Maybe build a shelter and hide for a few days if this feeling I have doesn't pan out. Then decide our next move."

"More climbing, I am not looking toward it," she said with a groan.

"You'll live. As my old drill instructor used to say, 'walking builds character private Shultz! So, get to building!'" I laughed at the old memory as I mimicked my first DI, wishing I could remember his name. "Some days, I miss being a green recruit with no responsibility other than to do what I was told."

"You have funny words you use. The world magic cannot translate some of them since there is no equivalent."

"Really? Who trains your troops here?"

"Adepts mostly, they give commands, and they expect the men to follow. Other than the medical wagons, I did not have that much experience, though. The men marched, the Chosen rode horses. The men were the fodder and the infantry while the Chosen rained down their power on the enemy."

"Huh, I'll have to find out more about how you do war here when we get back to civilization."

We walked up the steep grade, sweat poured off of us from the warm day. "Is it summer right now?"

"The end, cooler weather could hit us at any time."

"So, four seasons in this part of the world?"

"Yes, the effects lessen as you go south past Riven Hold, but the weather here can get quite cold in the winter. We do not want to be in these mountains for too long without a proper shelter."

It was my turn to nod. Useful information to have. We really needed a better plan than following the feeling I had.

We got to the top of the outcropping after an hour of hiking. "Alright, keep your head down and stay here. I am going to crawl over to the ledge and peek down the mountainside. I will be in sight of you the whole time."

"Okay," she said, and I noticed she was picking up some of my words.

I pushed myself up onto the rock and slowly crawled my way to the ledge, creeping forward. When I finally got to the edge, my view was spectacular, able to see for several miles down the valley.

"Crap," I said, as I saw the valley below.

I stayed there for several minutes, letting my eyes pick up on movement throughout the valley that branched off in several directions through many passes in the mountains.

Eventually, I pushed myself back to where Tyla sat against the rocks.

"Do you want the good news or the bad news?"

"I... I don't know, one sounds horrible without the other and I am not sure what would make me feel better first."

"Uh, it's kind of a rhetorical question, anyway. I will go with the bad first. There are at least three search parties out there. I saw a couple of campfires which look like base camps, too."

"Oh, gods!" She blurted out, but covered her mouth instantly.

"There is some good news though, there are so many passes going through this jagged mountain that they will still have a tough time finding us, I saw several parties going into the wrong passes. So, it doesn't look like they picked up our trail."

She seemed to relax at this.

"But that means we need to pick up our speed, they will eventually see one of our camping spots and figure out which way we went. So, we are going to jog hard every day with lots of walking breaks and see if we can't break off somewhere on the other side of these mountains or something."

"What do I need to do?"

"Just keep up, if you need a break, we will slow down, but we are going to keep up a hell of a pace while also doing what we can to break up a trail."

"I'm... I'm scared Derrick."

I reached over to her, putting my arm around her. It was really feeling right to hold her like this... almost like Jessica felt. A pang of sadness rocked my chest for a minute before I put that back in its bottle. "I know, I won't let them get to you, promise."

She sniffled and nodded. "I believe you."

I smiled, hoping I hadn't just lied to her.

Then we started running.

CHAPTER 10

— o —

INTERLUDE – THE DEN OF SEX AND EVIL

"State your business," the guard said to the man that approached.

"Seir summoned me, Edmund Stern reporting."

The guard nodded and opened the door. "You are expected."

Stern noticed the strange glyph on the guard's forehead that looked like an upside-down triangle with one point dead center inside a circle. The guard used to be one of the Matriarch's personal guards; the mark was new.

As he walked in, he was almost shocked at what happened to the former receiving room of the Matriarch of Blackrun. The smell of the room was nothing but sex and depravity, if he was to give words to it.

The once august hall was now a den of people having sex or watching it. A man sat on the throne with two women servicing him in front of the entire court, of whom lined the walls. Every single man and woman not engaged in the pleasures had one of those glyphs on their foreheads and stood against the walls, waiting to be summoned while watching the... entertainments that were available.

Other women were present as well, several he did not know or could not see their faces, but the rest were ones he identified as Chosen. None of these women appeared to have the mark on their head. The few he recognized either had a power dampening collar on their necks while chained to one of the myriads of sexual looking torture stations or, the ones without collars, were busy giving pleasure to another of their ilk from a mound of pillows built on the side of the room.

The contrast was clear, if you joined the new regime, you were treated well. If you did not, well, things were not in your control.

He then noticed a regal woman who sat in the smaller throne next to the man being pleasured. She was someone he had only heard of in his service to the Matriarch... or at least the former Matriarch of Blackrun.

Speaking of the former matriarch, Stern sighted the woman tied up on two crossed wooden boards in the shape of an 'X'. She was directly in front and facing the two new sovereigns, her hands tied above her head and her feet tied to the bottom so that they spread apart and displayed her intimate parts to all the world. Her head hung low, and she had a gag in her mouth and collar on her neck. She was obviously the prominent display in the room.

Stern became guarded, but she approached the man on the throne, took a knee and bowed.

"I am Stern, my liege, reporting as ordered."

"Ah, the tracker, I have heard good things about your skills," Seir said. His smile never left his face as one of the beautiful women shoved her mouth down on his cock repeatedly from his side. Her red ponytail bobbing back and forth from the motion, sharing the duty with the other, younger woman who focused her tongue on the base of his shaft and his balls. "My darling wife says you were one of the best in the territory."

Seir turned his head over to the woman in the other chair, lifting his arm to show he was speaking of her.

"The Matriarch of Nitre is most kind," Stern said and bowed his head to her, trying to avoid looking directly at the two topless women servicing his new lord.

The matriarch smiled at him, her solid black shoulder length hair encasing her face. The smile was more suited to that of a predator than a woman. "You have served my former lover and friend well over the years and she has spoken well of you until we had our... falling out last year. Haven't you my dear?" Josephina asked.

A moan came from the woman on the crossed boards. She lifted her head and eyed Stern as if begging for help and his heart felt sadness when he saw her, but he would survive and do what he must.

"I was a... slave to the former matriarch, nothing more," he said. Any hope left in her fled at his words, her expression became one of hopelessness and tears began misting at her face.

He felt shame... but did not want to end up dead either.

"You see!" Josephina said. "Oh, my dear Patricia, you have no love from those you led, no one left to save you. What remains of your army will soon succumb to our forces when we catch up to them. Your precious daughter will not escape us for long. Just give in to Seir's demands and all the suffering can end, we can even be lovers again."

Josephina got up from her chair and walked over to her former friend, standing right in front of her. "The pleasures are surely worth more than the suffering you are enduring now. Look how happy Miranda is!" She pointed over to the older yet still extremely attractive red-headed woman with Seir's cock down deep in her throat. Her large breasts rocked back and forth as she licked and sucked on him. "Tell her."

The former Matriarch of Riven Hold stopped her work and removed her mouth from Seir's phallus; the sound of an audible pop, as her lips released his head, was heard throughout the chamber. The girl sucking the bottom of Seir's shaft took over at the top without missing a beat, exposing him to open air for only a second.

"I... was wrong to fight it," Miranda said, wiping drool and pre-cum from her mouth. "I have never been as complete as I am right now. Give in Patricia, accept Lord Seir as your master and you can join me."

"What do you say, Patricia?" Josephina asked, reaching up and removing the gag from Patricia's mouth.

Patricia's eyes teared, and she shook her head. "I... Can't... won't let—"

Her words cut off when Josephina placed the gag ball in her mouth. "Not yet, my dear Patricia... but soon."

She walked back to her throne smiling and sat down, spreading her legs wide she said, "Come here Miranda!"

Miranda jumped up to her feet and hurried over to Josephina, kneeling in front of the woman. The Matriarch of Nitre then hiked up her dress and exposed herself to all those present, "Begin," Josephina said.

Miranda bent forward and started lapping at the soaking folds in front of her. Josephina closed her eyes and soon started a light moan. "Mmm, you do that so wonderfully, my dear. If you are a good girl, I may even let you pleasure yourself later."

"Mmm hmmm" Miranda mumbled and nodded, going faster and more aggressively, putting her face as far into the woman's crotch as she could go. Josephina put the top of her dress over the woman's head, covering it, and glanced over at Seir. "Thank you for this gift, husband. She is a wonderful treat."

"I give generously to those who serve me well and you were the first to join me of your own free will. You will always have a place at my side." He reached over to grasp her hand, so both of the rulers were being serviced by a woman's mouth as they held hands.

Seir's focus then turned back to Stern. "You... Stern, was it?"

Stern nodded, still on his knee, completely at a loss to the situation that was going on about him. He did not want to be there, but could not leave either.

"You are familiar with the former matriarch of Blackrun's daughter, yes?"

"Yes lord. I have been a... servant to the family for years."

"If I asked you to hunt her down, would you take the job?"

"Yes lord, I... have no love for this family, they treated the men like servants even at the best of times and I was no different." He hoped they believed the lie.

"Good. For me to hire you for this most important task, I would need an oath of loyalty from you. Are you prepared to take it?"

Stern thought for only a moment, he never had a problem with Tyla. She was always nice to him, and he had a history with her mother that was kept hidden from most. He would do what he had to do though, so he nodded. "Yes, My lord."

"Come forward."

Stern got up and approached the throne, the woman servicing Seir did not move even as he was almost standing over her, she went about her task of swallowing the man deep. She was a blond girl he felt was familiar based on the part of her face he could see, her negligee bottoms revealing a curvy ass and her perky breasts were exposed.

She never stopped bobbing up and down.

Seir reached his hand out and placed it on Stern's forehead. "Do you swear to serve me in all tasks for as long as I have need of you?"

Stern hesitated, not sure what was going on. "I... I do."

A pain erupted through his forehead, it felt like someone seared a cattle brand onto it. "Ahhhhhhhhhhh," Stern yelled and collapsed to the ground.

He moaned for several minutes before the pain finally receded. No one came to aid him or check on him. As it finally receded, he felt a leaden weight settle over his soul as he reached up and felt his forehead. A scab had formed where the burning sensation came from, he rushed over to the nearby water basin and looked down at his face.

A symbol, just like the other servants in the room, had been burned into his forehead. Stern now understood what it meant, as the knowledge flooded directly into him.

"Yes, Stern," Seir said, not looking at him anymore, but down at the woman still sucking his cock. "You are mine too, but not like Susan here."

He shoved her mouth all the way down and held it until she gagged before releasing her. She coughed once, then went back to going up and down on him.

"Mmm, well done, Susan. I am glad I chose you as well," he said to the woman before glancing up at Stern, who was panicking. "Fear not, I dislike the men of your species in that way. Instead, you will do my bidding in other ways. While those like Susan will service my... baser needs. I love having flesh and blood again. It had been so long that I had forgotten what the pleasures of the flesh felt like, and now I find myself rather enjoying them."

He pushed her head back down all the way, a grunt escaping his lips as he climaxed into the back of her throat. When he finally released her, she collapsed at his side, swallowing his gift and gasping for breath.

"Thank you, my lord." Susan got out after a couple of breaths.

Seir returned his focus back to Stern, not even bothering to pull up his trousers. "You will track down Patricia's daughter and bring her to me unharmed. I have promised her to one of my lieutenants for services he provided. Do not fail me."

Stern no longer had a choice. He knew without a doubt that any attempt at rebellion would equal pain he did not want to experience. "Yes lord. But she is a witch. How will I deal with her powers?"

Seir snapped his fingers and pointed at Susan, who was still wiping the contents that had escaped off her lips and licking it off her fingers. "You knew Tyla, did you not?"

She finished licking and looked up at Seir. "Yes, my lord, I was her roommate and best friend before I agreed to serve and service you," she said proudly.

"Excellent, go with them. Your power over fire should be enough to counter her."

"Yes, my lord, I was much stronger than she was, and she was more comfortable as a healer than in combat." She got on her knees in front of Seir. "Would you like me to clean you off before I leave?" Stern noticed she did not put her shirt back on and her large breasts bounced from her giddiness as she spoke.

"No," Seir said and looked over at Patricia. "I think I will have a volunteer for that after you leave. Now, go with Stern and give him a counter to anything she might do. Stern, take command of some of the mercenary rabble I hired to find her. I need most of my army to finish the last of Patricia's before I can move south and consolidate. That is all the support you will get."

"I will see it done, my lord." Stern said and stood, waiting for Susan to put on her clothing and join him.

I could hear a sob from the woman on the wooden cross.

"Do you fear for your daughter, Patricia?" Seir said.

Patricia did not make a noise but tears now flowed from her face freely.

"I can make things easier for her... transition if you agree to join my bed. It could even convince me to find another for my lieutenant and have her join us. Would you like that?"

Stern could tell that Patricia's will was about to break. She shook her head, but he did not see any real fight left in her actions. Susan stood next to him, now fully dressed in a silk shirt that amplified her large breasts, and skin-tight pants that hugged her ass.

"Let's go," he said and walked for the door, hating himself for the decision he just made, but knowing he had no choice but to carry it out now.

CHAPTER 11

DISCOVERIES

We slowly skulked through the woods, following the grunting sounds. It had been two days since we had left the rock outcropping overlooking the valley and we were out of jerky and hungry. Our speed made stopping for food before now next to impossible.

Then we spotted its trail.

I lifted my hand in a stop motion. Tyla froze. We now knew how to communicate silently after much practice over the past... four and half days?

I glanced back at her, pointing to where the animal would head if I missed. She nodded and moved in the direction shown; her spear held so she could stab into the target should it come her way.

I inched towards the small clearing, looking over the wall of leaves downwind of my target. There it stood, pushing its snout into the ground, looking for whatever it was that it ate.

I picked up my spear, using that term loosely since it was still just a stick with a knife corded on to it, and pulled back to throw for all I was worth.

Just as I started forward, it surprised me when my perception of time slowed. I wasn't sure how it engaged only when it mattered. I had no control over whatever was making the time slow, or my brain speed up. My body also reacted so much faster than normal as well, so it might just be my brain doing it.

I used that extra time to adjust my aim as my arm moved forward, going for the wild pig with bull horns on top of its head. Tyla told me it was a wild bull pig, one of the most unimaginatively named creatures I had encountered, if you ask me. In her defense, it was a translated name for what the elves told them. So, it could have been a super-fly wombat for all I knew.

The spear flew true this time as it left my hand, my daily practice sessions paying off now that I understood its drift better, hitting the pig right through the neck. It dropped instantly, not even squealing.

"Got it!" I said over to Tyla.

"Yes!" she said and jumped up and down before running over. She dropped her spear and jumped into my arms, giving me a tight hug and putting her legs around me. "I am starving."

She pulled back just enough to smile into my face and kissed me on the lips. It was sudden and unexpected, and I never had the chance to consider the ramifications of what it might mean.

So, I did not fight it. I just kissed her back. We locked lips and our tongues tentatively invaded each other's mouths. I just gave into the hormones and the moment.

It was one of the best kisses I could remember, and I savored it.

We broke after only a few moments, our breathing heavy, and peered into each other's eyes. Rather than saying something stupid like I normally would, I just nodded at her and kissed her again quickly on the lips, much more chastely this time at least. "Let's go get our food before something bigger than we can handle comes by."

She nodded as a smile formed on her face, reaching her eyes. She picked up her spear, then grabbed my hand after she got back to the ground.

We approached the pig, and I saw that the knife at the end of the stick almost went clean through its neck. The stick itself had broken in half.

"How is that possible?" Tyla asked, pointing to the stick. "I know you are not weak, but that seems like it should take more strength than any man possesses. To break a solid piece of wood like that? I know earth wielders that can do it, but outside of them, even the rest of the Chosen are not so strong."

"I'm not sure... don't really feel any stronger. In fact, I feel weaker in this b—than I used to before waking up here. I tested the wood out and it felt solid, but maybe it had a flaw I was not aware of."

"Then how did the dagger and hilt almost go through the pig's neck? These beasts are known to make strong leather from their skin."

"Honestly? I am as confused as you, but it will have to wait. I am going to field dress this kill so we can transport it somewhere and camp for the night. While I do that, could you dig a pit so we can bury what we leave behind? Then, look for another stick for me so we can carry the thing when I am done?"

"Yes, I can do that."

"Thanks," I said as I pulled out the other dagger I had and got to work cutting up the animal that would feed us tonight.

"And ready to go, you up for this?"

"The Chosen have some boosts in strength with their power, strengthening us more than a man of our size would normally be. While it does not give me an enormous advantage, I should be able to carry my end for a time."

I smiled. She was fairly tiny, "Alright, on three. One, two, and threeeee."

I lifted by myself, the unexpected weight difference making me stumble for a second.

"Crap... uh, why didn't you lift?"

"Oh, was that what I was supposed to do? I did not understand what you were talking about."

I set the pig down and was about to cover my face with my palm before I realized I still needed to wash them. "Fine, yeah I should have expected that. I'm so used to you by now, I forget we have different backgrounds. I need to wash off my hands anyway," I said, going for a water bladder.

"Oh, here..." She jumped towards me in her excitement and grabbed my wrist with her left hand and pointed to it with her right finger.

She closed her eyes just for a second and a stream of water sprayed out of her finger and hit my hand like a water faucet.

She grabbed my other hand and did the same thing, and soon my hands were clean.

"That's handy. Can you always summon water?"

"Well, umm, no and yes. I am not that powerful and only have an extremely limited reserve. Like I said, I am better at healing and internal magic. With the external, it uses up my power rapidly. When I poisoned that man back in the clearing, it drained me and that is why I collapsed... I did not say anything at the time, but my threat to you was a bluff. I had nothing left," she said, some shame on her face.

I laughed. "Well, I believed you, so when you need to, you can be plenty scary."

This got her to laugh. "I have never been what I needed to be. My mother is... was strong. I have always been afraid and quiet."

I put my arm around her. "Hey, none of that talk. You are a strong beautiful woman, and I think you are about to bloom into your best... And make an excellent towel," I added as I used the back of her shirt to dry off my hands.

"Stop!" she said and laughed, turning and pushing my hands away. "I have been living in filthy undergarments for days! Use your own shirt and leave mine alone."

We laughed, the byplay feeling good. Knowing we might get some actual food soon felt even better.

"So, you can use your water to hurt people? Can you turn it into steam or something and burn them?"

"No, I have power over the water. But I do not have the power over the states the water assumes. I can manipulate steam to a degree, but I cannot change the temperature of it to make it into water unless I move it so fast that it cools on its own. I would need the fire element for that. My roommate could add or remove heat from my water. Oh, I hope Susan is alright. She was in the battle line when I ran..."

She drifted off for a second.

"What is it?" I asked.

"I... just can't believe I forgot about Susan. She and I were... close. Best friends and... more." She turned red again.

"Lovers?"

"Not... no, not really. I could never have men around alone, so we kind of... experimented? With each other when we were alone. It is common among the Chosen to prefer a woman's touch to that of a man. I... find that I prefer the man's, though a woman's also pleases me." She brought her eyes up to mine.

I resisted the urge to kiss her... if only barely.

We had work to do, and we could relax later. I still wasn't sure if I should let it go any further.

I let the subject die for now and changed it. "Ok, I think we should head up those hills and see if we can find another traveler tree for some shelter and cook this pig. I hope we have enough distance to spare a night to eat and recover."

Tyla smiled. A small look of disappointment crossed her face for a second, but she still nodded. "Ok, let me guess. This time, when you count to three, you want me to pick up at the same time?"

"Yeah, that's how that works." I smiled.

"On three, one, two, and three" this time we both lifted, and it worked as planned. "Put the stick over your right shoulder and I will put it over my left, that way we can use one hand to keep it on our shoulders while we walk—" I was about to point to the tree line in the hills when a sudden urge made me point in a direction ninety degrees to my right towards a tight canyon in the hill's leading much deeper into mountains. "That way?"

"What?" Tyla asked, confusion on her face. "Why that way?"

"I... don't know, that pull I have been having got really strong and wants me to go there."

She glanced at the canyon, then back at me. "Lead the way."

I smiled inside. Her trust in me and this nonsensical feeling felt fantastic. Even if it was probably a bad idea to walk into the obviously dead-end canyon where we could easily get trapped if our pursuers caught us. Rather than listen to my own self-doubts, I just nodded back to her and said, "alright, let's go."

❦ ❦

"Is that a cave?" Tyla asked as we rounded a bend in the canyon.

"I... uh, think so. It's not like any cave I have seen before. It looks more like a door."

As we approached the opening, the rounded hole in the solid rock was lit from an illumination coming deep from within the cave.

"That is definitely where we are supposed to go though, I can feel it."

"If you think that is best," Tyla said.

I looked back at her, "You stay here, and I will go inside."

"You are not leaving me out here alone with a dead pig."

My response was simply a raised eyebrow.

"Every scary story my older sister told me started with a kid staying by themselves in a secluded space or separated. I would rather get mauled by the scary monster with you than by myself, thank you."

I chuckled. "Do any of them involve a man in a mask with a knife or something similar?"

"Actually, a man with a sword and a fiery skull for a head. He removed the heads of the little girls who did not stay in their homes at night."

"Really? That actually supports a theory I have," I said without thinking.

"What theory?"

"Huh? oh... It's hard to explain but has to do with where all the humans came from. I think we have the same origins because that is a story we hear in my land as well."

"You will tell me your secret one day, right?" Obviously not believing my cover up.

"I honestly don't think you will believe me, but I will later."

"Promise?"

I sighed. "Yes, but for now, let's check out this cave. Keep the pig with us but keep a hand on your dagger and we drop it and run if anything too big jumps out... but I feel we will be safe in there. At least it looks well lit."

"Ok."

We walked inside and followed the straight path back into the cave. "What are these crystals?" I asked.

"It's Panzite, a rare crystal that provides illumination on its own. Precious and rare, we might be rich if we can extract some without breaking them. They store magic currents which make them glow. How it happens I am not sure, but they can also lose the magic if improperly handled."

"Could you use them as storage for your magic?"

"You can, but it's... complicated. They store little, and extracting it is very inefficient and may not be compatible with the Chosen's power."

"Ah, ok," I said.

We walked into a large room at the end that looked more like a temple than a cave.

"Ok, someone has definitely been here before. That hole in the ground is big enough for three or four people to fit in and looks like it used to hold water based on the drains that come from the wall. Even has a place you can sit."

Tyla nodded. "I think this is a temple to the gods, or at least one of them. There have been rumors that some gods used to have sanctums in the world, but they are exceedingly rare and only spoken about by the elder races and in fables."

"So, we stumbled upon a god's temple in the middle of the mountains?" I said, looking at her dubiously.

"I am just guessing. I do not honestly know what this is."

"Well, this hole is too big to fill up by ourselves, but it would make an awesome hot tub," I said jokingly. Of course, it fell flat on my company.

"What is a recreational bath? You mean like a bathhouse?"

I sighed and shook my head. This world magic was almost perfect, but occasionally something slipped by that got lost in translation. "No, uh... It's a tub you fill with hot water and relax in, fantastic on sore muscles."

"I can see how that would be nice. I love a hot bath myself and am desperately in need of one. If your muscles are sore though, I can help with that."

"I really keep forgetting that you can do that. I may take you up on it later, but first let's start a fire to cook the meat and... see that basin over there? Do you think you have enough power to fill it with water so we can at least wash clothes, then bathe without wasting our drinking water?"

"I can do that!" Tyla said happily as we put the pig down on the ground and started making this into a temporary home.

"This is definitely a hearth right here in the center. I think I can go back out and get some firewood and we can cook here. Maybe I can find something to use as a spit roaster."

"A what?" she said, having finished filling the water basin. Sweat dripped down the side of her face from the exertion.

"Uh... might be easier to show you if I can get something that might work. Have to find something that will hold the pig up and we can spin it. Okay, let's go back out and see if we can find what we need."

Hopefully, we could stay here for a day and recharge before getting back on the road.

CHAPTER 12

BONDS

"That should do it, just have to keep turning it now that it's mostly coals."

"I have seen something like this before at my mother's estate. I never knew what it was called."

"It's a spit roast... well, as close as I can get to one in the woods. My strong suit was never the survival side of things. I'm just kind of winging it here. But we just have to turn it, so the meat cooks evenly, so if it's stupid, but it works, it isn't stupid. Right? You want to clean up and wash your clothes as best you can while I do this. I can look away while you do."

"Umm, sure, but it will take a while for the clothes to dry."

"Yeah, it's going to be awkward, at least it's warm enough in here with the fire. I will look away as much as I can."

"No, it's something we will have to deal with. I... do not mind if you see me without clothes." She said as her face flushing.

Smiling, I said, "Yeah, we really can't avoid it. A dire wolf ruined my one change of clothes. Still, I will focus on this, and you can get clean. Make it the least awkward as possible. Then we will switch off and just... adjust and adapt I guess."

She nodded and went to the back of the room with the washbasin. I heard her disrobe and place what little clothing she had on the ground. I did my best not to turn around.

"We need to get back to civilization at some point and get supplies. We can't last much longer like this. Is there any place safe to go?"

"I don't know anymore. We can go to the Riven Hold if they have not fallen. Their Matriarch was with my mother, but she had left her eldest daughter behind. We should be able to find sanctuary there for a time. There are also many small towns and villages we can hide in."

"Do you know what this Seir wants?"

"We do not know what any of the Demigods want besides power. In the west it is said that they gain power and then war between each other as a sport. We had hoped that they had no interest in humans or the gods protected us. But we were wrong, obviously."

She stopped what she was doing after she said this, causing me to look over to see what was wrong. I caught an eyeful of her perfect ass bent over the basin where she was washing her hair in the water, but had stopped. I pivoted my eyes back to the pig, a surge of blood going to my groin.

Not helpful there, buddy, I thought, while looking down at my crotch.

I watched out of the corner of my eye as she finished washing her hair, using the small bar of soap that I had in my bag along with some twigs that you brushed your teeth with using this jar of minty tree sap, which made morning breath slightly less of an issue, at least.

Redoubling my efforts to not peek, since my little marine was now at full attention, I knew he was going to make my own bathing later as awkward as possible. I thought I had grown past such concerns in my youth, but I was living through them again.

I sighed loudly.

"Are you fine over there?" Tyla asked.

"Yeah, just remembering something I thought was behind me."

"Like what?"

I snickered. "Oh, nothing... How are you doing over there? There going to be enough soap?"

"Plenty. I am almost done, then you can bathe, and we can wash our clothes last."

"Okay," I said, closing my eyes as I turned the pig by hand, trying to count numbers backwards from one hundred.

"Finished, your turn." She said, surprising me by standing right next to me, eliciting a small jump. "Did I scare you?"

I could hear the chuckle in her voice.

"Uh, sorry. Had my eyes closed and did not hear you walk up." I glanced at her nude form and noticed the fire was not putting out enough heat diverting my eyes back up to her own. I was fairly sure from her smirk that she had caught me.

"It's fine, Derrick, get used to it and it will be less awkward, at least I hope." Her own face was still a little red, to be fair.

Nodding, "Yeah, it's awkward. I am not used to it, but we will adapt. You are quite beautiful, though..." I drifted off, not knowing what I was going to say.

"Thank you. I will take over the turning while you clean up. How long should this bull-pig cook?"

I snickered at the name. "Uh, about an hour for every ten pounds, I guess about thirty pounds, so let's say three hours?"

I let her have the sticks I tied together to use as a crank and went over to the basin, disrobing from my meager shirt and pants.

As I took my pants off, I thought I heard a gasp and turned to see Tyla looking away from me, but her hair was still settling as though it had whipped around. I smiled at this. At least I wasn't the only one sneaking glances.

Clean and with our clothes drying near the hearth, we finally sat down next to the fire to enjoy the pork from the pig.

"It smells fantastic," Tyla said, her mouth watering.

We had finally adjusted to our nakedness and could look one another in the eyes again.

Mostly.

"This stone should be ok for serving. Wish I had more than one plate though, we will just eat with our fingers off it, together."

She scooted up right next to me, so that our exposed thighs were touching each other, and I sat the plate down in front of our knees with the freshly carved meat.

Tyla picked up a sizable chunk and blew on it while I did the same.

She put the food in her mouth when it cooled. "Oh gods, I was so hungry."

"Don't eat too fast, it will make you sick. We should have enough to last a couple of days before it goes bad, though. Wish I could smoke it or turn it into jerky. Hell, we don't even have salt."

I stopped to eat my own. She was right, this was damn good.

We just sat there and ate for a few minutes before I finally brought up what I wanted to say.

"So, about my past. I'll tell you, but you might think I am crazy."

She pushed her shoulder into my side. "I won't, I... trust you. Completely at this point. I probably shouldn't, but I do."

"Well, you may still think I am crazy, we will see," I said with a laugh, as I pushed her back. I hope it was not the stress of the situation, but I would swear I was falling hard for this girl.

I thought I knew the difference between lust and love, but the lines blurred again now that I was younger again.

"Alright, so I told you I woke up in the forest, right?"

She nodded.

"Well, let me tell you about the last memory I had before I woke up there...."

I told her my story. Her eyes widened further and further as I went. She never interrupted me once, whether she did not know what to say, or just was shocked. I couldn't tell.

Eventually we finished eating, and I stood to put more logs on the fire, finishing my story.

"So, my first memory of being here was that dire wolf coming at me in the clearing."

"You actually came from the world of the ancestors?"

"I think so. I can't prove it, but I believe it to be true, yes."

"And who were the beings in the... Ships?"

"Yeah, I call them ships. Cubes? I don't know, either what they were or who they were."

"But we were told the gods moved us to this place."

"For all I know, they are the same. From my perspective, I was on the street, looked up, and all I saw was a big black cube of death and a purple beam. I don't think our military defenses even had a chance. I actually wonder what happened to old Admiral Jackson though, he was in command of the fleet on one of our flagships, I doubt he went down without a fight."

"You can't fight the gods," Tyla said, looking at the fire with sadness on her face.

"Hey, none of that. You said yourself these Demigods got cast out by the gods. Making them mortal as in they can be killed, right?" I walked up behind her and gave her a hug, careful to not put my hands over her breasts.

She nodded and leaned back into me. I had to shift, so she was not putting the top of her butt to my groin and feeling my... reaction.

"Yes," Tyla said. "The Matriarchs of the elves killed the first few that came over. It wasn't till they began turning the Chosen that they had enough power to win."

"How do you think they turn them?"

"I... have only heard rumors, but Josephina supposedly asked to bond with Seir for power. Or he came to her with an offer of power. We are not sure. But she wanted to be bound to him."

"Her and my mother had a... disagreement or something. I do not know the specifics. But they argued over how to expand the Matriarchy. Josephina wanted to march the army and conquer the lands to the north, expanding to where the tribes live in the wilds."

"Who are they?"

"Humans who ran from the civil wars hundreds of years ago, they raid our lands from time to time. My mother thought we should leave them alone while we slowly expanded our cities and towns with colonies and built up our defenses."

"So, you don't think I am crazy?"

"No, I believe you. It... feels true to me. Like something is telling me to believe you."

Her comments triggered a thought. Specifically, it made me wonder if one of these gods was pulling strings in some way. I had this feeling I was a mouse in a maze hunting for the cheese and that bothered me. However, I would have to hold on to the thoughts, as there was nothing I could do.

"Ok, it's late and we're exhausted. Let's clean up and get to bed. I have more questions, but they can wait. Our clothes should be dry by morning, and we can get a move on. Maybe we can try to curve back south for the free towns you mentioned. I honestly still do not know what drew me here."

We split up and cleaned up our mess, protecting the food the best we could, then I put a few more logs on the fire. The single sleeping roll was just wide enough to fit us both, but it was... snug, to say the least.

"Uh, you want me to sleep outside the bag since we don't have any clothes on?" I offered.

She shook her head as she got into the sleeping bag. "Just join me... please?"

Her eyes, big, brown, and beautiful, looked up at me as she asked the question.

"Ok," I said, swallowing hard, and slipped in next to her, turning around so that my back was to her.

We didn't really have pillows and had been using my ruined clothes for that purpose, so I tried to get comfortable on the ground with my arm and closed my eyes. The bluish glow in the cavern was not so bright that it would make it too hard to sleep.

Tyla rustled next to me, trying to find a comfortable position, before she turned over to face me. "Can I use you as a pillow?" she asked.

"Uh, sure." I rolled over onto my back and let her get into the crook of my arm and chest. She snuggled next to me as I tried to get comfortable, putting her breast to my side while her head lay on me. I was really hoping she did not notice the rising problem I was having down below from her movements. Just as I said that, her right leg pushed up and onto my knee, only inches from my manhood.

She adjusted, touching it with her knee, causing it to twitch and go to full hardness. When Tyla finally settled, I relaxed, hoping the... rising problem would go away soon. I took several deep, slow, and steady breaths to calm my raging needs.

Just as I was getting them back in control, Tyla shifted again, this time pushing herself up and over. She was suddenly straddling me, looking down. She looked at me only for a moment before pushing her face into mine for a deep kiss, her ass right above my now instantly re-hardened shaft.

She cut off the kiss and sat back up, straddling me just above my groin. I was in awe of her beauty, silhouetted by the soft blue glow of the various crystals throughout the cave. My heartbeat increased very quickly, and my breath hitched as I looked at the brunette beauty above me.

I lost my ability to resist.

"I don't want to wait anymore," Tyla said, with a confidence in her voice that typically wasn't present.

She wanted this.

It was my turn to take the initiative, rather than speak, I reached up and pulled her into me. Our faces came together, and our tongues met once again.

Her hardened nipples poked into my chest like diamonds, and I could feel her dampness where she sat on me. We kissed like this for a few minutes before she pushed off.

"Do you... want me to put it in my mouth?" She asked.

Her question reminded me she was still young and inexperienced, allowing me to get control over the caveman inside of me, if barely. "Have you ever been with anyone before?"

She shook her head, "No... well, not with a man, just Susan... and me."

"Let's take this slow to start and discover what we like together. I have... had experience from my life before, so let's focus on you. Would that be okay?"

"But what about your needs?"

"It's fine. Let's focus on you first, then me later."

She smiled at this and nodded.

I grabbed her by the sides and turned her over, so now she was laying down on her back. I lifted myself away from her now soaking crotch to look down and her naked form. Her breathing started picking up again as her excitement increased.

I kissed her on the lips, our tongues again intertwining, but I broke it off after only a few seconds. I butterfly kissed her right check and moved over to her ear, pushing her hair out of the way with my right hand and using my tongue on her earlobes to see if I got a reaction.

Her back lifted just a bit, combining with a hitch in her breath, telling me she liked this sensation. I used my wandering hand to explore other parts of her while I did this, tracing lines down her chest towards her breasts with my fingers.

She reached up and grabbed my hand, put my finger directly on her nipples, telling me where she wanted me to go.

I kissed down the side of her neck as my hand traced circles around her fully erect nipples. Her back arched again, more this time than with the ear, and she started gyrating her hips up and down. Her own hand drifted towards her wet opening as she whimpered in need.

I stopped her from pleasuring herself. "Nope, let me find the spots, I will take care of you, I promise," I said, stopping my trail of kisses to peek up at her.

She nodded, and bit her lip, putting her head back down on the bedroll, looking up at the ceiling and taking a huge breath.

I continued my studies, now putting my mouth around her right nipple, sucking, then licking, and finally just lightly biting to see how she reacted to each.

"Oh, gods!" she gasped, as her back arched when I did my first hard nibble with my teeth on her nipple.

I smirked and pulled away, my teeth holding on to her tiny and hard tit for a second before I let go. She squeaked, then moaned in pleasure as her tit popped out of my mouth. Then slowly, I started kissing my way over to the other nipple to repeat the process. My right hand gradually tracing down her exposed belly towards her wet folds.

I tenderly massaged the areas around her opening, not yet touching the slit in the center. Her breathing intensified and her hands balled into fists at her side.

"Touch me there... please?" she asked, pleading. "I need it!"

I gave into her request and moved my hand to her center, lightly gliding a single finger up and down her pussy.

She pushed her crotch into my hand, wanting me to go deeper. Instead, I let go of her left nipple with another snap, again using my teeth. I kissed my way down south, slowly and surely, eventually replacing my finger with my tongue in her slippery canal.

I have never noticed a 'flavor' with women in my life before. While everyone was unique in their way, I just did not differentiate them like that before. Tyla was different. I could taste a hint of cinnamon in her as I investigated her depths with my tongue. I honestly don't know whether this was because of my new body, or there was something different about the Chosen of this world, but I didn't care. She tasted wonderful.

I added my finger back into the mix of giving her pleasure.

"Oh gods, oh gods, don't stop," Tyla said after a few minutes. Her legs, now lifted over my head, clenched down on me. Her hands reached up and grasped my hair as she gripped on, like she was afraid of falling off.

Her body then tensed right before her scream in ecstasy, while I pushed my tongue deep inside her sex.

"Ooohhhh goddsss!" She screamed as she came.

She finally relaxed, her body momentarily going limp on the bedroll, which unfortunately was a little damp below her ass now.

"That was... wonderful..." she said through her excessive breathing as I inched my way back up her body, only giving a few light and playful kisses this time. Eventually lying next to her as she basked in her after orgasm glow.

We kissed again. She put her hands to the side of my ears and held me there. "Can I... I have you inside me now? I know I promised—"

"Whatever you want is fine," I interrupted. "You are the most important person right now. It can be my turn later."

She smiled at me, then kissed me again, pulling me back on top of her. My rock-hard shaft screamed at me to take her now and shove myself inside of her without mercy.

Instead, I just pushed the tip right to her still wet entry and stopped. I used my hand to push it around the entrance, lubing myself up and... hopefully, making it easier for me to enter her the first time.

"I'll go slow, let me know if I need to stop."

She nodded at me, a light groan parting her lips as I entered her pussy with the head of my cock.

Her eyes scrunched down at the sudden sensation.

"Does that hurt?" I asked.

She shook her head, "No... yes... a little, but it feels good to... Don't stop but keep... ohhh gods... keep going slow."

I kept at it, entering her an inch at a time, pausing at each step forward to take another step or two back. Allowing her to adjust to my girth.

Before long, I was fully inside of her, and she relaxed.

"Please," Tyla said. "Fuck me. Hard."

Shocked at her sudden use of curse words, I almost lost my train of thought. I didn't remember her ever using less than proper language before. But the thoughts soon left when I agreed with her needs and began lightly pushing forward and back into her extremely tight but wet canal.

Her breathing increased and her moans became louder as I picked up speed. I grunted as I pushed inside her faster and harder.

"I am not... going to last... long," I said in between thrusts. My rock-hard shaft had been unused since I got here, and I had almost no endurance right now.

"Just fuck me!" She said, lost in her own passion. Her head bounced around from the thrusting and her eyes were almost glazed over. She moaned repeatedly in pleasure.

"Fuck... fuck... fuck!" She said every time I rammed into her.

I had intended to pull out as my climax neared. However, just as I was about to yank my cock out of her and come on her stomach... it felt like something took over for my actions.

A glow came from my core, right above my stomach, and I could feel a... power, like an electrical socket suddenly connecting to a plug, which reached out from me and into Tyla.

I could not control or stop it.

When the energy and light extended from my core to my groin, then into her, it consumed her whole body so that she was glowing brighter than the crystals in the cave.

I grunted loudly as I exploded inside of her, shooting my seed deep into her womb.

Tyla's eyes opened in ecstasy as she came at the same time. Her eyes lit up like they were light bulbs, loudly screaming "Yes, I accept!" as she orgasmed at the same time as I did. Her body convulsed in pleasure.

An explosion of energy exploded from our bodies, brightening the entire cave like a flash from a camera.

I collapsed on top of Tyla and couldn't move. A feeling of immense power flooded through me, and I felt a connection directly into Tyla's core for a moment. Like I knew everything about her, who she was, and who she wanted to be just for a moment.

We could not move. My semi-erect cock still nestled inside her, her arms and legs wrapped around me. Our eyes gazed into one another's as though we could see the very essence of our souls through them.

Then darkness consumed us as we passed out.

CHAPTER 13

GODS

My dreams came to me, disjointed, constantly switching between the sounds of people screaming out in pain while cursing my name. Then shifting to the sounds of them cheering me and thanking me for their salvation. It was confusing and the worst dreams I have ever had in my life... either life.

Then suddenly, they stopped.

Then I found myself in a room, a gray cell with no windows or doors. The room was lit, but I could not identify a single source of the illumination. Not even a chair decorated it.

I was alone, spinning around slowly as I tried to figure out what was going on. The silence in the room was almost deafening. The absence of any smell that I could detect, alarming.

Then a swirl of light unfolded in front of me, a being several feet taller than me, with a cutoff cone shaped head, and the body of Hercules formed from the various motes of light.

"Derrick Shultz, formerly of Earth," the being said.

It was a statement, not a question, but I answered it anyway. "I am."

He dipped his head slightly. Not a bow, just an acknowledgment.

"I am Vex, assistant to the Controller of Fates. One those on this world would call a god. Those from the world you hailed from would call me an alien. However, for our purposes, you may call me your benefactor. This will be the only time we can communicate freely while you are in my sanctum on Timeria."

"Benefactor? I take it you are the reason I showed up in a world where my people are being enslaved by those that you cast out?"

"Your information is incomplete. Yes, I picked you when your world fell for a purpose. A contingency of mine, to be precise. The Demigods, as you call them, are my people who came to this world by choice. What I am about to tell you is... sensitive and must not be repeated outside of your harem. Even the ones you bind to yourself through loyalty pacts must not be told."

"What? I don't have a harem and I have no idea what you are talking about," I scoffed at him, still trying to process what he just said.

"Yet," he replied. "It matters not. I am aware of what type of person you are. I followed your life before your species was saved. I saw your bravery when you jumped in front of that bullet to save your fellow marine. Your decision to be an enforcer of justice in your old world. You cannot stand by while evil walks. That is why I chose you."

I let the harem comment go for a minute. "Are you the one behind the death of my world?"

"I was its... orchestrator, yes, at the behest of my people and our ancient policies."

I tried to lunge at him, my hatred bursting forth, but my legs and arms wouldn't move.

"Peace, human. You are in both my sanctum on Timeria, and in a world I created in your mind. Here, I am in control and nothing you can do will harm me. This is your one chance to listen and take control of your destiny. Fight or flee after, it matters not. But I believe I know what you will choose."

I struggled for a few seconds, confirming what he said, it was pointless. Nothing responded to my commands to attack him.

Finally, I just nodded at him, the hatred still seething but my higher thoughts taking control... for now.

"Good. The Demigods are my people, yes. They are mostly from the lowest castes. We are an ancient race, with a history of over a million of your years. Several thousand years ago, when our science was at its apogee, we discovered the secret to immortality. With our medicines, we were long lived, but still mortal. This allowed our entire race to transcend that mortality and be like the gods before us. For we were not the first in the endless expanse of space to reach this height."

"What does this have to do with my people?"

"My race was a race of conquerors. We pushed out into the stars and enslaved those that were lesser. However, like all who live a life of luxury and excess, we became softer over time. Significant percentages of our society thought we should study the lesser races rather than enslave and destroy. Eventually, we created a new policy to judge the violence of a species. A minimal risk, or a subservient species like your cattle, we would make them a servitor species. An elevated risk, and we would eliminate the threat in a manner you would call humanely."

I sighed. "So, humanity was a high risk?"

"Very much so, one of the highest, actually. In the last several thousand years, the preservation protocols dictated that rather than destroy you outright, we would take a part of your population and put them on a living preserve, the rest, we would upload into a pocket universe, most of your population unaware of the transfer."

"I remember that transfer, as you call it, pretty vividly."

"That's because I let you keep your memories of that day. The woman and child you tried to save remember nothing out of the ordinary, living long and peaceful lives in a reality they could not tell from the one they knew."

"There is no way you are telling me this for no reason."

"You are correct, human, and I am not even telling you much of what is happening. Just enough to motivate you in the direction I need. The most important thing you should realize is that immortality is leading to the downfall of my species. I and the Controller must stop it."

"What do you mean?"

"My people have become bored, lazy, and entitled. The lower castes live forever, but they have no way of advancing in a society where no one dies. We do not have young to cultivate, we no longer expand enough to create new opportunities. We have stagnated. The purpose behind my people coming to this world is entertainment."

"So, you're telling me we are just a game to you?"

"Yes. Or so the ruling council believes, it's a way to weed out the most discontent and give them purpose. They will not age in this world, but they can be killed, which also eliminates the problem as far as the council cares."

I seethed at the information, but I was powerless here against this... thing.

"So, I guess that you need me to do something for you?"

"Astute human, yes," Vex said dryly. "I need you to be the instrument of your people's salvation. I want you to kill my people who come here, to deter this experiment from expanding to other worlds just like it."

"How am I supposed to kill one of these Demigods? They are too strong for even the super powered women here to deal with."

"Because I have made you just like them."

"You what?"

"Made you one of them. You have the same powers they do. Actually, you have more power than they do. My benefactor has created a special ability, a blessing if you will, just for you to give you an advantage over my people here."

This was all coming at me too fast. I was having problems processing the information. "Wait... so you're telling me I need to enslave women to fight them?"

"I am not telling you how to do anything. You already have one of them bound to you, add as many or as few as you like. The more you have, the more power you wield."

"Oh God, Tyla?" I said, fear shooting through my body.

"She accepted the terms and bound herself to you by choice. You did not even manipulate her into it like Seir does his own slaves. She accepted freely."

"How can I release her?"

"You can't. Not without killing her. Well, there is another way, but I will get to that later."

My body slumped against the cold concrete floor of the room. I felt rotten inside. I just bound someone to my will, going against everything that I believed in.

"I must go soon, the power you generated in your copulation will soon run out and I cannot inject my own. It will be up to you to figure out the powers you have, but I can tell you briefly what you are now capable of, and the extra blessings my benefactor has given."

Unable to speak, shame filling me from top to bottom, I listened to what this bastard told me.

I woke up slowly, briefly forgetting the dreams I had. I was warm, and I wrapped my arms around Tyla. Her breasts pressing against my chest, her leg draped over me in the bedroll we shared.

For a minute, all was perfect, and I was content.

Then, the memories of my talk with the alien asshole came back to me and my eyes shot open.

The first thing I noticed was a blue glow coming off Tyla. It was very subtle, but it radiated out like a halo just over her skin. Something I knew only I could see. A gift, but one I would gladly return if I could.

She was smiling in her sleep, a whisper of a snore escaping as she breathed in and out. Her hair was a mess, tangled from our sweaty lovemaking the night before.

Rather than wake her, though, I just watched her sleep as I processed my inner turmoil.

What should I do?

I should release her... but she may not accept the cost that comes with something like that. I can only offer escape. I can't force anyone to take it.

I can feel the new power we shared coursing through my veins. It was like a current that I can tap into at will now. I need to know how it works.

I am not sure how long we stayed like that, but eventually the blue glow disappeared, and her eyes fluttered awake. When they opened, she spotted me and smiled up at me. Her deep brown eyes showed nothing but happiness.

"Hello my love," she said.

"Wh... what?"

"What's wrong?" Her smile disappeared and her face became concerned.

"Uh, why did you call me that?"

"What?" she said, confused for a second. "My love? I am... not sure, it just felt right."

"Do you remember what happened last night?"

"I do, and it was wonderful... Wait, do you regret what happened?"

"I... No, but yes. Do you remember at the end, did anything happen?"

"You mean the offer?" Her eyes blinked a few times. "It was the strangest thing, I was... riding the pleasure you gave me, when I felt a question shoot into my mind, almost as if I could read the words in front of my face. It asked me if I would be yours. I accepted it, then the pleasure exploded inside me more than anything I had ever felt before."

I sighed. "I need to tell you something and I don't know how you are going to take it. They tricked you."

"Who did?" She asked.

I went over my conversation with Vex. Everything he told me, but rather than be upset or angry, she seemed calm and accepting through the whole thing.

Finally, when I finished, she spoke. "It's okay. Oddly, I do not feel any different... or that this is a bad thing."

"How can you say that? They... I... we took away your free will. Wait, it's the... geas or control magic or whatever, you probably can't control it. I am going to put my hand on your forehead, please do not resist me."

She nodded.

I did what Vex had told me about, focusing on my ability to release her.

Her face contorted in pain from my touch. "It... it really hurts."

"I know, and I am so sorry. Just try to hold on for a few minutes. If this is working right, it should disrupt the hold I have over you temporarily. I can offer you your freedom from my control, but there is a catch. You will lose your power and become a normal human again. Please, consider this... I don't want you to be a slave because of my poor decisions," I said, almost pleading.

She shook her head; the pain obviously became unbearable. "No, I will... stick by... my choice. I will be yours. Please, stop."

Releasing the disruption, I sighed. I had failed. Vex told me you only had one shot to release someone from the geas, and if they did not take it. "I am so sorry, Tyla. I—"

I couldn't speak anymore, just laying on my back, head now on the floor, and closed my eyes. Not sure what to do next.

A few moments later, Tyla recovered from the pain. She climbed on top of me, her legs straddling the sides of my chest, still naked. She gazed down into my eyes. "Don't do this to yourself, it was my choice. I may not have known exactly what I chose at the moment, but I am not angry that it did. Even when you... disrupted this connection between us, I felt my place was with you. This way, they can never turn me into one of Seir's servants. I know you will always keep me safe. I felt it when we connected last night."

I almost argued with her. I wanted to tell her the difference between love and lust. What may have been a survival instinct that cried out she needed protection, or a thousand other things people convinced themselves it was love. But none of it mattered anymore. She may have made the choice, but I still enslaved someone to me.

Even if she had a point about her being safe from anyone else doing the same.

Noticing my hesitation, she reached down and pulled my face so that we were again making eye contact. "Derrick, this is my choice. I want this." She said, her words almost forceful.

"I... understand. Give me some time to process this, though. Okay?"

She nodded and leaned forward, kissing me briefly on the lips, then shifted so she was laying down cuddled up against my side.

I was going to have to live with this, but I promised myself that I would treat her with the respect and dignity she deserved, although she would probably do anything I asked of her.

CHAPTER 14

— • —

POWER

Tyla, deciding she was not having any of my poor mood, experimented on me using her mouth to cheer me up.

I must admit; it worked. She was not the most skilled, but she made up for it with an enthusiasm that spoke to the Neanderthal DNA in my nature.

"How do you feel?" Tyla asked after getting dressed.

"Better... but I'll be honest, free will is important to me. I spent years with a personal vendetta against manipulating assholes and I hate that I became one... even unintentionally."

"Derrick," she said, "If not for you, I would have been captured and enslaved against my will. Not to mention what those men would have done to me before that. I have felt freer with you running through the forest with no food than I ever was in my mother's estate where I lived in a gilded cage."

She came over to me and encircled me with her arms, looking up at me with a smile.

"I'll... get over this eventually," I said. "Just might take a while."

Tyla lifted on her tiptoes and kissed me on the lips. "Good."

"Alright, let's clean up. I figure we can spend a day here training before it's time we head to civilization and stock up. Stay in a city or town if we can, run if we need to. First, I am itching to try out these powers I have."

Tyla nodded. "I have never felt so much power flow through me before... I may now know why Au—I must remember she is not my aunt anymore. Why Josephina may have sought out Seir. This is almost... no it is addicting, like it rewards me with serving you in any way you desire."

I felt odd at her statement and ignored it for now. Instead, we cleaned up and moved over to the empty hot tub looking hole in the ground. "Vex did not explain how to do this, just what it was. Can you tell me how it works?"

Tyla walked up next to me, putting her hand out in front of her. "There are two types of water magic, as they have taught me in the academy, the internal and then external."

I nodded. "Is there a difference in how they work?"

"No, not really, at least not with water. I can't say about the other types. I was always good with the finesse, not the brute strength, so I could easily use the already high concentrations of water inside the body. It was much harder to get the water in the air to do my bidding. However, with this newfound energy I feel... let me try it."

She closed her eyes and put her palm over the hole. Soon, water appeared to pour from her hand into the bottom like a faucet. It was only about an inch wide, but she held it for several minutes before stopping.

I caught her before she fell. "You alright?"

"Hmm?" she shook her head. "I mean yes, I just... exhausted myself. That was probably ten times what I could have done last night if I were to guess. I can actually feel myself recharging already, much faster than before."

I closed my eyes. "Yes, I can feel the small drain of power going from my core into you. Minor, but it is there."

"We should be careful in the future then, until we can study how much you have to give."

"Vex wasn't specific, but he said it increases with each of those who... bond to me. Though I don't plan on adding anyone to test it."

"Derrick, you should really reconsider. While a man with multiple women is taboo in this world, I would be fine with it, especially if it leads to you getting stronger."

"No promises, it's not that I am against multiple women... Where I came from, everyone talked about being monogamous, but most wanted multiple partners, at least in secret. My problem is with the cost that comes with it, to those that would join. I cannot see myself letting someone make that choice to be a slave to my whims."

"I understand, just... keep an open mind to the possibility."

Rather than answer, I changed the subject, "So tell me what to do to make water shoot out of my hand."

She shot me a look but let me have my way.

"Let's first start with the water in your body, it's easier to start with and you can heal yourself if you need to with it. Then you can learn to manipulate it in others, and we can worry about the water in the air later."

I shrugged, "Fair, is that how they taught you?"

"Yes, I am actually excited that I have the power to use what I have been struggling with in school." She smiled at that last bit.

"What do I do first?"

"Let's sit down, touching my knees to yours first."

I sat, crossing my legs like I did as a school kid so many years ago. Our knees touched, and we smiled at each other.

"Close your eyes," Tyla said. "First, I am going to push my power into you, and I want you to sense it, see how I use it to move through your body. Do not do anything yet. Just sense, we do not want you to accidentally create a blood clot or something. But this will allow you to see inside yourself using the water magic.

I felt it as the tingling returned to my body. Unlike before, I could tell what she was doing with it rather than just a general sense of it being present. I followed her power as she moved it up my arm and into my chest. She slowly made her way down my stomach and then to my...

"Whoa, there," I said, opening my eyes in shock.

She was looking at me with an enormous smile on her face.

"Sorry, I couldn't help it,"

"Where did this girl come from?" I laughed. "Funny, but let's do some training first. We have time for the rest after."

She nodded with a smirk, "Sorry, I don't know if it was because it was my first with a man or what you flooded me with, but... I cannot stop thinking inappropriate thoughts. I will try to focus."

We closed our eyes again. This time she did not use her senses to feel me up, but I promised myself to return that favor as soon as I figured out how.

"Now focus here on this blood vessel in your foot. I want you to use your own senses to bring it into your mind's eye. It could take a while, but this is where we shall start. It is just a minor part in your extremity, easily fixed if we should mess up."

I nodded and focused, letting my mind wander into the sensation. After several minutes of trying, I seemed no closer than I was before.

"This took me a week to master this exercise when I first started," Tyla said. "Do not let frustration slow you down, it takes as long as it takes."

I took a deep breath and settled in for the long haul.

"Are you ready to go?" I asked, putting the bag on my back and tugging onto the straps.

"I am. How is your arm?"

I sighed, grabbing the bridge of my nose. "You could have warned me before you cut me, you know."

She laughed. "Then you would have over-thought it. Half of our magic is the ability to do it without thinking. Besides, it was just a minor scratch with a knife."

"You call that a scratch? Fine, but it still sucked. On Earth, that would have needed stitches at the minimum."

"You did very well. I am astonished at your speed of learning. You did in a day what I took weeks to learn."

"Honestly, I think our connection is giving me more than just access to your power, it's like the connection between us is... building."

"Yes, I can't explain it either. I can almost sense you... feel you when I am not looking."

"Well, we are pretty much stuck with each other now." I reached over and grabbed her in a hug. "Thank you for being so understanding."

We kissed, and it started building.

"You are going to make me take off your clothes again if you don't stop." She said when we came up for air.

"Mmm, you're right, this is worse than the last time I was in my early twenties. Let's hike, it will give us something to look forward to when we camp next."

I spent the entire day yesterday practicing my newfound magical skills... and other things of a more intimate nature with Tyla. I finally figured out how to push the cells in the affected parts of my body to heal faster.

It wasn't quite my idea of magical healing. Things did not just glow and then heal like a video game. However, being able to heal a cut to perfect skin in ten minutes was better than several weeks of natural healing.

The water molecules themselves did not really heal the wound, but because water made up every cell, I could... convince it to return to the way it was before the damage.

Honestly, it made little sense to me either. It really was me focusing enough to tell the cells to go back to their former location and shape, and they somehow did.

"So, does a water... mage?" I said, looking at her in question as we walked towards the cave exit.

She shook her head. "Since you are the first man... Well, you are a Demigod, but let us not tell anyone that just yet. Those with magic are women, so they are all Chosen, not mages. I am not sure what we would call you if that term would not apply without saying Demigod. The Chosen are classified by training and power. It goes Apprentice, which is where I was before you... filled me up." She said and smirked at me. "Then initiate, adept, lady, mistress, and finally matriarch. Though the commoners tend to just call us all witches. Most Chosen consider it a derogatory term and some of them will beat a commoner for saying it in their presence."

I rolled my eyes at her joke. "I heard what you said there. Anyway, does a water mage, and yes, that's what I am going to call it, live forever? It seems my skin is the same as it was before the cut. The color even matches."

"We can live longer, and others seek us for age rejuvenation and can actually make a lot of coin doing that. But we are not immortal like the gods, or even ageless mortals like the Demigods. My grandmother, the former Matriarch of Blackrun before my mother, she was also strong in the water element, lived to be one hundred and forty before she died. She looked much younger than that, but even the magic fails, eventually."

"Good to know, honestly I should have asked Vex if I was going to age as a human or demi." We reached the entrance to the cave, and I peeked out of the opening. No movement caught my eye, and I moved forward. "Keep your spear out and ready just in case—" A snap sound came from somewhere up the canyon behind a tree.

"Down!" I shouted, and pushed Tyla back into the cave.

Time slowed for me as I saw the arrow coming towards me. It was still moving fast, but like a slow ball rather than a speeding bullet.

I stepped to the side and knocked it from the air with my makeshift spear staff.

"Hold! Gods damn it! No one shoot!" a male voice said as he stepped out into view.

"I am not here for you... they should not have fired that arrow, and I am sorry for that. I want the girl, give her to us and you can go free with a reward for her capture. She is a wanted fugitive by the new lord of the human territories and the Matriarchs of Nitre and Black-run."

When he finished, I noticed two more archers step out of the trees and pointed their knocked arrows at me. Four of them, two of us.

Ah fuck.

CHAPTER 15

— ◦ —

AMBUSH

I put my back to the cavern entrance as I gazed around at each of the four men. Each had a peculiar tattoo on their forehead that looked like an upside-down triangle in a circle. My gut told me that it was a Roxannez symbol, but I could not be sure why I thought that, or what it meant.

"Stern? Is that you?" Tyla called out from the cavern before I could reply.

"Don't come out of the cave," I whispered.

The man who had spoken stepped forward. "Yes, apprentice Tyla, I am sorry about this, but Lord Seir has tasked me with tracking you down and apprehending you."

"You would betray her memory so?" Tyla asked.

"I have not betrayed her. For she is alive and issued her own order personally besides Seir's before I left. I must tell you she is in his service now."

Stern bowed his head, and I could see a little shame on his face.

"What?" Tyla asked.

I quickly backed up into the cave to grab hold of her and keep her back.

"Stay here. We will figure this out. Just don't give him what he wants."

"He corrupted my mother!" she screamed.

I struggled to keep her back with one arm while keeping my guard up in case any of the men tried something.

"They have ordered me to guarantee your safety on pain of death should I fail. Your mother stated she will accept you back with open arms and ensure your... transition into Sier's service will be painless."

Tyla was breathing hard, she stopped struggling and was now staring at the ground. I wasn't sure she was in a state to be much help.

"Tyla," I whispered. "You are not going with them. I'll deal with this, but I need you to promise me you will stay in the cave. Can you do that for me?"

"I... Don't... Order me to do so... please! I am not sure I have the will on my own," she pleaded.

I hesitated, just for a second.

Do I cross that line?

I swallowed hard. "I order you to stay in the cave, unless your life is in jeopardy, then you can use your best judgment."

A shudder went through Tyla's body. "Yes... Master."

I hated that term, but I didn't have time to correct it. "I'll be back soon."

I stepped back out to the mouth of the cave, relieved to see that no one had changed their position or charged me.

"I am going to have to refuse your request. The lady does not want to work for Seir."

The man nodded, as if expecting that. Was that approval on his face?

"I will give you one last chance to reconsider," he said. "I have been told to use whatever force is necessary. You will not survive."

I reached into my pocket and cupped an item in my right hand. shifting the spear into my left while I did so.

"Not happening," I replied, then lowered my stance.

Ramping up my newfound ability to affect my power, my perception of time slowed just a bit compared to before. Hopefully, I could use it in the entire fight.

Stern's voice slowed in his response. "So... Be... It... Fire!" he yelled, his voice slow and deep from the time dilation.

As he sounded out the last word, I pushed off the ground and threw the object in my hand to the nearest archer, adjusting my throw along the way to line it up.

One of the Panzite crystals I had removed from the cave rocketed towards the archer and hit him in the face.

BOOM!

"Shit," I yelled as I hit the ground in a roll, my ears now ringing.

I had not expected it to explode like that.

The archer dropped to the ground without his head as I started healing my ear drums.

The other archer on that side took cover from the explosion with his hands over his ears, but the last one on Stern's side pulled back the string and fired.

The arrow came at me with a twang and sped at me like an average little leaguer's fast ball. Not slow enough for me to knock down, but I evaded it easily enough.

I countered by taking my spear and throwing it as hard as I could at him, my increased strength sending it forward like a bullet.

It hit him dead center, and he folded forward in half from the impact and his body flew backwards.

I pulled my dagger and spun, putting the archer and stern on my left and right. Releasing my power of time perception for a moment to talk to them.

"You two want to run away, or should we keep playing?" I asked.

Hoping they ran for it, I used my tricks and now it was a little more dicey to guarantee my win. I was hoping the shock and awe would send them scattering.

"Fuck this!" the archer said as he dropped his bow and ran.

He stopped after half a second and reached up to his head.

"Arghhghh!" he screamed from pain, rolling around on the ground.

What the fuck?

"It's the symbol on our heads," Stern said, somehow standing there the whole time and staying calm. "It ties us to Seir making sure we cannot bend or break his orders without extreme pain. If it doesn't kill him, he will wish he was dead for several minutes at least. It is to remind you of the cost of displeasing your lord."

He sounded somber, as though having experienced it.

"Are you a Demigod too?" he asked me with a smile on his face.

"Does it matter?" I replied with a question of my own.

He shook his head. "No, she is still coming with us, and I still have to kill you."

"You seem pretty confident in that."

"Because I know something you don't,"

A whoosh coming from behind me was my only warning as a fireball slammed into my shoulder. I spun from the impact as the pain spread throughout my body.

I had to focus on the water in my shoulder so that it told me how bad it was. It burned me all up and down my back. The pain was so bad that it threatened to send me into a blackout.

I rolled on the ground to put out the fire, pushing myself up against the rock face near the entrance to the cave. The stench of burned skin invaded my nose, and I knew I was in trouble.

I gazed at where the fireball came from, where a woman with dirty blond hair stepped out of the underbrush.

I was honestly not sure how I did not know she was there. Her greenish dress, with a leather vest I would have to struggle to call armor, only really served to amplify her rather massive bust.

How did I miss her?

"Impressive... for a man," the slutty woods-woman wanna-be said as she put a device back in her satchel.

"Susan!" Tyla called. "Is that you too?"

"Yes lover!" Susan replied giddily. "Come out where we can see you."

"I... cannot. I am sorry. Why are you here?"

"To bring you to your new lord. Seir is most... generous to those who serve him well. I have learned this lesson entirely," she said, a knowing smile on her face.

"Did he turn you too?" Tyla asked, despondent.

"Turn me? No, he freed me! I never knew the power and pleasure I was missing out until I met that man."

I could hear the sobbing in the cave.

I tested my shoulder, able to move it once more. If they could keep talking for just a few more minutes while I focused...

"Come Tyla, he promised your mother you would join our harem. We could be together again. I know how much you loved what I did to you those nights we were alone."

Stern walked up behind Susan and stood next to her. "Miss Tyla, please come out, or I'll have to kill your protector out here."

A blast of water the size of a bowling ball exited the cave, striking Stern in the chest and sending him backwards.

Tyla marched out of the cave, a grim look on her face. "You will not harm him!"

"My little Tyla has grown stronger, I see," Susan said, an evil smirk on her face.

"I have grown in a lot of ways since we last sparred."

Tyla shot another ball of water at Susan, who jumped back and put up a narrow wall of flame to eat up the projectile of water. An explosion of steam, the result of the two forces meeting.

Out of time, I jumped up, intense pain running up and down my left shoulder, but it was the best I was going to get. I slowed time once more but could feel my energy depleting to zero. Hopefully, it was just enough to give me the edge I needed.

I rushed forward and tackled Stern to the ground before he could launch his crossbow bolt at Tyla. I heard the crack of the crossbow hitting the ground and the single arrow firing with a twang in the small canyon.

A shriek sounded from a woman's mouth, and I panicked for a second. Looking over, expecting to find the bolt stuck into Tyla.

But it was Susan on the ground. A bolt rammed through her back angled so that it pierced her heart and lungs. She had dropped to her knees from the impact.

I looked down at Stern and hit him on the side of the head with my elbow. He went out instantly and I stood up in pain.

Turning around, I found Tyla holding Susan's nearly lifeless body in her hands, which were glowing from the power she had pushed into the woman.

I walked up gently and watched as the life drained out of Susan's eyes. "Don't go, Susan! He can give you back your life."

Susan let out a single smile before she released her last breath and died.

"I... couldn't save her," Tyla sobbed through her tears.

I reached out and grabbed her shoulder, letting her know I was there as she cried and not bothering with any words as I focused on comforting her and healing my wounds.

CHAPTER 16

INTERLUDE - THE CARRIAGE RIDE

"I believe they will not last more than a month before we force them to surrender, my lord," General Taimana said.

"Excellent news, General. No need to risk your men in a direct assault, use siege equipment only. This is the last of the human armies that oppose us, and we will teach them the price of resisting my rule. So, ignore any offers of surrender and let them starve to death. None come out alive, do you understand?"

"I do, Lord."

"Carry on." The general saluted and pulled out of the window before stepping off the moving carriage to go about his duties.

The large carriage they were in continued its rocking on the cobblestone paved roadway on its way to the capital of Nitre.

"Does it bother you I am about to let your only remaining husband die of starvation, Patricia?" Seir asked the woman in the seat across from him, an evil smirk on his face.

With no hesitation, Patricia said, "No, my lord. Your happiness is all that concerns me now."

"Good." He smiled, taking pleasure in her subservience. "Take off your dress and service me with your—"

Pain gripped Seir. He turned pale as he grappled with it.

"What is it, husband?" Josephina asked with alarm from the seat next to Patricia.

Seir gasped for a few more seconds, and he pushed the feeling of pain away. It was a feeling he did not like in the slightest.

"Susan is dead," he croaked.

"What does that mean?" Patricia asked, the pitch in her voice rising.

"It means," Seir said through his heavy breathing. "That we either underestimated the power of your daughter or Susan was a stupid twit that is better off dead. Now follow your command, Patricia!"

Patricia did not hesitate as she began untying the ties that held her dress in place.

"Get me, Albris!" Seir yelled out of the window.

"Yes, lord!" a male voice sounded and ran off.

Seir pulled his cock out of his pants. "All the way to the base this time."

Patricia nodded and got to her knees while she tied her long black hair in a ponytail. "Yes, lord," she said before she put Seir's still soft manhood in her mouth.

The carriage rocked as a man climbed up onto the sideboard. "You summoned me, Lord Sier?"

The body builder of a man poked his head through the carriage window. Glancing around at the occupants, only briefly stopping on Patricia before focusing on Seir.

"Yes, Albris, the concubine I sent after this one's," He said as he patted Patricia's head, "daughter has failed and is dead. The tracker I sent is likely dead as well. I need you to find another tracker and go after them."

The large man brushed his hand over his closely cropped hair, flexing his muscles as he considered this. "Do I get to keep her this time like you promised?"

Seir felt the sensation as Patricia gagged deeply on his shaft, a knowing smile formed on his lips. "No, I have promised that I would take her as my own. However, you can pick any three you choose from the holding facility at the academy as recompense."

Patricia became enthusiastic in her bobbing movements, bringing her hand and encircling the base of his shaft to let Seir know she approved of his words.

"Yes, lord. I will hunt her down and bring her to you immediately."

"Mm-mm," Seir moaned, unable to help himself. Finally starting to relax after the shock and anger, he continued. "Good, thank you. You may go."

Albris left the same way that General Taimana did without another word.

"You coddle her," Josephina said, reaching over and caressing Patricia's shapely thighs before reaching up and rubbing her womanly folds.

"Mmmmmm," Patricia moaned deeply, then backed her ass back into the wandering hand as she was caressed by her lover.

"Only because you asked me to, though." Seir paused. "I have to admit she is an immensely powerful addition. My power grew significantly when we added her to our harem... and you were right, she is also excellent at using her mouth. Very relaxing."

"I did. Speaking of, may I?" Josephina asked as she sat back, hiked up her dress, and spread her legs, exposing herself.

Seir nodded and pulled Patricia up from his manhood and pushed her towards Josephina.

Without a word or complaint, Patricia wiped her mouth of the drool that fell off her chin. She then moved to the other side of the carriage, sticking her tongue into the waiting slit that was presented to her. She followed quickly with a shake of her butt to announce she was ready for Seir's attention.

"May I join you, my lord?" Miranda's voice called from above the carriage.

"Not this time. Keep watch. You will have your turn later," Seir replied out the window as he got out of his seat to line up to his new target.

He thrust inside of Patricia's waiting womanhood, eliciting a stifled moan of pleasure from the brunette woman.

"Thank you, my lord," she said when she pushed away from Josephina for just a moment before diving back in.

"I take care of my concubines. Be prepared to turn around and give me your mouth for your reward," Seir said with a smile as he pumped hard and fast into Patricia.

"Mmm-Hmmm," Patricia mumbled and nodded since her tongue was quite busy.

Seir gazed into Josephina's eyes while they both enjoyed their new toy. Susan was but a fading memory.

CHAPTER 17

CLEANING UP THE MESS

I cut the man's throat without a second thought. Try to hurt me or mine and you die, that simple. The archer was still out from the pain earlier and didn't even scream as I killed him.

Whatever this pain compliance thing was, and whoever thought of it was an idiot.

I walked towards Stern, intent on doing the same thing to him, not even bothering to wipe off the new knife I gained from the archer. Much better than the shit daggers we had before.

"Wait, master!" Tyla said as I grabbed his hair to pull up his head and end his life.

I froze.

She got up, setting her former friend gently on the ground before doing so, and walked towards me.

"Tyla," I whispered. "I am not sure I am comfortable with you calling me that."

"I am sorry m — Derrick," she said, still sniffling. "I did not even realize I was saying it... but it felt natural to me. As if I get pleasure from calling you that."

I shook my head, still holding Stern's hair with my knife, ready to cut his throat. "I... dislike the way this came about. Eventually I'll adjust... but you are too important to me to see you as anything but an equal. Please try?"

"Yes, my love," she said.

"I can live with that. Why did you want me to stop?"

"Stern was my mother's concubine. It was a secret to all but a few. She was very fond of him, though. If they coerced him into his loyalty to Seir, maybe we can free him?"

"V—our contact didn't say anything about the loyalty oaths, which I believe this mark on his head represents." I barely stopped myself from saying Vex's name aloud.

"All I am asking is we wait for him to wake up and then try. I just find it hard to believe that he would betray my mother willingly."

"Ask him yourself. He has been awake since I lifted up his head."

Stern sighed.

"Fuck," he said. "I... can't say anything without risking the oath's curse, the only time I tried, I was out for an hour from the pain." He spoke the words slowly, as though testing each one before he said it.

"Fine. I am going to try something. It will hurt... a lot. If you resist, I'll kill you."

"I understand. I kept telling myself that I was waiting for my chance to strike, that keeps it at bay. Please hurry."

I nodded. "Tyla, would you get me the leather cords out of the bag?"

Tyla did as I asked. Without another word, I tied up Stern. His eyes closed the whole time while he hummed.

Satisfied my knots would give me a few seconds to work with, I spoke. "Okay, do your best not to resist. This is going to suck for you."

I reached my hand out to his forehead and pushed my power into the symbol on his head, hoping that was the best way to go about it.

"Arghhhhhhhhh!" Stern screamed and struggled against his bindings.

Tyla pushed him back down and held his arms. Finally, I felt my power come fully into contact with another. Stern moaned in pain but stopped struggling as the two powers fought over his very soul.

My will battled the Mark of Seir, for I now knew that is what it was. It was Seir's will, pushed into a mortal that agreed to serve him, or at least the representation of his will. Not as powerful as the Demigod himself, but stronger than anything I had ever experienced.

Sweat beaded on my forehead as I focused on the mark. In my mind's eye, I saw a glowing ring clamped down around the midsection of a standing representation of Stern, holding him in place and leaving him no room to move on his own. He was screaming silently in pain in this dream state I found myself in temporarily.

I redoubled the energy and imagined myself pulling at the ring, trying to break it in half. But no matter the effort, it resisted the attempts I made. Knowing I only had seconds to figure this out, I panicked a little.

In frustration, I reached back and used all the metaphysical body weight I could manage to punch the glowing ring dead center, putting every scrap of energy I could muster into the swing.

It shattered into a thousand pieces... and I blacked out instantly.

I awoke with a start a few minutes later, ready for a fight. Tyla pressed both her hands on me and pressed down, stopping me at the sitting position.

"Calm my love, he is still out, the glyph on his head is gone."

I blinked my eyes and looked at Stern, his body had all the signs of passing out this time. I relaxed a bit.

"That was rough," I said. "Not sure doing that regularly is going to be possible."

"Unless you get stronger."

"I, uh... you know how I feel about adding more people. If it was just a sex thing? Maybe. But the cost..." I trailed off.

"I know, I... part of me likes the idea for purely selfish reasons, you may need the power to free my mother."

I sighed. She was right. If just freeing a man from an oath took more than I had, how was I going to break free a bond that strong? Stern's oath was just a fragment of a percent of Seir's power.

"You have a point. I promise not to close the door on it, but the circumstances would have to be... perfect. I am sorry."

"Don't be. I understand. I will try not to push."

She leaned forward and kissed me on the lips, lingering. Even with Stern passed out three feet from me, it took willpower to resist taking her when I pushed away.

"Later," I said, letting her know with my eyes that I meant it.

"Not sorry," she said with a smirk.

"You seem different, Tyla, almost more confident since we... joined."

"I..." she began then paused, looking pensive for a moment. "You may be right. The part of me that always tells me that I am not good enough or not strong enough has been absent lately. I have not thought about it, but now that you have mentioned something, I feel almost, and this will sound odd, free."

I reached out and grabbed her chin with the crook of my finger, pointing her face towards me. "I don't like what I did to you, Tyla, but no matter what, with me you are always free."

She nodded and squeezed her eyes, a single tear escaping. Before I could ask her what's wrong, a smile broke out on her face. "Thank you, my love. I can feel you mean that... here." She tapped her hand on her chest.

We kissed one more time, a show of affection and happiness rather than passion. We broke apart much easier, both of us smiling.

"Good. I want it to stay that way. But now for business, I need to watch Stern when he wakes up, would you gather anything that might be of use from the bodies... and I am sorry about Susan, we will give her a proper burial, or however that is done here. If you want me to take care of that."

"Burial is the accepted practice for most commoners, then a few words to the gods usually follow. However, for the Chosen we usually burn the body. It's about becoming one with the gods once again."

I nodded. "I don't know if that is a good idea. We don't know how many more search parties are still out there."

"None," Stern said with a moan following. "Oh, gods, that hurt."

He paused for a second and pushed up on his elbows, looking like a man after an all-night bender. "Seir or his lieutenants recalled the other search parties to quash minor uprisings and hunt other Chosen that escaped the academy. They judged us as... sufficient to hunt down a half-trained witch. None of us thought she would be with you."

"That's good news but... I have to admit I am still not entirely sure I can trust you Stern."

"You shouldn't," he said simply.

"Derrick?"

"Yes?"

"May I test him for truthfulness? I want to believe him, but you are right, that we should be sure."

I smacked my forehead. "You're right, I forgot about that. I trust you. You don't need my permission for such things."

She wrinkled her brow. "I actually think I do. I don't think I could touch another man intentionally without your permission given the... changes. But I thank you for your trust."

She reached forward and placed her arm on a very confused Stern. "What did you mean by that? Wait, are you bonded to him?" Stern asked.

Tyla closed her eyes and simply nodded at the man.

"You really are a Demi?" Stern turned to me.

"Yes, and no. I am human but have been granted a—" I searched my brain for words "Boon? Or something like that which lets me share some of their abilities."

I stopped to give him a hard look. "I warn you, though, I am only telling you that much because if you fail her test, I will kill you where you stand to keep that secret. I may yet anyway because she is that important to me."

He nodded, his eyes wide. "Yes... Lord?"

"No, none of that. I am just Derrick, well I actually prefer Derk," I said and gave Tyla an eye, even though hers were closed.

Even without seeing me, she smiled. "You could order me... Master."

I laughed and shook my head. "I am glad you can still be a brat at least. That makes this easier to accept. Speaking of orders, how did you leave the cave when I ordered you to stay?"

"They were going to kill you... if you die, I die. You told me to use my best judgment to save my life."

"Glad I did. You saved our lives today."

"Thank you, my love."

"I am sorry to interrupt. Do you... want me to swear an oath to you as well. Like I did for Seir?" Stern said, the confidence he had shown before now totally gone.

"I..." I stopped and considered it. I knew little about the process, but I had a feeling deep down that I could do it. "Not sure yet. Let me think about it. If I can figure out a way for it to just ensure that you keep our secrets, with no other side effects, we can try it. So far I know little about what I can do or even if I can do it for you once I remove the mark of Seir."

"I understand."

"I am ready, my love."

"Okay, Stern, are you loyal to Seir?"

"No," he said simply. Tyla nodded, her eyes still closed.

"Did you betray Tyla's mother?" I said to gauge him.

"Yes," he looked down in shame. "I was afraid and knew I couldn't help her. I wanted to, I... think it was me that caused her to give in to Seir's offer. When I turned my back on her—" He sobbed.

"She gave up because of me. I saw it in her eyes... I am why she turned into Seir's plaything." He finally finished.

I stood there in silence, waiting for Tyla to answer.

"You are telling the truth, I... don't blame you, Stern, though I might have before I met my... love." Tyla added, catching herself from using the word I disliked.

"Do you intend to betray our trust?" I asked Stern.

"No, I will keep your secrets to the grave."

Tyla nodded one more time, and I gently shook her shoulder, letting her know I was happy with what we had.

"Okay, Stern, you get to live. Congratulations. The question is, what do we do with you now?"

"If I may make a suggestion?" Stern asked.

I nodded.

"I will give you most of our supplies here and at camp up the ridge where we stayed while waiting for you to come out. Then, if you will allow me, I would really like to head back to Black-Run and get my sister out of there. Provided I can survive that, I could meet you in the south, it should remain free for a while at least."

I snapped my fingers. "I have a couple of questions now that you say that. First, why did you stay outside and not come and get us if you were there long enough to set up camp?"

"We... Susan said something was keeping her from entering. She did not know what it was or how. The rest of us did not want to risk a witch... I'm sorry, Chosen's power without her. So we waited after I tracked you here."

"Hmmm, that makes sense, I think. Next question. Why are they moving so slow and not blitzing the south? My military senses say that is stupid to let them prepare."

"It's mostly conjecture and hearsay about what Susan talked about. She overheard a lot and was always around him. First is that Seir worries about the factions of Demigods invading the human lands and doesn't want to spread too thin or waste manpower. The second is that the remnants of your mother's army refused to submit and fortified themselves at the old fortress of Maetrine in the Rochden mountains to the north."

"Who leads them?" Tyla asked, a note of hope in her voice.

"I don't know my mistress." Stern said, shaking his head. "Susan never spoke of people individually other than Seir. I got the feeling she did not think of anyone as individuals and only could focus on how she fit into his... harem. Most of what she said was how important to him he was, and he would ask her about these things. Complaining endlessly about missing his... comfort."

"She always was kind of selfish, even with me. But I cared for her," Tyla said somberly.

I wrapped my arms around her from behind. "It's okay, we can do that next."

Stern stood up from the ground, having untied himself. "What do you want me to do, lord Derrick?"

"Again, just Derrick, or Derk, really. I have an idea to ensure your silence and protect us just in case you're captured. Part of me is morally against this and the other part of me says she is too important to me to risk." I pointed at Tyla with my thumb when I finished.

"I understand and will accept your oath."

I took a deep breath, "Here goes nothing."

I reached out, not touching his forehead like a self-obsessed asshole, and instead reached out to the inner meaty part of his forearm and pushed my power into it.

Time froze, and I could see the mind's eye representation of Stern sitting in front of me. How was I doing this? I honestly couldn't say. It was kind of like breathing, it just happened if you let it and didn't think about it too much or over think it.

Someone told me once that ignorance is bliss, and my goal was to be a happy mother fucker about this.

Instead, I studied the representation of Stern. He was smiling in my image, and I could feel his happiness at being free of Sier's control. His... soul, if that was what I was looking at, was still bleeding in several spots from the damage my blow did to him earlier. However, it was mending.

I concentrated on the meaning of the word oath, on how it fit into my paradigm of life. The importance that it held to me every time I gave one. I thought of my oath to the Alliance Marine corps, back when I was a kid and didn't know any better. I just wanted to make a difference. I thought of my oath as a Boston Police officer, the drive to protect those that couldn't protect themselves.

I even made an oath to Tyla right there, to ensure that she was safe and as happy as I could make her for whatever time we had together.

When these feelings and thoughts coalesced in my mind, a glowing ball of light appeared before me.

It was what I could use to bind him to my will. Now that I studied the ball, I could see that it was my will and representation of my power.

Instead of making it a ring like Seir, I made it a small strap like a belt. Flexible, but tight fitted. If he betrayed me, he would feel a light squeeze that would warn him first, rather than incapacitate. But he would only get one warning. The light squeeze was just a small warning to a massive one. Designed to kill instantly. No pain, no further warning, and no mercy. I nodded at this.

If my understanding was correct, he would get a small squeeze in his chest if he did something that I would consider betraying my trust, and if continued, he would die.

I breached the time dilation and spoke to Stern. "Do you accept this oath of loyalty, to not betray mine or Tyla's trust? You will have one mild warning before death. That is the price."

"Yes," Stern said, and time froze again when I demanded it.

I knew I did not have to tell him as much as I did. All I needed was for him to agree to it and I could have done whatever I wanted to him.

But that was not how I operated.

I wanted safety, but I was going to be honest with it. I pushed the power around Stern, and it gripped him like a loose belt at the chest level. Right around his heart and lungs. He could bend it, which was a risk, but if he considered breaking it, then it would tighten into a ball faster than his heart and lungs would stop.

The belt, now properly in place, I had to set the anchor of my will. It would be a small sliver of myself I was leaving to watch him. Seir used those glyphs, but I did not have one myself. I just hoped something would happen, and I tried to finalize it.

Something happened, it just was not what I thought would be.

It... wanted me to design something. Again, this was hard to explain, even to myself. This one was more like knowing what your dog wanted just based on the way he barked at you. You know when they want out to go to the bathroom or are hungry without them ever speaking words to you. You just understood their behavior.

I willed it into a design that came easily to me. It was cheesy, if I were honest with myself, and more of a stick figure drawing than the art that symbol deserved, but I let it pass.

I don't think there is anyone alive here that would know what it was, and I don't think the gods gave a flying fuck.

I pulled out of the mental time and pulled my arm away from Sterns.

"It... it didn't hurt!" he said, relieved as he looked at his arm.

"I think I could have made it hurt, but I didn't."

Stern got red in the face. "That fucking asshole. He did it on purpose, then."

I couldn't help but chuckle a bit, not really at Stern's pain, but that this revelation surprised him.

"What is that glyph?" Tyla asked.

"It's... well, it's a stick figure of an Eagle and anchor and a globe," I said, tracing the lines I had used to stand for the eagle, or at least its wings. Then the cross with arrow shaped lines of the anchor. Finishing it off was a circle for the globe. "No chain. Unfortunately, it's the best I can do, apparently only simple shapes are allowed by whatever empowers me."

I glanced up at each of them. "I don't like that it is reminiscent of what an eight-year-old might doodle at school, but it's not like the dream state let me have crayons or anything." An old joke of eating them popped into my brain. I smiled.

Both Tyla and Stern looked at me with confusion.

Rather than answer their unspoken questions, I dropped Stern's arm. "Okay, do you have a map or something so we can plan?"

"I do at the camp L... Derk."

Smiling, I said. "Let's grab everything, then make a funeral pyre for Susan and then we can plan our next moves. We can stay another night in the—"

I froze.

"Where is the cave?" Tyla asked what I was about to.

"I... Don't know." As we all stood there shocked at its disappearance, now just a solid rock wall. The bag that Tyla left inside, along with the two slavers' batons I really should have equipped myself with, skillfully placed just outside where it used to be.

"Fuck," I said. "Guess we really are on our own out here now."

CHAPTER 18

— • —

ACKNOWLEDGEMENT OF TRUTH

"Before I forget, what was that shadow ball thing again?" I said as I cocked the action back, inspecting the appropriated crossbow.

We camped for the night in the cloak of another traveler's tree, and I really hoped these things were plentiful everywhere we went. They supplied a perfect place to hide from both people and the elements.

It had been two days since we burned Susan's body and a day since we split up with Stern.

"It's called the shadow's mantle. That one just happened to be using a ball of semi-precious metal as its focus. It is a construct of both the light element and the wind element. Though you could have had a simpler construct with just either. You could even use common items, but they won't last as long," Tyla said.

"How does it work?"

"I only have the basics. They do not teach specifics until your initiate year, but it requires a Chosen of at least the rank of adept, since that is when you can start imbuing objects with power. They specifically powered this one with both light and wind, so it took two people to make it. The light, which in this case creates darkness, shadows a person so they are harder to see. The wind will create a barrier of air that can dampen the sounds. It only has so much power, but anyone can use it, and it is usually awfully expensive."

"So that's how I missed her." I nodded my head, thinking back to when Susan surprised me, never even knew she was there.

"Yes, and it will help Stern get into the city without being noticed. Thank you for not questioning me, allowing him to have it, Master."

"Tyla, you know you don't have to call m—"

"Please? At least when we are in private? It... makes me feel... right? I don't know. Like I want to serve you and it gives me pleasure when I do."

"I am pretty sure that is just the bond."

"No," she shook her head. "Well, yes. But I have always had... fantasies about losing control to a lover. I just never had the courage to admit them to anyone. Until now."

"So, you like to be dominated?"

"Not... exactly, more like... I don't know, maybe just letting someone else in control? Just to make someone else happy by doing for them. They always groomed me to be a matriarch someday, and I hated it. I would rather let someone else be in charge and make them happy."

I sighed, but relented. "If it will make you happy when we are in private. I am not sure if it will be comfortable for me, though."

"If it still bothers you after a while, I will stop. My pet name for you almost makes me feel the same."

"My love?" I asked.

"Yes." She smiled at me.

I was silent for a second as I considered it. "Okay."

"Thank you, Master," she said and scooted closer to me, hugging my side as she laid her head on my shoulder. "Do you... love me, Master?"

"Huh?" I asked, surprised.

"You have not said it, and I was curious."

She was right. I hadn't said it, but not because it didn't cross my mind. "It's... complicated. I have been on this world for seven days. I have feelings so strong for you it makes what I felt about Jessica almost disappear. Everything from my previous life tells me that it should just be infatuation and lust."

I paused as she let me think of the next words before I continued. "I stop myself and wonder what is real. Is this me in love with you? Or is this me being forced to play the game of a supposed god who presided over the death of my world... and who knows what else."

I set down the crossbow and put my arm around the beautiful woman. She adjusted a bit and pushed into my side.

"You worry your love for me is created by another, and that my love for you is the same?"

"Yes... No? I... I don't know Tyla, I really don't know." I sighed in frustration. "That is not a reflection of you, it's just the situation I find myself in and haven't resolved in here." Tapping my head.

"Does it matter?" she asked.

"Does what matter?"

"Does it matter if it's real? I mean, to me it feels real. The love I feel for you is so strong that I would do anything you asked. I was beginning to feel this way before we bonded, then it only magnified a thousand-fold after we bonded. Is that a bad thing?"

I deflated. She was right. "No, I guess it doesn't. I... I do love you Tyla, I can't deny it. Nor do I want to. I just... don't like the idea of being used as a pawn in some chess game by beings so powerful they call themselves gods."

Tyla smiled and lifted off my shoulder, facing me with her pretty face and beautiful eyes. "Good, my Master, it's fine to hate the idea of being treated as a caged rat. But accept our love for what it is, even if it is forced. Love is too rare to waste, my mother would tell me as a girl." She leaned up and kissed me on the lips.

As our lips parted, I smiled. "You are beautiful, brilliant, and I absolutely do not deserve you." Which got her cheeks to glow the slightest hint of red as she smiled.

She kissed me again, this time going deeper, and pushed me back into the blanket we had set on the ground under the tree. Her fingers started wandering down my fresh shirt and light leather armor, plundered from the camp of those men we killed. She unwound the cords of each of the straps, never letting her lips lose contact with me.

I moved to help her.

"Nuh uh," she mumbled, shaking her head through our kiss before pulling back. "Just relax, let me take care of you."

"As you wish," I said, an image of a cheesy ancient movie going through my brain.

She undid the front of my shirt and then moved down to my pants, unleashing the drawstring to pull my rising monster out of its lair. Pushing my pants down just enough to give her unrestricted access to it.

She licked the tip of my cock and swirled it around. Teasing me with just the tip of her tongue, causing me to moan.

"You like that?" she asked.

"You know I do. This isn't the first time you've done that."

"It is not? Oh, then I better try new things," she said, a mischievous smile on her face.

I pulled the pack I found when I awoke in this world over near me and laid back on it, sitting up because I did not want to miss this show of her affection.

She licked my shaft up and down with her tongue, not putting it in her mouth, my toes of my bare feet curling from the sensation. As she did this, she shifted around so that she was now kneeling in between my widened legs, with my cock in front of her face.

Without further warning, she lifted and plunged her mouth down on my moistened shaft, engulfing almost three quarters of my length.

"Oh fuck," I said, the pleasure of the sensation flooding through my groin to my body.

I opened my eyes from their involuntary closure to see her looking up at me as she gagged around my girth.

She came up for air, a bit of drool hanging from her lips, and smiled. "Was that something you enjoyed?"

"I... did, immensely in fact."

"Good." she said and went back to it.

She did not go as far, but she continued to bob up and down on my shaft as I lost myself to the bliss that she was giving me. My neck lost its ability to keep my head lifted, and I set it back on the bag. I felt nothing but the sensation of her sucking on my cock.

Before I was ready, I felt the end coming. "Tyla, I am about to..." I tried to warn her, reaching to tap her on the head to give her a physical warning. She just kept going until I felt the explosion coming from my loins.

"Oh god!" I cried out as my seed blasted into her throat. Tyla pulled away from me, unable to hold it all in as it dripped from her lips. She wiped it off with her arm.

"Oh god, you came... a lot, Master," She said after she could speak again.

"I'm sorry. I tried to warn you."

"I wanted to. The other girls always said it was a weakness for a Chosen to consume the seed of a man. I... wanted to rebel a little, to be honest. Though I did not think it would actually taste... good."

"It does?" I asked, surprised. "That's... not what I have heard before."

"You taste good, a little salty, but it also creates a pleasure when I swallow it."

I laughed. "It's probably something the gods did to make you addicted to being bonded."

Tyla licked some of it off her hand and shrugged. "Either way."

"Come here," I said, and she climbed up my chest and cuddled with me. "Give me a second to recharge and it's your turn."

She snuggled into me a little more and nodded.

"Tyla?"

"Yes, Master?"

"Before we go much farther, and I realize we did not have a choice the first time, but is there birth control in this world?"

"You mean like a plant or a medicine? No, there is not, but it is incredibly difficult for Chosen to conceive a child. One joke at the academy is that we are so... needy for sex to increase our chances of getting pregnant. My mother and fathers had sex regularly. I, uh, heard them all the time in their tent when we were traveling together."

"All three together?"

Tyla nodded.

"Mind if I ask an awkward question that I shouldn't?"

"How do we know who the father is when a child is born?" she said, knowing my question before I asked.

I chuckled. "Yeah, fairly obvious, right?"

"Water magic would tell us at birth, from a Mistress level Chosen or above. Though when I was conceived, my mother only was with my father for months until it happened. To ensure his bloodline passed to at least one child."

"That makes sense. Though, to be on the safe side, I think I should... we called it pulling out on my world, does that translate?"

"Yes, do not put your seed inside me when you release."

"Yes, at least until we figure out some kind of stability. We don't need you pregnant right now."

She nodded. "Some water blessed Chosen like me can make good coins, helping women prevent children they otherwise would not want. It must be done within the first weeks of conception unless you are at the mistress level or above. As it requires significant amounts of power, something the gods put in place to ensure a healthy population. Before the fall, the Matriarchs and queens of the human lands also frowned upon it, as they wanted more children to help push our species into the unoccupied lands, at least before the other races did."

"I am really amazed at how many things the elemental powers you have can do. I really need to learn this water magic. It saved my life in the fight but... if I could have controlled it better, I could have gotten right back up when she hit me with that fireball."

"Susan was a year senior to me and close to adept. If she had mastered that, she might have been able to imbue an arrow with fire. It would have been much worse." Tyla shuddered at the thought.

"You can imbue weapons?"

"Yes, I was told it is much more efficient than direct casting. With water, it does not really do any good to imbue an arrow, but with fire, you can make an arrow a thousand degrees without burning the shaft to cinders. With air you can coat it in electricity so that even if you miss you can still stun. It gets more brutal with the more power and control you have. Not to mention that Earth elements can increase your strength and you can send it farther and faster."

"I really need to figure out how all this works. Can we spend some time each night going over it? After training in fighting and power use?"

"Yes, Master," Tyla said as she smiled. "We will also get some books when we get to Hills Crest."

"You said it was just a small town we were going to meet Stern and his family in. Will they have that kind of stuff?"

"It should still have some books and other supplies we need. We have enough coin now that we should be able to get plenty, even there. If not, then Riven Hold will definitely have it."

"Guess we will find out when we get there. Stern's map said we should be able to make it in about six days at a fast clip."

"Yes, Master," Tyla said, pulling down her shorts without preamble and climbing on top of me. "You promised me we would sate my needs next. May we begin?" she said sweetly.

She was right, even if the gods forced this upon us, it still felt great to be in love with such a sexy woman.

CHAPTER 19

— ⁘ —

HILLS CREST

We woke just inside the tree line across the clearing from the town of Hills Crest. No fire and only prepared rations, something else we had liberated from our would-be captors.

"Thank you for warming me this morning," Tyla said, a subtle blush on her face.

"You deserved a pleasant wake up, though I should have considered the noise."

"I'm sorry, Master, I didn't mean to be so loud." Her sly smile contradicted her words.

"Nymph. You regret nothing."

"If you want, we could..."

"No," I blurted before I could consider her words. "I want to get into that town as soon as they open the gates. Well, what they call gates anyway, from the looks of them they barely keep out the wildlife."

"Hills Crest is just a way station between Blackrun and Riven Hold. Technically neutral and historically protected by both. It has, well... had, a small ruling council of three Chosen, I do not know if they are still in charge. They may have come north with the Matriarch of Riven Hold's army. I don't remember."

I finished tying the straps of my light leather armor. Not a perfect fit, but I was hoping to get something else in town.

"Okay, let's ditch the makeshift spears and put the crap daggers in the bags. Also, glad we got rid of those cheap batons, I don't think they would have been worth much and they were heavy, and we never wanted to use them. Let's decide what we keep and try to sell."

"All the cheap knives, Susan's blade is the best and... I would like to keep that?" she said, looking at me. I nodded, and she continued. "Then the crossbow is built well and the bow, but after our training, I think the crossbow is better for me."

"I agree, it's easier to point and shoot, but longer to load. Hmmm. Yeah, keep it, it packs a punch in a pinch, then you can use your element as needed. Speaking of, let's refocus your training to do smaller shots of water for distraction rather than actual damage. If you can keep a few people busy long enough for me to take out individuals in the future, it might make all the difference."

"Oh, I never really considered that. I think I can do that. My power will last longer too."

"Let's sell everything but your dagger and the crossbow." I thought for a moment on the items in front of us. "What about Susan's Rapier? It's serviceable and we could probably keep it on you as a backup... Hell, I have never really used a sword in my life, knives sure, but not swords. Thoughts?"

"I... agree. The Susan I knew always thought I should have studied the martial arts more. My use of them is very rudimentary. For my memory of what she was, not who she became, I will do so."

I reached out and grabbed her hand, bringing it to my lips for a kiss. "That's a good way to remember her."

"Thank you." She wiped her eyes. "Sell the rest, then?"

"Yup, even the clothes then buy new stuff. Susan had all the wrong measurements to fit you properly and everything she had was like a slutty Halloween costume."

"A what?"

"Nothing, just something from my land on Earth...." Her look made me continue. "A holiday where people would dress up as something they are not. Sometimes to scare others but mostly to party and act like something they regularly weren't."

"Interesting. I can't think of anything like that. You don't like... slutty?" she asked.

"OH, I love slutty when it's in private and done for your partner as a turn on. I guess I mean provocative more than slutty, but that's in the weeds." I smiled. "Though if you are single, it's fine. I guess if that is how you want to attract someone. For me? Sexy in public is okay, but I always thought slutty sent the wrong message when you were in a committed relationship like we are."

She smiled. "So, no others will join us? You have decided?"

"No men, for sure. Just not my preference. I promised you I would be open to women, but the conditions have to be right, and they have to be fully aware of what they are getting into."

"Thank you, Master. I have no desire for other men, but for you to have power. I want to add other women for you... and somewhat for personal reasons, I enjoy their touch as well."

"Nymph," I teased.

"Yes, Master, I guess you bring it out of me."

"I am going to make you prove that later."

"Please?" She grabbed my finger and put it in her mouth, softly biting it.

"Mm-mm," I stopped. "All stop, or we won't leave. I want to stick to the plan, and I see the guards opening the gate. You are going to get it later, though."

Tyla released my finger, stood, and turned away, sashaying in front of me. "I am yours as you please, Master."

I smacked my hand to my face. "She is going to kill me. I have awoken a sex kitten, haven't I?"

"Yes!" she called out over her shoulder as she brought the hood of her cloak over her head and donned the pack.

"Down boy," I said downward, as she started walking. I picked up the rest of the gear, following my woman to town.

"State your purpose!" the guard said, an older man with long hair and a pot helmet. A well maintained but old spear at his side. His breath was rancid even from the four or so feet that separated us.

"Travelers from the north, passing through."

"No more refugees. If you want in, you have to pay the town entry fee." He pointed his finger at a sign I couldn't read.

"Not refugees, looking to stay a couple of days, pick up supplies, then head south to Riven Hold."

"Fee," he said, holding out his hand.

Tyla spoke beneath her hood, only part of her face visible. "The entry used to be free, why the three coppers?"

"Since the defeat of the Matriarchs and their swearing of loyalty to Seir, we have had a lot of refugees, Ma'am. We can't hold no more." The guard said, showing respect to Tyla.

I forgot that women had run the world before Seir.

"Pay the man," she said.

"Yes, mistress," I said, assuming the role of protector and bodyguard.

I pulled out the three coppers, handing them to the guard.

"Thank you, mistress," the guard said, ignoring me.

Without further word, Tyla walked in through the gates like she oversaw the world. I followed in her wake, smiling at her without being able to stop myself.

"I find it easier to act like I should have for all those years." She said, as if trying to explain.

"I am so proud of you right now. I can't even describe it. You didn't even hesitate."

She pushed back part of the hood and looked back at me, smiling.

"I recommend we go to the Inn first, mistress and get you comfortable, then I will take care of the shopping." I stayed in the role in case anyone took notice of us.

"It's better if I accompany you, less likely to get cheated," she said, mimicking my intent.

We walked down the main street of the town. The main road was built of cobbled stone. Wooden shops and stores lined this section of town. Branching off from the main road were less well-maintained paths of crushed rocks that lead down streets towards more residential houses. It gave me a real medieval vibe to the place.

Even the wonderful smell of outhouses.

I saw a leather shop, but it looked like it was just a storefront, otherwise the smell would have been worse. Next to it was a weapons dealer, but I could not make out what they had in stock. There were no window displays, as most of the shops still had their wooden shutters covering them and were not open.

"What time do the shops open?" I asked.

"I am not sure, probably not long, though. We can ask the Inn."

I nodded as we continued down the street.

The Inn was the largest building in town, calling itself the Witch's Haunt.

"I thought the term witch was derogatory?" I asked.

"This inn was built by a powerful matriarch many years ago. She retired from the politics of the south, somewhere in Casting's Harbor, and wanted to get away. Rumor was it was a play on words, and it stuck. You can see the original building in all the stone, the wattle and daub extensions are more recent, I think. Though it might still be the original glass, as my mother told me she was powerful in the fire element."

"Nice," I said, studying the structure as we approached. It had two doors in the center that opened apart from each other for a wider entry. To each side of the door, it had glass bow style windows that looked like they sat tables on the other side. Two chimneys stuck out of the wooden roof over the gray stone central building. On each side of the main were the wattle and daub constructed extensions Tyla mentioned. Small wooden shutters closing each of the windows and several pipes billowing smoke vented out to the flat roof on top.

We walked into the inn, and my nose picked up the smell of cooking. My mouth watered. I was so sick of the jerky and fruits, I wanted to drop everything we planned and get food first.

"Master, can we eat first?" Tyla leaned over and whispered the question to me.

"I was thinking the same thing. Yes," I whispered back to a smiling Tyla.

"Can I help ya?" A young woman with red hair came out from the door to what I assume was the kitchen.

Tyla stepped forward. "Yes, I need a single room for me and my... companion. We would also like breakfast and meals for the few days we will be staying."

The young woman glanced at Tyla, then studied me, her eyes staying on me a few seconds longer than was usually proper. "If ya pay in advance for seven days, I can make it a large copper. No refunds if ya leave early, though. Baths and all meals included."

"Lovely," Tyla said and waited.

Taking this as my cue, I reached into the coin bag in my shirt and pulled out a large and small copper for a tip. "Here you go. Miss?"

"Tasnia," she said. "Tasnia Baird. This is my father's inn. He handles the afternoon crowds." She held out her hand to take the coins. Her accent was odd to me. The translation magic almost made it normal but some of her words sounded odd, like an Irish accent.

I put my hand out with the freshly retrieved coins, but as our hands touched, it was like a static shock went through me. Both of our eyes widened, and I saw a red hue come over her skin. Subtle but visible.

"What was that?" she asked as she pulled her hand back, the coins in her hand.

"Not sure," I said, shaking my hands. "Felt weird, though."

"Is everything alright?" Tyla asked.

"Yes, some kind of shock when I touched her." Without another word, I stepped back. Tasnia did not seem to notice the color on her skin shifting. I held my face in an impressive expression.

She is a Chosen.

❧ ❧

"What was that?" Tyla whispered when we sat down at a table built into the window where we could watch the town wake up as we ate.

I looked over my shoulder to make sure that Tasnia had gone back to the kitchen to get our food. "She is a fire mage. She lit up to me for about a minute."

Tyla glanced at the kitchen door, as though she could see the red-headed young woman through the wall. "She is about my age. With all the troubles she may have missed the testers. They usually come to all the small towns to see if any of the women have an affinity just once a year. She probably doesn't even know yet. Powers rarely develop on their own until our early twenties, without training and focus. The testing stone is how we identify them early enough."

"How does that work when they are untrained?"

"Usually violently, if she is a fire elemental, or mage as you call them, then the next day she gets furious could be the day this inn burns down."

I nodded, not sure what to say to that.

"We should..." Tyla stopped as Tasnia came back out to our table with bowls of soup on a tray with hunks of homemade bread. My mouth watered.

"Here ya go," Tasnia said, her eyes glancing at Tyla, then lingering on me for a moment. "It's only breakfast porridge in tha mornings here, but I have tha bread, some butter, and honey ta help. Ya want wine or beer with that?"

"Wine, please," Tyla answered, and looked up at me.

"Er, do you have anything without alcohol? Ever heard of coffee?"

Tasnia looked at me as if I was mad. "That's too expensive. I could bring ya some hot tea. Ya don't want to drink tha water that hasn't been boiled."

"What kind of tea?"

"Breakfast tea, it comes from tha south as well and isn't always in stock, but we have a little left."

"Tea would be good. Thank you, miss."

Tasnia smiled. "Just Tasnia, or Tas, as most people call me here. Comin' right out."

She walked away. Without thinking, I glanced at her shapely backside, catching myself and putting my eyes back on Tyla, who was smiling.

"She is pretty. I love her green eyes, not as grayish green as yours, but pretty," she said.

I rolled the eyes in question. "Don't get your hopes up, but she is beautiful, yes."

"Do you think her boobs are bigger? It's hard to tell by her dress." She smirked at me as she pressed hers together.

"Okay, stop making fun of me. Yes, I am a guy and yes, I stared at her butt and saw her boobs. I did the same to you when we met. It's a species imperative and I can't control it sometimes. I think yours are slightly smaller but perkier. Her pale skin is beautiful, but your tan skin is what I prefer. That satisfy you? Or you want more?"

"Yes, Master!" she said excitedly, barely keeping her voice down.

I could see the humor on her face and hear it in her voice.

Tas came back and served Tyla her wine and gave me my tea. It smelled like English breakfast tea. It wasn't coffee, but it would do.

"Your rooms will be ready in a couple of hours. Ya want a bath? We only have the one but it's open for now."

"Please!" Tyla said. "We will take a bath after breakfast."

"Only one at a time. But if ya want an attendant, I can help ya miss since I run the bath in the day. I'll get tha cook to watch tha counter, and my father should be down soon."

Tyla nodded. "Yes, please. After breakfast. Do you want to go first, then?" She said, looking at me.

"No, go ahead. I will take mine after."

Tas smiled and left while I took my first sip of tea, looking forward to the new version of caffeine once more.

CHAPTER 20

— • —

THE BAIRDS

I was sitting and enjoying my tea, relishing the caffeine that came with it but still dreaming of coffee.

"Are you one of the new guests?" A voice came from behind me.

I turned towards the large man. His hair was red, but had some gray in it. A beard adorned his heavy face, and his body was massive, though a gut was pushing out of his belt, showing he may have softened recently. His muscled arms and the way he stood, though, that put me on guard. That was a killer's stance if I ever saw one.

"Yes Sir. Are you Tasnia's father?"

The man nodded. "Yes, I saw her leading the other young woman to the baths. She looks... familiar to me and I was hoping to get your names."

I stamped down on the alarm that flooded through me. "I don't know what you mean?"

"I have seen her here before. I think she is someone important."

I shifted my legs to put myself in a better position to leave the seat quickly. Trying to prepare without setting him off.

"None of that son, I don't mean you any harm."

He was a killer, or at least trained, if he noticed that movement. So, I relaxed as best I could. "What do you want?"

The man sat down at the table across from me, putting both hands out and flattening them against the table in a non-threatening manner.

"That's Tyla Russel, isn't it?"

"I could waste your time and deny it, but I won't. I will just warn you I will protect her... violently if you threaten us."

"I would normally smack a young pup like you for such words, but your eyes speak to experience beyond your age."

I just glared at him.

"Good." He nodded. "My name is Roman Baird, and I know Tyla's mother and served her grandmother in my youth. Her mother and my wife were friends... long ago. Tas's mother was close to most of the nobles. Not Chosen herself, but from a long line of them. With the changes we are hearing out of the north... I... worry for my daughter. Please tell me if you are running from them?"

"If we were?"

He let out a breath. "The rumors are they are turning all the Chosen into demented sex slaves to the Demi's. I know Tyla, or at-least I knew her mother before... She joined him. I don't know you though and that is my problem."

"What are you asking?"

"I... don't know," He deflated. The killer in him turning off and the father turning on. "I want to send my daughter away before they get her. I have been around enough to know some of the early signs of being Chosen."

"What signs?" I asked, curious.

"I was part of the personal guard for Tyla's grandmother. The young women who would become Chosen all showed certain signs before their test day at nineteen. The guards all knew what to look for, so we would inform the Matriarch. Who would prepare them as soon as possible without them knowing? They kept it secret from the young women, but it was never really a surprise who would be Chosen or not.

"In Tasnia's case... periodically she would do things like grab a pot from the fire without gloves, never recognizing it being scalding hot. I don't think she ever thought about it, but I noticed it. Other things as well."

I would not tell him about my abilities, but that was useful information to have. "Have you told her?"

"No, I... don't want to take any actions until I set a course. If you know what I mean. I just don't know what will happen if I move too quickly."

"We are going to be here for a few days, at least while we wait to meet up with someone else. If at the end of that time, you feel you can trust us, you and your daughter can come with us."

"That's the problem. I can't go. Promised Tas' mother, I would look after the place when she died. I don't think that Seir will give two shits about an old, retired war horse like me, but I can't risk her being here when they come. That is why I want to get to know you. If you are protecting Tyla, you might be worthy enough to get Tas out as well."

"I make no promises, I don't know you either... yet. But I will consider it."

"Fair, I will pay you, though. I am assuming you were a bodyguard as well. You have the look, and Tyla with you gives me hope."

That explains his willingness to trust me. He thinks I am a kindred spirit, I guess. In a way, he was not wrong, he just did not have the right specifics.

"Something like that. It's complicated though, and I can't really explain. If what you hope comes to pass, and we let her come with us, I will protect her till my dying breath. That I can give my word on. Do you understand?"

He smiled, "You got a spine kid, or an old soul. Because no one who hasn't killed to protect another should have that look in their eyes. I understand. Do you need anything while you're in town?"

"Supplies, we have a couple of items, but we need basic armor. I need to get a sword or something more than a knife and supplies to get us down to Riven Hold at least. I actually think farther than that, I have a feeling it will not stay free much longer either."

"You take my daughter with you and promise to get her safely away. I will give you one of my swords. My first one. It's of a fine make and has a lot of experience behind it. Given to me by Tyla's grandmother when I became one of her protectors, as a matter of fact."

"If we come to terms after a day or two, I will accept. You should also tell her your suspicions."

A sound to my right got me to turn as a beautiful and freshly clean Tyla walked out of the door in a robe. Tasnia was right behind her. They were whispering softly before they saw the two of us sitting together.

Tasnia jerked. "Father! What are ya doing?"

Tas's father laughed at her reaction and glanced over at me. "Just talking to the bo—" He caught himself. "Young man here. Having a polite conversation since it's so slow I got nothing better to do. Anyway, your room is ready, you can take your stuff up and get settled, the bath will be clean and ready for you when you come down." He tossed a room key with a number '12' on it to me.

"Thank you, Sir," I said formally. "My name is Derrick, by the way, or Derk, if you prefer."

We shook hands. He reached for my wrist and clasped rather than my hand. I had to adjust quickly, and he looked at me oddly because of it.

"I will be by ta wash your clothes while ya bathe. Just ring the bell when ya are in tha bath," Tasnia said.

"Thank you," I said and stood, looking to Tyla. "Let's go get settled."

We left the father and daughter who began whispering behind us in a heated exchange. I could tell Tyla wanted to speak to me as well.

"What was her father talking to you about?" Tyla asked in a whisper just as the door closed.

I placed our gear in the corner, grabbing the few sets of clothes I salvaged or saved since I got here. Piling them up on the small bed. The room was just four walls with a small table two people could eat at. No glass in the windows, but it had a wooden shutter which was open to let in the light. Several candles adorned the room in brass fixtures on the walls and a chamber pot was in the corner.

"I am going to miss plumbing, I think."

"That word did not translate."

"Hmm? Yes, sorry, distracted for a second. It was nothing. Though that reminds me. Why are Tasnia's words coming out weird to me rather than translated?"

She sighed in frustration because I never answered her question. "Sometimes when you first meet someone, you hear what you expect to hear rather than what is being said. It is common with the other species, but I did not notice her having an accent. And no, I do not know why or how that is. But please master, may I know the answer to my question?"

"Hmm, I guess her looks made me think of an Irish bar wench from my world. That might have done it. Never heard an accent with her father, which is why I thought about it. I wonder if it will go away now that I know or ⎯ "

"Master!" Tyla hissed in the loudest whisper she could manage.

I laughed. "Sorry, but that's for teasing me earlier. Fine, he knew who you were and wanted to send Tasnia with us."

"So, she was right!" Tyla said, mostly to herself.

"Your turn. Spill."

"Spill what?"

"The... never-mind. What did you two talk about?"

"She did not know who I was, but she suspected we were running from the north and that I was a Chosen. Her dad has been acting strangely lately and talking to all the travelers that have passed through. She did not know why."

"Because he knows she is also Chosen and wants to get her out of here."

"How... would he know that?"

I explained to her what Roman said to me about the signs and that they kept it from the younger generations.

"Why would they do that?" Tyla asked.

"No idea, but in my world, young women tend to talk and ruin the surprise. Young men too, for that matter, so they probably waited until maturity before they told you all the secrets."

"How come I never noticed them?"

"No idea. Probably just played them off as weird, but normal. Humans are weird that way," she said, giving her a shrug of my arms. "Anything else from your talk with Tas?"

"She is extremely sweet when you get past her gruff exterior. She gets approached by the men in town constantly, so she is usually on guard."

"That sounds like most men I know."

"None of them in town are really her age and they pester her a lot, but her father keeps them back. It has gotten worse since the Chosen in this town left for the north."

"So, they were captured or killed like you thought?"

"I am afraid so. One of them was like a mother to Tasnia."

I winced. "If she mentions it, I will give her my condolences. You will be alright by yourself up here while I bathe?"

"Yes, I finally feel at least a little safer, though I don't want to be apart from you. I think that is more the bond than my fears now... Oh, she was very interested in you, and asked a lot of questions about us and you specifically."

"Of course she did, but are you sure she did that? Or are you just projecting on her what you hope? This isn't a romance novel, Tyla."

"I'm sure. Doesn't seem attracted to women, which is disappointing, but I think it's more about not having any men her age anymore. She said that the few younger men in town left north with the army months ago. She has only been nineteen for a few months."

"Why is nineteen important here? Is that the age of adulthood?"

"Sort of, it is when the choosing stone can be used with guaranteed results. While it sometimes works on those that are younger, at nineteen, it has never failed to be accurate, and each stone can only work on a single person once. So that is the age of majority for both men and women, in the human lands at least."

"You have mentioned this choosing stone before. What is it?"

"A matriarch will imbue an object, usually a precious stone, with power. It must be a matriarch because it takes such a massive amount of power and control that only a woman on that level can do it. It is the last test before achieving the rank, if not the position that goes with it.

"The type of power does not matter, but the object then becomes sensitive to other types of magic so that it glows when contacting someone who has it. It's the only method, besides you, to know for sure that someone is Chosen or not."

"Interesting. So, the titles are like the ancient nobility on Earth. You can be a matriarch, but you may not be a landowner like your mom was. Now it's making more sense to me. Alright, I am going to go get clean now. Come get me if you need me."

She rose from the bed and came and kissed me. Pressing the pile of clothes against my chest as we did.

"See you soon, Master. I will sort our stuff so we can sell it later."

"Good." I left the room, heading down to the bathing area.

I sank slowly into the steaming water with a combination of pain and joy. Almost too hot, but I did not care. I could feel the tension bleed away as I sank up to my neck in the copper tub.

"Fuck, I missed this."

The room smelled of summer flowers if I was to place it, the soaps much nicer than those I found in my bag when I arrived in this world.

I reached up and pulled the cord above the tub. A bell rang in another room somewhere. I was guessing the front counter.

I closed my eyes and just relaxed. Trying to let all the worry and tension that had built up over the last few weeks leave my body.

"Sir?" a voice called, along with the knock at the door.

"Yes, come in."

I could hear the door open but could not see Tasnia enter. The privacy screen blocked the tub I was in from the entryway and laundry station.

"I will clean ya clothes while ya soak and we have a robe if ya did not bring an extra set. We do not offer any... extra services to bathers at our inn."

"Thank you... for the clothes and I will take the robe. I was not planning on inquiring about anything else," I said, as I noticed that her accent had reduced from earlier. Just the slightest hint of an Irish accent on just a few words now. This world magic translation thing was weird.

I sat back in the water and let my mind drift again. Tuning out the sounds of Tasnia washing my clothes.

"Is... is what my father said true?" Tasnia said after a few minutes.

I hesitated before answering. "What did he tell you?"

"That I might be Chosen and that ya can get me to safety?"

"Uh... I can't really promise that Tasnia. I can promise we will try, though. If you come with us, I will say that you are Chosen. Don't ask me how I know, but I do."

I heard a sniffle on the other side of the cloth screen.

"It's kind of funny," she said. "I always wanted to be one since I was a little girl, before mom died. To be important and noble and all that. Now with the Demigods turning them... us, into their slaves, I find that it scares me out of my mind."

"I..." I said and stopped. "It's fine to be scared, Tas. I don't know what you're feeling, not exactly anyway, but Tyla and I are going through something similar. We can't predict tomorrow, but I can promise that should you decide to come with us, I will do all that I can to both protect you and teach you to protect yourself."

"But ya can't teach me to use these powers, can ya?"

"It's... complicated, but I think Tyla can. Or at least start you on the path."

She did not respond and instead hung my clothes up on the string to dry. "Your clothes are as clean as I can get them. Some will never be clean again, though."

"It's been a rough couple of weeks. Going to sell most of them if we can and get some new ones," I said with a chuckle. Standing to get up out of the bath and move over to the rinsing station to finish washing off.

"Here is yer robe—" she cut off as she placed it over the divider. I looked up to see her eyes peeking at me through the slit. Her face suddenly red when I spotted her. "Sorry, I'll go now."

She turned and sped out the door, slamming it shut.

Oops.

CHAPTER 21

NORMALCY

I used the water and rag someone left at the door to our room to clean myself off as Tyla finished getting dressed. After a week on the ground, the bed we slept in last felt like magic, even if it was not the best bed I had ever slept in. It was also nice to conduct our more intimate activities with something soft underneath us.

"Stop staring," Tyla said as she looked over her shoulder at me.

Caught.

"Sorry... No, I am not. You're gorgeous... But I do need to finish so we're not late," I realized I had stopped wiping myself at some point.

"Tas said she will meet us in the dining room at breakfast. Her father suggested she spend time with us the next few days to get to know us better."

"That's good, you know it's scary times when a father has to trust strangers to take care of his daughter. Did I ever tell you about my kid back on Earth?"

Tyla stopped with the last strap. Staring up at me in shock. "You... had children already?"

"Just one, technically, but I was a horrible father. I... met this girl when I was twenty-two and her name was Angela. She got pregnant and had a boy while I was on deployment. I did all the responsible things, sent money and such, but we were only together for a night, fueled by too much drink and poor decisions. Never meant for a long-term commitment. I was just working on building that relationship with my son before the end of the world." A pang of regret hit me at the thought.

Tyla walked over to me and sat on my lap. The feel of her leather shorts was almost uncomfortable on my exposed skin. "I am sorry, Derk." she said as she hugged me.

"I lived a pretty normal life in those days to be honest. It just so happened that normal was full of regret for most people. Like I said, I was not a good father, and regretted that when I got a little older. I visited a few times as my son was growing up, but really did not commit to it till I got released from the colony project. If we... ever have children, I will not make that mistake again."

Tyla smiled and kissed me on the lips. Pulling away, she got an evil smile on her face. "You make me happier every day. Now, let's go seduce the innkeeper's daughter!"

I snickered. "Nymph. Do not push her into this. I said I was open to it, but if I think she is being pressured, then no deal. Understood?"

"Yes, master!"

She got off my lap and swished her hips as she moved over to hand me my clothes.

"What happened to the pretty and passive girl I met?"

"She became happy," Tyla said. "Though I still feel a little anxious around strangers."

"I noticed that last night when we ate in the main hall. I want you to be who you are, Tyla, don't try to be someone you're not."

"Thank you," she said, "You do not know how much that means to me to hear you say that. My whole life was the opposite."

I finished putting on my clothes, not wearing any of the armor as we wanted to sell it, but strapped on one dagger. "Okay, let's go eat."

I ate the breakfast that was in front of me. The same porridge as yesterday, topped with a few local fruits that looked like raspberries but tasted more like strawberries. The fresh baked bread, honey, and butter were a good balance to the otherwise bland oatmeal like bowl.

"The bread is fantastic," I said, complimenting Tasnia who had joined us.

"It's simple, but we only do grand breakfast when we have visiting nobles... which hasn't happened in some time... oh sorry, Tyla, I didn't mean—"

"It's fine, Tas, I am not a noble anymore. I am probably closer to an outlaw now."

"Which is why we are going to be leaving soon. Are you still thinking you want to come with us?" I asked, looking at Tas.

"Father wants me too, and I really enjoy hanging out with Tyla. In fact, you both seem so nice... I just... I don't know what the future will hold, and it scares me."

Tyla reached over and placed her hand on Tasnia's. "I know, I am scared too, we will make the best of it."

Roman came up to the table and interrupted our conversation. "Morning to you three."

"Good morning, Roman," I said. "The dinner last night was excellent."

"Just steaks and potatoes, all locally available. Our cook has been with us for ten years now, she is getting older, but I was just about to hire some new kids to help... since I may lose my best employee soon."

"I can stay if ya need me, Father."

"No, I worry too much about you, and my gut says I can trust them. It breaks my heart, but your safety is paramount. Are you still planning on getting supplies today?"

We all nodded in response.

"I have something I would like to show you Derk, it is the sword we talked about yesterday. Would you like to let the women go out and we can let you test it out in the back?"

I gazed at Tyla and Tas to get their opinions. They both nodded.

"I think that would be fine," Tyla said when I raised my eyebrow at her.

"That sounds good, my experience is with knives, spears, and... ranged weapons, so I could use some time to get used to it."

"You never learned the sword?" Roman asked.

"It's... complicated, but it was never a part of what I trained on."

He nodded. "In that case, you and I will spend a lot of time together. I will teach you as much as I can."

"That works. Can we borrow something to measure with so Tyla can get clothes that fit me?"

"Sure, I have some string at the counter. Tas, go get Becky to man the front for us today?"

"Yes, father. She might not be happy about being up so early."

"I warned her you would be busy the next few days, she agreed to be available as needed and I would pay her extra."

"Yes, father," Tas said and got up from the table, picking up all our dishes then going to the kitchen.

"Is that the woman who sang last night?"

"Yes, she has also been working here for years. We are not rich, but we treat the staff like family and let them live here. That's why most of them do not care that I am a man running the place."

"Her voice was delightful," I said.

I needed to remember to ask Tyla how the words seemed in perfect pitch to the music, even though we were not singing the same language. Though I was fairly sure the response would just be a shrug and her telling me it was magic.

I smiled at my internal joke as I got up and followed Roman up to his office. I looked over my shoulder. "Be safe Tyla, you know where I will be."

"We will be back soon, my love."

"Roman, while I appreciate this, I was picturing more of a one-handed model. This thing is huge," I said as I held the two-handed beast up in front of me.

We had gone to the back of the inn, two old wooden posts with a crossbeam halfway through sat away from the building. They looked unused with the amount of dirt still on them, but the many cuts in each showed that they had seen plenty of practice in the past.

"You showed me your knife skills and they are... good, but a one-handed short sword will not protect my daughter from men or Chosen in every situation. This sword will protect you from spear and other swords much better. Only way a short sword is better is in a shield wall."

The sword was a great sword, which was about as much as I knew. The handle was about sixteen inches long and the blade about four feet, if I were to guess. It was only a few inches shorter than me.

"I don't even know how I would carry something like this."

"Practice," he deadpanned. "This isn't even the largest I could have given you. It's a balance between two-handed brute strength and portability. But you can one hand it if you have need. You also don't seem the type to want a shield getting in the way, so two hands."

I nodded, but still wasn't sure. "I can try it. I never studied HEMA, so I don't know."

"Studied what?"

"A... Ancient martial art about great swords where I was... trained."

"Look, Derk, I figured out you were not part of the Matriarch's guard, but you have skills... and my gut tells me I can trust you. I won't ask about your past but tell me the truth when you do."

"Thank you, it's probably better if you don't know. Let's just say my training focused on hand-to-hand knives, two handed weapons, and a type of projectile weapon that you don't have."

"Which is why we are going to focus on a weapon that will complement your close quarters fighting with some range. A short sword won't give you anything more than a long knife. So, we will get you a good knife as a backup and focus you on the long sword for the next few days."

"That makes sense," I said, then sighed.

"I warn you kid, if I only have a few days to get you to where you can protect my daughter, every day you will hate your life."

"I have never been afraid of hard work."

"You will be when I am done. First, we go over the stances and grips," he said as he brought up his own version of a great sword. "Your grips are good, but a sword differs from a knife. You have to be able to move the sword fluidly and account for its weight while still being relaxed."

He showed me, gripping the handle so that his weak hand was at the bottom grip above the pommel, and his dominant hand was at the top, near the tang, in an open grip.

"Fast, loose, and flexible is the key to any sword. Do not grab the pommel or you will lose control." He moved the sword around in his hands. "With this first grip, you can be two handed and move the sword wherever you need it to be easily and still have the power to strike."

He launched forward and hit at the rightmost of the two targets on the field. A solid strike reverberated through the wooden post, making all the dirt and dust fly off it.

"Now, you grip just like I showed you, and we will go over just those forms today. Then work on the next tomorrow and start blending them together. I can't teach you everything, of course, but I think I can get you a solid foundation in a few days with a little sweat and blood."

"Oorah," I said with a smile, thinking back to days gone by.

"Another thing I do not understand."

"Oh, something the soldiers of where I came from used to say as a motivator."

"Oh, we have something similar, yes. Now, first stance. Hold your grip just like this with your feet slightly more than shoulder length apart and at an angle like this."

I followed along, studying and mimicking each of his forms. Each was simple in their way, just like every other form of fighting I had ever learned.

Simple but efficient beat complicated and flashy most days, so I settled in to learn what I could.

"Holy shit, you feel amazing," I said, followed by a deep moan of pleasure. "I know I could really just do this myself, but you doing it really feels so much better."

"Wait till later tonight," Tyla purred into my ear as she massaged the muscles in my back, applying just enough of her power to heal the damage from today's training.

"That man has put me through hell today. Pretty sure I would be dead in my old world."

Tyla leaned forward and nibbled my ear. "You will love my training later... just wait. Tas is also coming along with her training, we worked on it all day after we ordered what we needed. Fairly sure she is asleep. Thank you for letting me teach her."

"She'll need it and no reason not to. I noticed she is getting along with you, and I find I enjoy her. But I have spent no real time with her yet. I don't honestly know if what you hope... will end up happening."

"My plan," Tyla said, "has been to not to push anything. If I judged her worthy of joining us, then I will tell you and you two can make the final decision together. I have spent all day with her now, and I think we will become close friends regardless of if she joins our bed. She is infatuated with you, though. She denies it to me, but she constantly volunteered to bring you water today."

"In my old world, a woman in your position would be quite jealous."

"I... may have been before our bond. Not now though, it's an imperative in me to increase your power, even if I did not also have an attraction for her."

"Wonder if it's another suggestion the gods wrote into their mind-fuck matrix thing. Another reason I am against adding more women."

"Even if you are right, master, I can't change the will of the gods, nor would I want to, based on how I feel right now. I think you should spend some time with Tas and decide for yourself if you want to tell her the truth. Then see if she is interested. I am done by the way." She said as she finished rubbing my back and turned away.

"I love you, Tyla. I no longer care about how it happened or why. You know that. But... putting someone else through it... I still am not totally convinced it's the right thing to do."

"I know, my love. Just promise me you will consider it."

"I will. We can spend some time together, the three of us tonight after we eat."

Tyla smiled and nodded.

CHAPTER 22

— • —

LAST VESTIGES OF A PEACEFUL LIFE

"Your father is trying to kill me," I said to Tasnia while Tyla worked on my battered muscles.

We had been at it for four days, and I had been beaten black and blue by Roman.

"He can be relentless," Tas said and looked at me. Her cheeks pinked slightly, and she refocused on the pot of water before her. "He wanted a son to teach, but never had one. He tried that with me, but... I never had the skills."

"Thank you, Tyla," I said as she got up from the chair behind me.

I put my shirt back on. "I don't think I would have made it if not for your ability to restore me like that."

"You are welcome, my love," she said and went over behind Tas. "Bubbles at the bottom! Excellent work, Tas. That shows you can transfer enough heat into the pot that the water is close to boiling."

Tasnia let out a breath of air and let go of the pot. "So close, but I couldn't hold it anymore. That is so exhausting. How ya hold the power in your mind long enough to boil, I don't know."

"It takes a while to build up the endurance, and the power comes with time and practice. I was not able to do half the stuff I could now before I met Derrick."

Shit, I thought, and looked to catch Tyla's eyes.

She held a hand up to her mouth. "Oh..."

"What?" Tasnia asked. "Why would meeting Derk make a difference?"

"He uh..." She looked at me.

"Tas, there are things that are different about me and Tyla. Our relationship, it's... complicated, and we want to keep it a secret. If you decide to stick with us long term, maybe we can tell you. But until that happens, I hope that will not bother you."

Tasnia stopped and became pensive for a minute. "That reminds me of something my father said. He mentioned to me he does not understand how ya can go as long as ya do in training. He has been pushing ya to get you to the edge and complained that he couldn't. Says it's almost unnatural."

"That is part of it. Yes."

"Then the other night, when we went out together, ya helped that man with his broken cart, changing his wheel. Liftin it by yerself almost so he could put the new one on. I have seen a lot of other strange things about ya the past few days too, Derk."

"You should just tell her, Derrick," Tyla said.

"It's too much of a risk."

Tyla walked over to me and whispered in my ear. "People will eventually find out. We should find out where she stands so she can decide if she really wants to come with us."

"Please tell me. I... won't betray yer trust."

I stopped and thought for a minute. Slowly concluding that we should take the risk. "I... Okay. I have only been on this world for about three weeks now."

"Ya what?" Confusion was written all over Tasnia's face.

"I was born on another world... Earth, to be exact, roughly about two hundred and fifty years ago. The same planet everyone here originated from, actually."

"I... the world of the ancestors? I don't understand. How is that possible?"

I explained it. Mostly. I told her of the fall of earth, how the aliens powerful enough to be gods put humans into this world and how one had brought me to her world. I left out the technical parts but gave her the gist of the information.

"So, yer saying yer a Demigod?"

"No, I am human, or was... just given the same powers."

"So ya and he?" Tasnia asked, looking at Tyla and pointing at me.

"Yes," Tyla said. "We... did not know at the time, then we... bonded, and I became his in body and soul."

"So, yer telling me this so you can add me—"

"No!" I blurted out. "That's not what is happening here. We are telling you because you will travel with us and will eventually figure out that I have powers, too. This way, you can decide if you really want to go with us or take your chances elsewhere. You are absolutely free to decide what you want."

"But... wait... all those things ya said about him. Were ya trying to convince me to join ya?"

"What are you talking about?" I asked as we both glanced over at Tyla, who was turning red. "What did you say?"

"Uh... I am sorry master, I might have... mentioned we wanted to experiment with another person to see if she was interested."

I sighed, putting my hand over my face for a second. "I'm sorry, Tas... We... she was not supposed to do anything like that, and I apologize if it made you uncomfortable. Being completely honest, we discussed the possibility, but only if you were interested and had all the details. I am actually against the whole thing because of the bonding process."

"So, yer not going to try and make me a slave?" Tas asked.

"Absolutely not! I regret how it happened to Tyla. If I would have known, I wouldn't have..." I trailed off for a second and shook my head. "Regardless. No. You are and forever will be your own person. Even if you did volunteer for that and we accepted, you would be your own person, just like Tyla is to me. But now, I am sorry I even considered the idea. We will take you to wherever you need to go and protect you as promised. Nothing more."

Tasnia nodded. "That's fine. I... know the ugly stories coming from the north about the Demis, but you don't seem like that at all. And really, she only made a couple of comments when we had... uh... girl talk. Nothing like what you are thinking, so don't be mad at her. I will trust you to keep yer word, and I will keep mine and not tell anyone, even my father."

"Thank you, Tas. Again, you nor anyone else will ever be pushed into something like that, by me at least. You are welcome to stay with us as long as you want, though. Or leave when you feel you can."

I stood and held up my hand to shake. "Still friends?"

Tas smiled and stood, dusting off her hands before reaching out and grasping my wrist. "Yes."

Tyla walked over to Tas. "I... am sorry. I... just wanted to make it work... and help Derrick."

Tas reached out and hugged Tyla. "I know. Ya have been the closest thing to a friend I have had in a long time. All the other girls in town are small-minded twits. I forgive ya."

Tyla walked her to the door I had opened. "Good night. See you for breakfast?"

Tas smiled and nodded. "Sure, see ya then."

The door closed. With Tas gone, I looked at my wayward nymph. "Tyla?"

"I was only trying to help!"

I knew, and I reached over and pulled her into a hug. "But we can't do that... that's not who I am or what I want to be."

"Can I make it up to you, master?" she asked, reaching for my drawstring and tugging on the loop.

"What am I going to do with you?"

"Anything you want."

A creak sounded from the door frame, and I turned towards it. "Is someone there?"

The sound of feet running down the hall was the only thing we heard in response.

"I still think we have a chance with her." Tyla whispered into my ear as we both guessed a certain someone was eavesdropping.

"Don't push. It's her decision, but at least it is in the open. It's a risk, but we have to trust people at times."

"Yes, Master."

"I am going to make you stop calling me that. I think it's creating issues."

Tyla laughed as she continued to untie the leather strap holding up my pants.

I held the heavy sword up in a guard position, waiting for my opponent to strike. Sweat beaded down my face from the exertions of the day.

My opponent lunged at me with a long spear. Turning away and lunging forward at the oblique, my arms came down as I struck down hard on the spear. Sending it to the ground with a clang and a small rebound.

Resisting the call of my power to speed up my perception of time, I pushed forward with my padded elbow and struck at the heavily padded gut of the man trying to skewer me.

Then I pushed off him with a swing towards the head.

A heavy thunk sounded from the helmet as my wooden sword stuck home and the man dropped the spear and held up his hands.

"I yield!" Roman said.

I stopped from delivering another strike and let my training sword drop to my side. We both removed our helmets at the same time.

"Bravo!" yelled the girls, both Tasnia and Tyla clapping for my victory.

"About time I got one on you. Too bad it was a spear, not your sword," I said as I clasped wrists with Roman.

"Son, I have been fighting with a sword for thirty-five years. I would hope I can still beat you after a week of training. But you got me with the spear, and the spear is a more common weapon for a soldier. Not my best weapon, but I know it well. You did good."

"Thank you, Sir," I said, meaning in my voice.

"Here, Derk," Tas said as she handed me the jug of water.

"Thanks, Tas," I said as we gazed into each other's eyes for just a fraction of a second longer than was typical. I jerked my head back at Roman after taking a long drink. "Dinner tonight, still?"

"Yes," he said, a look of question on his face. "I want to wish you two and my daughter off with a delicious meal before you go."

"I'm sorry we can't stay longer. It's just getting too risky, and our friend still hasn't shown up. I fear something may have happened."

"If they come here, I will send them on to you, as we discussed."

Nodding, I watched as Tyla and Tas walked arm and arm up the steps back into the inn. "I'll do my best to protect her."

"Derk... Are you interested in my daughter?"

"I... am honestly not sure how to answer that. I am already with Tyla."

"I know, and men having more than a single woman is against the law in most places, but she has been talking about you and Tyla non-stop, just like her first crush a few years back. I... worry she will try to get involved with you two."

"Sir, your daughter is exquisite, and if I was not with Tyla, I would be extremely interested in courting her... with your permission. But there are some... complications that prevent us from even entertaining the idea... Even if it was a choice. So, you can sleep peacefully at night about that."

He relaxed. "She is willful when she wants to be, just like her mother. If she wants something, she finds a way to get it, and always has. Make sure you remind her you belong to another. Her mother was quite... aggressive with me back in the day, even though I was seeing another woman. It was a bit of a scandal."

"I don't think she is interested in me, at least beyond a schoolgirl crush. It probably is more about the lack of options for her. I am sure that will change when we get to Riven Hold."

He nodded. "Thank you for being upfront with me. I have been happy to teach you these past few days. If you were not with Tyla, I would have given you my blessing if you had asked."

"That means a lot to me, Sir. Thank you."

"Saying that, I expect you to approve of anyone she meets, or I will find you and punish you. Do you understand?"

"I... uh... yes... absolutely."

Roman smiled and clapped me on the back, directing me towards the door the women used. "Let's get clean and eat."

"So, we entered the room, I was right behind Major Trino and we threw in a... small explosive that causes a lot of light and sound to distract anyone that might be inside."

"How does that—"

"Father, stop interrupting. He has said repeatedly they use different weapons, so ya just need to enjoy the story."

"Fine... go on."

"So, we throw in the flash bang... as it's called. And we go inside in a line. Major Trino moves in first and turns to the right and I am right behind him, about to go left. We have these... projectile weapons like a small crossbow that fire multiple shots. We enter the room and there was this man about to open the." I stopped to think about the words I should use.

"He was about to kill them with the use of a machine in the room. All he needed to do was press this button to activate it. When we came in, he turned and fired his bow at us. Aiming right for Trino, who was facing right as he went through the door. I saw this before I went left and jumped in front of the arrow with my... chest plate and crashed onto the floor.

"Luckily, I still had my weapon pointed at him and fired right into his head. Trino turned and fired as well. Honestly, to this day, we are not sure who hit him first, but we shared the credit. I think he punished me for a week after, for going against the plan with cleanup duty." I laughed at that last thought, even as it brought a pang of sadness with it.

"That is a... fantastic story," Roman said.

I shrugged. "It loses a little without some context, but it was my one claim to fame in my homeland. The man we saved ended up leading a grand expedition to a new land, the woman that was with him was his wife."

"So, in your land, the men run things?" Tasnia asked.

"No, well, not when I left. For a long time, though, yes, it was that way, but things had changed to be more equal by the time I... left."

Roman smiled. "That explains the dynamic between you two a little more. I was wondering why Tyla seemed to ask your opinion so much. It's not normal for a noble to be so... informal."

"Yes," Tyla answered for me. "I have agreed to follow his customs since he saved my life."

Nodding, Roman went on. "I am not saying anything negative, mind you, but men have always been second rate in the Matriarchies. Here in this town, we did not see that as much, for which I am grateful to my wife's memory for bringing me to her ancestral home, but when you go to Riven Hold, expect to be treated like a brute and bodyguard, nothing more, Derk."

"I understand. We won't bring attention to us."

"That might be different soon with the changes coming from the north... Sorry Tyla." Roman said.

"It's ok," she said sadly. "We are in no position to do anything about it yet. I will make do with what I have. At least she is still alive, so there is hope."

Silence consumed Roman and Tasnia as, as far as they knew, the stories all said it was impossible. I had not mentioned my ability to Tas.

"Well, kids, I am off to bed. I will see you at breakfast to wish you off. Tas, don't stay up too late with them."

"Yes, father."

He kissed Tasnia on the cheek and gave Tyla a hug. Shaking my hand last before he left us in the private dining room alone. The hearty meal of steak and potatoes followed by apple cobbler for dessert was excellent.

"I am sorry about yer mother, Tyla." Tas said.

"I have faith we will break her free."

"But the rumors say that—"

"Tas, there is more to Derrick than we have said. He may have a way of freeing those who have been bonded. Please keep that as another secret."

Her eyes widened at me. "Ya can do that?"

"I... may. It's about a battle of power, and I may not be strong enough. But we hope that someday we can," I said.

"So ya say that if I were to join ya, that maybe ya could be strong enough to free yer mom?"

"No, that is not what I am saying. You will not be joining us if that is your reason. Would the power help? Probably. But that is not happening, not for that reason alone. You join us because you genuinely wanted to spend the rest of your life with us? Maybe. No other way. Understand?"

"Couldn't ya just release me afterwards?"

I froze at the thought, not having considered it. "Yes... I guess that is possible. But to get to that point requires certain... acts. That I will not do for simple convenience. I just... can't. Please do not mention it again."

I stood and walked to the door, a little angry at Tas for her comments and leaving the two girls behind in the dining room.

Making my way to our room, I just barely kept from slamming the door and sat down on the bed, staring at the wall.

"I will not fuck someone just to achieve a goal. I have never been that person and I never will be," I muttered to myself.

I sighed and tried to relax, feeling bad because Tasnia had probably not meant it that way. I wasn't even sure she knew how the bond happened.

A knock at my door broke me from my thoughts, and I got up to answer it. I opened the door to see Tasnia standing there by herself.

"I wanted to apologize if I upset ya," she whispered.

"It's not you, Tas. I am the one who should apologize. To be honest, I probably overreacted. Want to come in?"

She nodded and walked through the door. "Tyla said she would give us a few minutes."

She sat on the bed, and I took the nearby chair. "Tas, I get you don't know everything yet, but the... bonding is a very intimate process. I didn't create it, the gods did, but there is no other way that I am aware of."

She looked at me and nodded rather than ask more. I guessed she had figured out what it meant, or Tyla had told her.

"If it was as simple as saying, I promise?" I continued. "As I can do with just a simple bond? I would totally do what you suggested... but I... to me, being with someone in that way has to mean more than that. Or I might lose myself."

Exhaling a deep breath before continuing. "When I was in my old world, I used to believe casual sex without meaning was perfectly fine. Many people did, in fact. That was until that sex ended up with a kid I never got to know and me being a father who was not around. I promised myself I would treat any woman I ever met in the future as more than just a passing fling, and I plan to stick with that."

"I understand. I just wanted to say that you and Tyla are so great together. I find myself envious of what you have and part of me is open to being part of it."

"I get it, but your dad has sheltered you in this place for a while. I think you may confuse curiosity for... other things."

Tas grew a little red in the cheeks at this. Before we could continue the topic, Tyla walked in the door, peeking inside before she finished coming in.

"Why did you hesitate?" I asked.

"Just wanted to make sure nothing was... happening." She smiled.

"Nothing is going to happen. Between her dad and this, I am fairly sure this will not work."

"What did my dad say?" Tas asked.

Fuck me and my big mouth.

"Nothing, he just... wanted me to look out for you. Look, it's getting late, and we are leaving in the morning. Let's all make sure our gear is ready to go so we can pack up and move after breakfast."

Tas stayed on the bed like she wanted to ask more questions, but Tyla grabbed her hands and pulled her up, giving her a hug. "It will be fine, Tas. We can talk in the morning."

Tas smiled and kissed Tyla on the cheek. "Thank you," and walked to the door. I got up and moved to it first and opened it for her. She also reached up and kissed me on the cheek. "Thank you both for being... so kind to me," she said, then walked out the door.

"Was she alright?" I asked after the door closed.

"I think she might be a little sad that you shut her down like that."

"It's just a little crush on us. She can't possibly want to take that kind of step."

"Maybe, Master. We will see," she said as she undid the tight-fitting dress she was wearing.

I watched as she undid the clasps and ties, causing the entire thing to pool to the floor at her feet. She took a step towards me and swished her hips as she did so.

Suddenly, my mind focused on what was before me rather than on my other problems.

CHAPTER 23

THE SACKING OF HILL CREST

In my dreams, I could see a ball of light floating in orbit around me. It has a bluish light that felt familiar to me.

As I studied it, I noticed a small thread of energy breaking off from it and winding down, attaching itself to my chest, dead center where my heart was found. Where it was attached to me, the bluish glow seemed to defuse inside of me, spreading throughout my body in a way that looked like the pictures of the human nervous system I remember from school as a kid.

The light inside me was still mostly white, with just the slightest hint of the blue that entered.

I reached out and touched the thread, taking hold of it and pulling the ball of light towards me. Gently placing my hand on the watermelon sized sphere.

Tyla...

I am not sure how I knew it was her, but it was. Every fiber of my being believed it so strongly. As I pondered, it felt that I could move power between me and it. Taking or giving it in equal measure, almost no restrictions were binding me in what I could do with it. It was an intoxicating feeling and a dangerous power to give anyone. I could drain her dry and take it all for myself if I wanted.

I shuttered to think what the Demigods did with it.

Wondering what would happen, I tried to push some of my power back into the ball.

Suddenly, the brightness increased, and I had to turn my eyes away from the sensation.

A moaning sound broke through my dream, and I wondered what was going on. I had to focus, then force myself out of the dream state.

My eyes opened, and I turned to see Tyla grinding naked body against my leg, moaning in pleasure next to me. Her eyes were closed, and she looked to still be asleep.

My own needs flared to life, even though I thought we had sated them sufficiently before bed. My cock became rock hard at the sight and feel of her gyrating against me.

I pushed her over onto her back, breaking myself free of her grip and shifting myself down so that my face was in front of her lower entrance. Without preamble, I licked her folds and buried my tongue as deep as I could.

Her hands reached down and grabbed my hair, showing me exactly where to go. Looking up, I saw her eyes were now open and glowing a bright blue color, the only light in the otherwise dark room. I sped up my motions, bringing my finger up to help me give her stimulation, pushing it inside her just below where my tongue now caressed her clit.

I never broke eye contact with the woman I loved.

Without warning, her back arched and her hands clenched my hair tightly, almost causing me pain as I forced myself to give her pleasure through her orgasm.

"Oh fuck, oh gods, ohhhhhh fuckkkkkk," she moaned, letting the last words out slowly as she rode the sensation. After a minute, she shifted. "Okay, okay," she said, while tapping the top of my head.

"What did you do?" she asked when she caught her breath. "I feel so full of... power right now. And oh, gods, that was the best I have ever felt."

I smiled as I pulled myself back up to her side. "Had a dream, though it felt like the time I put the oath on Stern more than an actual dream. I saw an orb that I... just knew was you. It was slowly pushing power into me, so I wondered what would happen if I put some back, and then I heard you... um... moaning."

"That was... I do not know how to describe it. I have never felt so powerful and... the feeling of pleasure that came through was... just so much."

Her color returned as her breathing stabilized.

"Can we do it again?" she asked, a sly smile on her face as she pushed me on my back this time, mounting me and grabbing my still hard manhood.

"I think that—"

Ding. Ding. Ding. Ding. Ding.

The rapid ringing of the bell interrupted us, coming from somewhere in the distance outside.

"What is that?" I asked.

"The watch bell, but that means there is an attack..."

With concern fueling me, I got up, stark naked, \ went to the window, and pulled the shutters back.

"Oh, fuck," I said.

"What is it?" Tyla asked, getting off the bed to join me.

"Fire at the edge of town, and I see soldiers coming in through the gate. I think we are out of time."

We rushed to dress and equip ourselves with our gear. I quickly put on my leather armor and buckled its front straps. It had an inner vest that was a lighter, more comfortable leather and an outer layer that included thick leather bands that overlapped and supplied an excellent range of motion.

Arm pauldrons, also leather, came out in the same bands down halfway along my triceps. Then a small space where you could see my shirt before the arm guards and vambraces made of the same type of leather. Each arm had a small metal spike at the elbow about an inch long. That was an atheistic choice, since I could not really conceive of a tactical reason that I would use it.

My pants were also leather, padded, and reinforced, but again, I went for speed and dexterity over protection. I fitted a long knife that we had bought on my right hip, and my great sword I had become so acquainted with lately, hung from a chest harness over my front, crossing over my left side down the leg.

As I was putting on my pack, someone knocked on the door. Tyla, who was also in a light leather set similar to mine but fit for her womanly figure, grabbed her crossbow and aimed it at the door.

"It's Tas!" came the voice from the other side.

Tyla lowered the bow only a fraction as I opened the door. Tas, by herself, walked in quickly. She had her bag with her and a rapier type sword at her side.

"I heard the bell. That means we are under attack... and I think we should get my father and flee," Tas said.

"Agreed," I said as I finished putting on the bag. "Did you see him?"

"No." She shook her head. "I uh... came here first."

"Let's go, then. Tyla, can you bring up the rear? Tas in the center. Keep in a line."

They agreed and got into position, Tyla grabbing her bag and hoisting in on her back. She also had Susan's rapier... her rapier on her side with the crossbow on a sling I had designed for her in front.

I opened the door and made my way towards the stairs. The few other residents of the inn were opening their doors and watching us move into the hallway.

"What's going on?" an older woman asked as we walked down the hallway.

"I think soldiers from the north are here. We saw them coming in the front gates, and I advise you all to run if you can," I said.

"They should leave us alone, right?" an older man, whom I was assuming was the lady's husband, asked from behind her. He looked like he was using her as a shield.

"Up to you, but I am not staying," I said and left them all behind, continuing for the stairs.

As we approached the bottom of the stairs, a loud crash came from the main room, followed by the sound of stomping footsteps.

I paused at the door, trying to decide if we should go out the back instead, when I heard a voice yell out.

"By order of the new King Seir, leader of the former Matriarchies of humanity, this town is hereby annexed and under his law. All women between the ages of nineteen and forty shall be apprehended to be tested for magical power. You have his word that we will release them back to your custody if they are found to not be Chosen."

"This is my inn, damn you. What gives you the right to storm into here like you own the place?" Roman yelled from the room.

"Fuck," I said to myself.

I heard steel being drawn and knew we were about to be in trouble.

"Last warning," the voice from before said.

"Go fuck yourself!" Roman yelled, and I heard a clang as sword engaged sword.

"Father!" Tasnia screamed, and I pushed her back.

"I go in first. You cover me, make sure I don't get surrounded. Tyla, you find a spot and shoot the crossbow and your water." I hit the quick release latch on my pack, letting it fall to the ground, and pushed through the door to join the fray.

Seven men were in the hall, three of them were engaged with Roman as the rest stood back, ready to intervene. They obviously did not think the older man was too much of a threat that it would take more than that, because the one guy with a crossbow just stood there smiling until he saw us enter.

The man raised his crossbow towards me just as a cone made of water blew through the room and took the man's head off. I could hear a loud splat throughout the space and the fighting ceased momentarily as we all looked at who let out such a powerful blast.

Tyla, a face set in determination, had her hand in front of her, glaring at the man she just killed, then glared at the others as though daring they try something.

"A fucking witch!" the man who had spoken to Roman said. "A fucking strong one."

I was curious where the hell Tyla got that much power from and wondered briefly back to when I pushed all that energy into her. Then remembered where I was and charged the men, pulling my sword as time went into its slow-motion dance for me.

I saw Roman re-engage the three men, while I drove towards the other three in the room. My sword knocking down the first spear that tried to skewer me with a quick jab.

I shoved it out of the way and turned into him, punching the sharp spike on my left elbow into his eye. A loud thwack could be heard, and my arm jammed into him.

Guess I was wrong about the spike.

"Arghagk," the man yelled out, his voice deep from the dilation of time. But my elbow stuck into him as I tried to continue my turn, and I stumbled briefly. Leaving me open to an attack from the guy that was right behind him.

This next man lifted his sword in a downward chop, intent on cutting me in half, not caring that the guy with my elbow was stuck in his way. A crossbow bolt hit him in the arm, accompanied immediately after by a blast of water that knocked him in a spin to the ground.

I punched the guy's face who had attached himself to my elbow with my free arm, trying to lodge him free. Immediately after my fist connected, I yanked back again with my arm. A sucking sound was the prelude to the now empty socket where his eye used to be, and I refused to look at what was now on my elbow. Some things were really better left unknown.

I looked towards Roman briefly to see that Tasnia had come to his aid, taking on one man's attention to let her father focus on the other two.

I faced the last man of the three in my way and noticed that he was looking at me in fear and had pissed the front of his pants. Just as I was about to approach him, he turned and ran, but before he made it a single step, a bolt of water struck him in the back of the head, and he hit the ground.

I strode over to him as he struggled to get up, lifting my great sword and chopping at his neck. Putting an excessive amount of force behind the swing.

His head simply fell off, like he was a French noble during the revolution of 18th century France, and my sword was a guillotine. With blood gushing out everywhere, I turned to help Roman and Tas.

Even with all my speed, as I turned, I realized I needn't have bothered. With only two adversaries instead of three, Roman dispatched one with a strike of his great sword and cut a great gash into the leader of the group. Killing him instantly.

The second guy fared little better as he tried to capitalize on Roman's apparent distraction from the strike to his comrade.

But Roman had expected this move and stepped to the side just as the man stabbed with his sword. The stab missed by a few inches and put him out of position with his arms extended.

Roman simply cut the man's right arm off with his sword. Efficient, even if not as clean as the strike I made earlier.

A second later, a bash to the head with the pommel of his sword ended the threat, and he shifted towards the man who was engaged in a fight with the much more powerful than she looked Tas.

Tasnia had not over committed to her fight and was instead focused on keeping him busy. Despite the man's size, she defeated each blow and countered the strikes cleanly with her own.

Looking like a dancer more than a fighter, she parried and blocked each blow that the much larger man tried. Countering just enough to keep him off balance, deflecting rather than blocking. I considered moving into assist as well. but stopped when I saw what was happening between her and Tyla.

Tas had skillfully led him away from the rest of us, and Tyla had moved to line up a shot on her reloaded crossbow. As soon as the man was in position, she shot.

The bolt struck right in his neck, and just like that. Our fight was over.

We each congregated in the middle of the room after checking to see if anyone was alive enough to deserve a follow up.

"Well done, Tas, I am very proud of you." Roman said then shifted his glare to me. "I am extremely interested in how you moved that fast, kid, but we have to run, so I don't have time. Let's pick up our stuff and go. I know a back way out of town that should get us out of here. Oh, and Derk, clean off your elbow, that's disgusting."

CHAPTER 24

—— o ——

SACRIFICE FOR THOSE WE LOVE

We moved out of the Inn and heard yelling and screaming as we passed through the area that we had used to train the morning before.

"Derk, would you be so kind as to take up the rear? I will lead us out."

I nodded at Roman and let him go out the gate first, followed by Tas, then Tyla, and finally me. I could see shadows flickering caused by the light from the burning buildings in the town, the smell of smoke thick in the air.

After we crept out the gate in the back, we turned through alleyways at what seemed random to me. Occasionally doubling back if Roman heard the shouting and screaming of soldiers and frightened townspeople on our path.

I left the route completely up to Roman.

Somehow, we made it to the edge of town without being seen. A slight break in the old wooden walls was in front of us, only about fifty yards from the main gate to the town.

The break was small; it was just a couple of collapsed wooden stakes that were blocked by shrubbery on the other side of the fence. Wide enough for us and our gear, even for Roman's larger frame, if barely. I found myself thankful for the town's lack of maintenance of their defenses.

Roman turned to us after peaking through the gap. "They have a large force at the gate. This will be tricky, but I think we can get you across without notice."

I shuffled forward and viewed it for myself. Soldiers in armor stood outside the gate. Mostly they looked bored while a few wounded ones got treatment by a Chosen woman attending to them.

"Surprised they are not patrolling the perimeter more for runners, I don't trust it," I said.

Soon, a large man with two women at his side walked through the group from inside the town. He felt off to me... it was hard to describe, like he did not seem like just another man. Even if he was larger than the rest and looked like a gym rat from back home. Something about him was making my skin crawl.

"Roman, do you know that man?" I asked, shifting slightly so that Roman can peer through the gap.

"The big one? No."

"Let me see," Tyla said, pressing against me and looking out from over my shoulder. "I am not sure, but that may be one of Seir's lieutenants. He has a few, but the colossal size makes me think of what my mother told me of Albris, though I cannot be sure."

"Okay, then we plan for a Demigod then. I only see two women with him and one that looks to be healing the soldiers. She does not have a collar so she may be with him as well," I said.

"Rumor was that Seir kept his lieutenants in line by making them earn their... Chosen. Albris is the newest of the Demigods to descend and is trying to earn favor. Though it was rumored, he prefers men and only takes a Chosen for her power."

"Interesting tidbit. But it doesn't help us. Roman, where are you going?"

"I can create a distraction. When it happens, you three run for the tree line and I will follow when I can."

"Father, no!" Tas said, almost too loudly.

I placed my hand over her mouth, and she nodded.

"I know, Daughter. But there is no other way. I will be fine, trust me."

She nodded but looked upset. Tyla reached over and put her arms around the red-headed woman, kissing her on the cheek and whispering something in her ear I did not hear.

"Okay," I said. "I... We trust you and will be ready to run. If you don't show up in fifteen minutes, I am coming back for you. So, you better not be bullshitting me about following."

"Bull—?" Roman shook his head. "Trust me, I will be fine. Be prepared."

He moved off quickly and quietly, leaving his pack behind. I picked it up and put it on my front, adjusting it so that it did not cover my sword. "Alright, Tas, like I said, we trust your dad. He is a tough bastard who knows what he is doing, let's line up, you two first, and we get ready to run."

We watched the gates for the next several minutes as women were brought out bound and placed into the back of several wagons on the far side of the gates from us. I could not see the details because of the darkness.

I grasped tightly around the hilt of my great sword, the coolness of the grip comforting me only a bit as I struggled with allowing this travesty to occur.

"Why are they taking so many?" Tas asked.

"I am not sure," Tyla responded. "There is no way so many could be Chosen. It only happens to one out of several hundred women."

"My guess," I said, my tone grim. "They are putting them in one place for testing later or will use them as pleasure slaves to keep the male troops happy. But the history from Earth that I know of could influence my thoughts."

My emotions were getting the best of me, and I was about to get up when Tyla pressed her hand on my shoulder. "Master, there are only four of us. There are at least fifty that we can see, along with a Demigod and his Chosen. Not to mention the soldiers in the town. I love your willingness to protect, but... we really have no chance against those odds. If you order it, I will go with you, but we will die and do them no good."

I let out a deep sigh. She was right, but I could hardly live with myself and was still considering it.

"Derk," Tas said. "I know it's not my place, but if we run now, we have a chance to build and do something for them later... hopefully."

She was also right. But I absolutely hated it.

"Fuck Vex, he knew I could not resist fighting his war. Fuck them and their stupid games. I am making this vow right now. I may not have the chance to help them now... but I will kill every fucking Demi that I can, just to see all the people of this world free." I pounded my fist into the palm of my hand.

"And we will help you, Master."

"I will be by yer side as long as you let me."

Both reached back to put their hands on my shoulders as they said this.

But before I could say anything to them, an explosion came from inside the town. So large that a fireball reached up into the sky from somewhere off in the distance and I could feel the ground vibrate. Debris from the palisades fell on the three of us, and more importantly, most of the soldiers at the gate went running towards the explosion.

"Run," I said and pushed forward on both girls to get them moving. I held back for several heartbeats to make sure all the attention was away from them.

Everyone was running towards or staring at whatever Roman did to make that explosion. I could see the last vestiges of the fireball's glow on the other side of the buildings fade away.

With the attention away from us, I ran, my pack on my back, Romans pack on my front. Gripping the great sword so it did not jangle too much. I did a low shuffle rather than a full sprint to keep my outline and, hopefully, my noise level down. Following the girls, the two hundred yards distance to the tree line.

When we got there, I hid behind the shrubs next to Tyla and Tas, looking back to see if anyone had seen us. No one at the gate looked in our direction. However, it was too dark for me to see anything beyond the torches that were set up near the entrance to the town.

"Let's head farther into the woods, find some thick underbrush, and wait for your father."

The girls nodded, even though Tas hesitated a bit, chewing on her lower lip. We worked our way through the thick brush to a point I figured we could be safe from casual observation.

A small clearing proved perfect for our needs, and we set down all the packs on the far side from the town.

"This should work. Put all your stuff over there so we can grab it if we need to run. How are you both doing?"

"I drained a lot of that power you gave me in that fight. I am not sure how much I have left. But it's not much. I went a little... overboard on the man who was going to shoot you." I could see her smirk, even in the darkness. The moon's light was just enough to let us see each other's outlines.

"It's okay, try to save it. I'll try to figure out how to give you more, but for now, I don't think it's a good time to go to sleep and try it again. Something we will have to work on. Tas?"

"I wish I knew more about my power. I felt so useless."

"You were a natural with that sword. You impressed me with how you handled that man," I said, putting my hand on her shoulder and making eye contact. "You did great."

"Thank you, Derk," she said, smiling at me.

Her pale face was easier to read in the darkness than Tyla's, and I could see the outline of her lips. I would swear that I could almost see her blush. But I may have been projecting that part.

"Alright, I am going to sneak back over towards the clearing and see if I can keep an eye out for your dad. You two stay here with the stuff and keep as silent as possible. I'll knock on a tree over in that direction before—"

A crash behind me in the brush got me to turn around as a hulking figure trampled through the brush. "There you are, little Tyla. I have been looking everywhere for you," the figure said.

I pulled my sword as I put myself between the girls and this current threat. However, he did not rush me right away, as I would have expected. Following him were three other figures that had much smaller silhouettes, likely women.

The man was closer to seven feet than six. Shirtless except for a single piece of thick leather armor on his left shoulder that was more decoration than actual protection. It had straps going down to his pants and held a war hammer from a thong on it. The costume, because that is what it really was, reminded me of old cheesy roman gladiator movies I used to watch as a kid, showing off the muscles more than protecting the body.

"Lord Seir has bid me to capture you and return you to your mother. Whom I am told is very much looking forward to getting you home. I promise to be polite should you come with us and allow no one to touch you." The man said. I was now sure it was the one from earlier, the same feeling of... not quite right, permeated off of his body.

I drew my sword up in a guard. "Sorry buddy, she is not going."

"Ha, ha, ha, little mortal. You may not know who you are dealing with, but I am Albris, Demigod and the right hand of Seir. You will not survive, but I am merciful. If you put your weapons down, I will let you go with your life."

"Really?" I asked. "You're going to monologue like a cheesy super villain?"

"What did you say, mortal? Your words make little sense. Are you insulting me?"

I rolled my eyes, even though I was fairly sure he could not see them. This guy did not seem the smartest, but he had size. That mattered too. "No... just saying that she is not going, I don't care who you are."

I hoped the girls behind me had prepared. Without further warning I rushed forward to Albris to take him by surprise, pushing all my focus into my time dilation perception.

I was a little disconcerted when his eyes widened for only a brief second and he moved, matching my speed in drawing out his war hammer.

A loud clang of metal meeting metal clanging throughout the night.

My confidence fell, however, now that I realized he could counter all my advantages I had relied on to that point.

Fuck it, I'll go down swinging.

I backed away from him after our weapons met and he took a swing with his hammer and his giant reach. I barely made it out of the way. The wind from the blow came hard into my face as it came within inches of turning me into a nail.

Then fire ran through it as it lit up, creating a light that we could all see by, which also ruined my night vision.

Now I was even more concerned. Not sure how I could handle the fire and keep it from burning through my defenses.

I swung the sword at him in an overhand blow, his hammer again meeting with a clang I could feel reverberating down my arms. The heat from his hammer made my palms burn a bit as it transferred its energy to my sword and then down to my hands. I pushed my water element into them to heal them and then tried to move it up into the sword to see if it could counter the heat.

Steam resulted from my success, but it did reduce the burn I felt.

Sounds of struggle were happening around us, even if that fight was happening in slow motion to me. As Tas and Tyla engaged the three women that had come with Albris.

I blocked another strike from Albris' hammer, again my arms felt like they were going to shake out of their sockets from the blow. I knew in the back of my mind we were in trouble at this point, and I started mentally struggling for a way to get out of it, but I was coming up blank.

I backed into a tree and stopped while Albris swung his hammer at me sideways. While he had great strength, he did not vary his technique much. I ducked and rolled underneath him as the hammer hit the tree like a supersonic jet. The tree blew out but did not catch fire like I had expected, as the debris rained down on everyone here with no flames.

Using the moment of chaos, rather than attack the big and ugly brute, I instead went for one of his companions. I got up and leaped at a dark-haired woman who looked like she had electrical wires coming out of her hands, about to attack Tas from behind. Before she even realized she was under attack, she died as I stabbed her through the chest and killed her instantly, this time twisting my sword as Roman taught me, so it would be easier to get out.

"Noooo!" Albris screamed

Each of them, his women included, all shuddered and took a step like they were puppets that had a single string cut. It was not enough to put them out of the fight, but I think it just put the odds from overwhelmingly against us to just significantly against us.

Baby Steps! I thought to myself just before the giant fucking hammer hit me in my right shoulder.

I flew sideways, and I was sure that my entire shoulder was just broken from the impact. I was an idiot that let his guard down for a moment and now I was paying the price.

I managed, just barely, to keep my sword in my hand when I landed.

I heard a scream of rage that sounded like Tyla, and I glanced up just in time to see her send a bolt from her crossbow at the now unarmed Albris. The bolt landed with a meaty thwack into his own shoulder, missing his heart with a last-minute dodge from the giant.

One woman rushed up to Albris and put her hands on him, obviously his healer from before. While the other woman's hands blazed a reddish orange as she prepared to cast what I assumed was fire at Tyla. Before her energy left her hand, Tasnia came up from behind and pushed her rapier through the woman's midsection in her stomach.

While I was proud of the girl, I noticed it wasn't an instantly killing blow.

"Off me, woman," Albris yelled and stood up. "So, you are one of us. I do not recognize you. What is your name and why do you not serve Seir like the rest of us in these lands?"

I had my shoulder mostly healed, but my power was running low. Not sure I could do that again, I decided stalling would be good while I figured out a new plan.

"I... am a rival faction. That is all I can say," I said, bluffing my ass off.

"A rival? But wait, does that mean... No, it can't be." Albris said, looking up to the air while he thought.

I did not know what he meant, but I was really hoping he would say more. Information was king of the battlefield. So, I just stayed silent, and I worked my way back to my feet.

"Do you serve Rilro or Takus? I offered my services to both of them, but they refused me."

"I am forbidden to speak more about it. I will, out of courtesy, offer for both of us to walk away while we consult our masters for further guidance."

God, I hoped he bought this line of bullshit and kept talking.

"Your offer is tempting, but I cannot," Albris said, shaking his head. "I bear you no personal ill will, but I gave a compact to Seir and I must keep it unless released."

Fuck!

I moved over, putting myself beside my girls again, who had gathered to one side, and his. The briefest thought of why I was suddenly considering Tas as mine nagged at me, but I ignored it.

"I understand. I am sorry the others did not accept you. They have... a little more honor to them than who you serve now."

A motion in the distance caught my eye, and I resisted the temptation to smile.

"I... agree. While I find Seir's methods cruel, he is also not the worst of them. As you know, what we call life in our society is rigid. The freedom granted to us in these worlds, the release of the rules placed on us, not to mention the pleasures of the flesh we lost access to when we accepted our ascension so long ago. I gladly accepted the first opportunity to leave."

"I understand, and do not disagree," I said.

"You did not give me your name yet. May I have it?" Albris asked.

I considered for a moment, but decided against it. "I wish I could, but I also have a compact, and it is not time to reveal that yet."

Albris nodded. "Understood. Shall we carry on, then?"

"If that is your wish," I said.

Albris picked up his hammer and the fire on it, which was almost dead now, came back to life. Lighting up the clearing once again. He looked at his healer and pointed at the bleeding fire mage. "Heal her. I will handle them."

"Yes, lord," she said, and went to comply.

Her face was void of any emotions that I could see.

"Let's finish this, and for what it is worth, you fought well," he said and took a single step toward me.

However, right as he did, a blur came out of the bushes and sliced down with a great sword. Albris had the advantage of being able to slow time just as I could, so he was able to dodge the sword. It only sunk into his shoulder, punching through the armor padding then bit into his shoulder an inch or two at most.

"You will not have my daughter!" the man screamed.

Before he could follow up with anything more, Albris elbowed him hard in the gut.

Roman staggered back from the blow, leaving his sword wedged into the giant, and I moved forward to deliver my own attack.

My goal was to finish this bastard off with a head strike from behind, but Albris stood unexpectedly, turned to me, and used his good arm to block my sword with his hammer.

He followed with his other arm, even with a sword stuck in it, to punch me in the chest.

The force was enough to send me flying into the dirt several feet away. Landing with a thud and a roll.

I lifted my head just in time to see Albris reach and grab the part of the sword that still stuck into him.

Pulling it out of his shoulder, barely grunting from the pain.

How he did not scream from all the damage I did not know.

The large man threw the great sword in the air and caught it so that it was now in his hand like a javelin.

He threw it as hard as he could right at Roman.

Roman died, never having a chance.

It impaled him right in the middle of the head, and I watched the man I grew to respect die right before my eyes. Hatred welled up inside me as I struggled to my feet. Promising myself that I would mount Albris' head on a fireplace somewhere and use it for darts.

I, however, was not the one that Albris needed to worry about.

"FATHER!" Tasnia screamed in a combination of pure sorrow and rage.

It was a scream that I am not sure could have existed at that pitch if I had not been there to hear it.

Tas' arms lit up with the glow the colors of hellfire, her eyes lighting up an eerie orange and red to match. The energy then traveled down her arms and pooled up into bright balls of light in her hands. She pointed both at Albris and his two remaining witches and in a powerful scream.

"BURN!"

Albris did the smart thing. He turned and ran, picking up both his women in his arms as he did so. The flames coming right on his heels.

Tas unleashed two torrents of flame from each palm, each the size of a basketball in width. They coated the ground and the foliage like napalm as they hit.

It was so bright; I could see nothing on the other side as the fire spread throughout all the brush in front of us like a world war two flamethrower. I did not know whether she incinerated her targets or not, as I had to turn my eyes away from the vivid light.

When the glow finally stopped, I turned back just in time to see Tasnia tittering on the verge of collapse.

I ran over and caught her, laying her gently on the ground. "Tyla! Grab the packs that you can. I will get mine and carry Tas. We need to run. I don't think we have enough left to go again, and we need to run from the fire." My voice barely made it over the roar of the flames, the crackling of the burning trees also making it difficult.

Our only salvation was that the breeze was pushing the smoke and some of the heat away from us but sweat started pouring from my forehead, anyway.

"Yes, my love," she said, and moved to comply.

I dragged Tas away from the flames, setting her down briefly to pick up my pack and my sword and put them on me. I had to leave Roman's gear to carry Tasnia, but I picked her back up in a bridal carry and we left the now blazing inferno behind us.

We ran as hard as we could, and just like that, I found myself once again in the forest, running for my life.

CHAPTER 25

INTERLUDE - SURRENDER AND FEAR

Seir sat on his throne, perfectly comfortable while waiting for his next guest. He sat in the highest tower in the City of Nitre, the room once was the bedchamber of Josephina. Now it was a greeting room used to impress visitors and conduct orgies with those he considered worthy. Usually, it was the same women that were in this room with him.

Because they were his property.

Even if he treated Josephina well, all of them who had agreed to join his harem were his forever. He was the one who wrote most of the rules that governed the process by which they forced these Chosen to serve their masters in whatever manner they were ordered. He designed the compulsions, ensured their quality, and arranged them so he could achieve his own desires when it was his turn to descend.

The only restriction placed on his creations was that they had to agree to their servitude with free will.

He enjoyed the power immensely and his... benefactor had promised him this position many years ago for the services rendered.

As the thought of what was now his drifted, he studied his current favorite toys.

To his left, Josaphina sat in a chair only slightly smaller than his. She was the only one he allowed to dress as she wished. She had never disappointed him, and a small part of him enjoyed rewarding her with some semblance of self-control.

Josaphina still played the part. She dressed regally and elegantly. Her slightly reddish-brown hair was done up and coiffed to perfection. Her legs crossed with one knee over the other, she waited patiently, just like him. She had a small and knowing smirk on her face.

To his right, kneeling on the ground, sat a completely naked Miranda. Her hands were behind her back, and she sat up straight, with her butt on the backs of her feet, ankles crossed behind her. She had a leather ball in her mouth with a matching tie strap going over her ears and around her head, tied simply. She could remove it, if she chose, but her own inner desire, mixed with the compulsion that Seir personally wrote so many years ago, made it the furthest thing from her mind.

She glanced over as he gazed upon her, a smile showing through the ball of leather in her mouth. It was a look that promised anything and everything he wanted, should he ask.

Shifting his head to the left, he saw Patricia. She was similarly positioned like Miranda with similar accouterments, or lack thereof. So far, she was his favorite acquisition, resisting him longer than all the others. Even with the compulsion, she fought for her daughter even as she gave into the desire to pleasure him. It took him weeks to break her of that, even with the compulsion.

Now, however, she did not differ from Miranda. She was a slave to his whims and only concerned with his needs.

He had three others, but they were on assignment. He only kept his favorites with him. These women were powerful, and he had decided that after Susan that quality was preferable to quantity. A lesson he should have learned previously in his five-thousand-year long life before coming to Timeria. But even Demigods made mistakes.

He had a tendency of thinking with his dick a lot more than when he was an ascended. As a full Roxannez, his baser instincts were suppressed, done so by the social propriety protocols forced upon his kind by the council and written into their matrixes.

But his needs and desires were always trying to break through. Driving him to want to be on this world so badly, that he became the pawn of his master and agreeing to achieving the Overseers goals.

A guard knocked on the door, and it opened, allowing a single female to enter the room.

"King Seir, lady Einestra of Casting Harbor has arrived," a guard with Seir's glyph on his forehead announced.

"She may enter," Josephina called out.

A beautiful young blonde woman entered the room. She tried to keep the bearing of a woman in charge of her fate, but Seir could see the signs of panic and nervousness all over her features.

Her breathing was rapid and the vein on her neck was pushing in and out rapidly. Clearly visible as it pulsed all the way down her flow cut dress which highlighted her magnificent breast. Her neutral mask was further betrayed by eyes that darted over everyone in the room several times, stopping repeatedly on Miranda and Patricia.

Part of her was aroused, if Seir was reading the signs correctly. Her sudden eye dilation when she glanced at the two subservient women followed by the release of pheromones she was giving off. They were wafting off her like a cloud of dust turned up like a tornado in a desert. Another advantage he had written into the ruleset for this world. However, this improvement was only for him, a personal gift from his master, along with a few others.

The woman stopped several paces in front of him. Saying nothing and standing erect, playing some kind of power game that she somehow thought mattered.

The only thing that mattered to Seir was power... and pleasure. He would play any game that resulted in both things for him.

"Lady Einestra, to what do we owe the pleasure of your visit? As we promised, I have given you safe passage to deliver your message and not forced you to wear a collar," Seir said.

Einestra took a breath, trying to do it slowly so her nerves would go unnoticed.

She failed.

"Lord Se—"

"King," Josephina interrupted, causing Einestra to fluster a bit.

"King Seir, my apologies," Einestra said, making her first genuine mistake of the conversation. "I have come to beseech you for power. I have heard that you treat those that come to you first..." She glanced at Josephina. "...better treatment than those you acquire through force." She cast her eyes distastefully at both Patricia and Miranda.

"Why would I do that?"

The look of surprise on her face told Seir that she did not prepare for that question. Another person so full of themselves that they could not conceive that anything they offered would not be accepted.

She again paused while she considered.

"Be... Because I am the daughter of the Matriarch of Casting Harbor, first in line to her title, and I can give you the entire matriarch if you agree to my terms," she said, nodding.

"You, however, are not your mother. My question is, why would I choose you? What do you bring me that I could not get from her?"

"I... my mother has locked herself in her castle. She has turned inward in abject fear of you and your fellow Demigods. The people suffer and she does nothing but fret. I am offering you myself for your power. With promises to deliver to you the entire matriarchy without having to resort to force of arms. I am of Lady rank to the level of Mistress. I can replace her and serve you with the same power as she. All I am asking in return is treatment equal to Josephina."

Seir put his hand on his chin and rubbed it, as though considering her offer seriously.

"No," he finally said, dropping his arm back to the arm of the chair with a plop.

"What? What do you mean, no?"

Her confusion was amusing to him, so he smiled.

Seir snapped his fingers once, and Miranda and Patricia stood in unison, taking out the leather balls in their mouths and dropping them to the floor.

Einestra lifted her arms and electricity sparked from her hands. Her hair lifted from an unfelt wind, and the curls in her blond hair rose.

"What is this? You promised me peace!" she said in alarm.

Seir reached out with his hand and made a crushing motion, using his power to neutralize hers. It was the other gift he was given.

"How did you do that?" Einestra asked, deflated and shaking in fear.

Seir did not answer. He simply snapped again, and Miranda and Patricia approached the throne he sat on. Bowing their heads in front of him, he watched as they worked perfectly in unison together to pull his pants down and expose his cock as though they had practiced doing that together hundreds of times.

Because they had.

As soon as they began servicing Seir's manhood with their mouths, he gazed back at the incredibly nervous young woman. "You see, lady Einestra, I know something that you do not. You may say you want to be treated like Josephina here..."

He glanced over at the woman to his left, who had now pulled up her dress and was pleasuring herself while watching Miranda and Patricia perform their duties.

"However, I do not need that. I may be willing to give you the power you seek, but you will agree to become just like these two here." He placed both of his hands on the heads of Miranda and Patricia. "Which I actually believe is your secret wish. But since I could be wrong, however, the choice is yours. You may leave and return to your mother just as you are, or take off your dress, get on your knees, and join these two in their duties. It is all completely up to you."

He relaxed his head, leaning it back on the throne as he enjoyed the two women moving their mouths in sync up and down his engorged cock. Each one had taken a side and was moving at a steady clip, their tonguing mingling together as they slathered him in their saliva.

"Choose," Josephina added, not looking up at the blonde-haired woman as she kept her hand in her womanhood.

Lady Einestra stood there for a moment in indecision, several times making like she would walk out but never fully committed to the motion.

Finally, she closed her eyes, took a deep breath, and reached up to undo the clasps of her elegant dress on each side of her shoulders. The garment lowered, exposing her supple and perky breasts. She then released the belt that held it all in place, letting the dress drop to the floor. She was left only in her panties and garter belts attached to thigh-high stockings.

"What would…" she began, her voice squeaking. She coughed to control it before continuing. "What would you have me do to you, my king?"

"Excellent choice. You may yet get all that you wish and more. Now, start with my darling wife. If you bring her enough pleasure and convince her of your sincerity, then I will make you an offer to accept of your own free will. Then you will get the power you hope for and take a place by my side."

Einestra took a step forward as she pulled her feet out of the pool of fabric that was her dress, undoing the claps of each of her garters slowly. When that was complete, she guided the underwear below her wide hips as she turned away from the king and bent over to guide them the rest of the way down. This provided Josephina and Seir with a perfect view of her wide and curvy hips and recently shaved nether regions.

She stood back up and faced Josephina, taking another noticeable breath before moving forward to kneel before the older woman.

Josephina smiled at the young woman, readjusting her seat to pull the entirety of her skirt above her hips and bunch it around her waist, fully exposing herself to the young woman. Then, placing each leg over an arm of the chair, she lifted her hand and gestured to her crotch.

"You may begin," she said.

Einestra, now breathing heavily in excitement and with a noticeable run of fluids running down her legs from her eagerness, bent forward to claim her prize.

She fully committed to doing the best job she could.

Seir had never left his chair the entire time, but now he grunted to control himself.

"Be prepared to accept my offer," he said through clenched teeth as he prepared to shoot more than just his power inside the young blonde-haired woman.

Einestra never responded. Instead, she focused on impaling herself repeatedly on his erect manhood. Facing away from him and towards the three former matriarchs who sat on the floor watching as the heir to the Casting Harbor throne debased herself on their king's cock.

Sweat dripped from her face, and her hands gripped tightly on the arms of the throne as she continued to undulate her tight opening into Seir's lap. The loud slaps of skin with every hard impact echoed throughout the chamber as Einestra struggled to keep up her pace.

"Fuck, fuck, fuck, fuck," she called out as she orgasmed again, but never stopped, even after the next climax passed.

"Kneel before me," Seir commanded.

She got off his cock and turned to face him, dropping on her knees.

Seir shoved his erect member deep inside her throat and shot his load deep inside.

"Do you accept my service?" he asked, grunting between each word.

"Mmm hmmm," Einestra mumbled while nodding as she frantically tried to keep his fluid from spilling out.

Power erupted from Seir's chest, through his groin, and suffused into the Lady Einestra. Her entire body glowed with a bright white light.

Einestra came once again from the flood of power, leaving a mess of bodily fluids on the floor beneath her as she did.

Then she passed out, her mouth slipping off Seir as she hit the floor like a sack of flour. No one moved to catch her.

"Miranda, take her and get her cleaned up. Patricia, make sure you get her properly attired when she wakes up and is ready to join you."

"Yes, my King," Miranda and Patricia said in unison as they got up to complete their command.

Josephina simply got up and moved to put her clothes back on.

"Thank you, husband," she said when they left.

"I love to spoil you, my dear. It is a guilty pleasure of mine. But that makes seven of you now. I cannot add anymore." He reached out and guided the back of his hand on the supple skin of her still exposed ass as she put the dress on.

"Though I doubt Patricia will mind as much now. But we can no longer add her daughter as we promised."

"She is fully in your thrall now, my King. As are we all."

"As it should be." Seir finished putting his own pants back on as a knock on the door sounded. "Enter."

The guard from earlier put his head around the door. "My lord, members of your guard stationed in Black Run have come bearing a prisoner."

"Bring them in," Seir said.

Seir sat on his throne and waited as four men escorted in a fifth with a hood over his head and fully bound. Something felt familiar with him, and he was giving off a strange feeling.

"My King," the senior guard said as he took one knee in front of Seir, the king's glyph on his forehead plainly visible. "We captured one of your servants. He was helping some witches escape from the academy holding grounds... we could not retrieve them. My apologies, my king."

Seir was confused at their use of the term servant. A servant could not betray him so easily, but he had to address the incompetence first.

"Who is responsible for this lapse?" Seir demanded.

"I... take full responsibility, lord," the man said.

Seir looked over to Josephina who nodded and lifted her palm. A beam of light put a hole right through the man's head, cauterizing the wound and leaving no trace of blood as the man hit the floor.

Seir moved his gaze to the next man standing. "Ensure that it does not happen again. Who is this man... he feels... familiar to me?"

"Yes, my king," the new leader of this group said, his voice high in pitch and breaking from nerves.

He reached over and pulled the hood from the man.

"Impossible!" Seir cried out, astonished and shocked at what he saw.

"King now? You have moved up since I saw you last, haven't you?" the man asked with a giggle.

"How?" Seir paused as he stared at the man's face, eyes swollen from the beating he had received, and marks and scars all over his body. The guards had not been gentle. "Leave now. The man stays," Seir said.

The guards who dropped the man to the ground and fled without a word, hoping to save their lives with a quick exit.

When the door closed, Seir continued. "How did you remove my Mark?"

Stern smiled through the pain from his position on the floor, unable to move because of the bindings and the broken bones. "I serve a new lord now."

He laughed briefly until he started coughing in a fit.

"That's impossible," Seir said, speaking more to himself than to Stern.

"Not anymore!" Stern said, somehow still giggling through the coughs while spitting out some blood.

Seir put his hand out in front of him and closed his eyes. He sensed for the telltale mark of power, but it was not in the usual place where one of his kind displayed such marks - prominent on the head to declare ownership. Instead, it emanated from the man's arm. He opened his eyes and pulled back the sleeve.

"Who did this? None of the others here would have hidden their mark in such a manner."

"Can't say. Sworn to secrecy," Stern said, still smiling.

Obviously, the man had lost his faculties.

"Josephina, kill this man and have Miranda incinerate the body. Send word to General Taimana to end the siege and take the fort by force, then get his forces back into the garrison. Bring me any important prisoners he captures and kill the rest. Start training and rebuilding his forces for a potential invading army of unknown composition."

"Yes, my King and husband," Josephina said, concern in her voice.

"I will speak to my benefactor. Have the women attend me when I am done... wake Einestra forcefully, if you must. I will have many needs to be filled when I am done."

"I... will see it done. We will relieve your stress in any way you command us."

Seir marched into the back door of the chamber without answering, entering his private study. Just before the door closed, he heard Josephina use her power to end that miserable Stern forever.

CHAPTER 26

TEARS, HOPE, AND NEW BEGINNINGS

I awoke to movement next to me. I had been sleeping lightly, even through the complete exhaustion, just in case.

We had found a traveler's tree in the early evening hours the night before. Having moved away from Hills Crest, into the forests from the early hours of the morning into the day. I am not sure how Tyla and I had the stamina, but we had traveled many miles that I would hope would give us enough space to get away.

Aided by the massive fire started by our new resident fire expert, we could still see smoke rising off into the distance when we finally stopped. She had created one hell of a tremendous blaze.

No campfire for ourselves, we had just laid out the bedrolls so we could all fit together and put a still sleeping Tasnia in the center. Then we had each taken a side when we went to sleep. We did not want to take a chance that she would wake up without those that cared for her in close proximity.

As my eyes finally adjusted to being open again, the dawn light streaming through the branches allowed me to see what was happening.

Tas was moving and wrenching in her sleep from a dream. Based on her rapid movements, I would guess it was a nightmare. She moaned several times in a way that made me think she was screaming.

I tightened my grip on her midsection and peered over at Tyla, who had also opened her eyes with concern at her friend.

"Should we try to wake her?" Tyla whispered.

I pondered this for a minute as I considered. I was not a psychologist or anything, but I recalled that dreams usually helped the subconscious process things so that the awake mind could deal with them better. There were a few technologies developed back on Earth before the end that would even let you learn things in your sleep.

"No, we can just be here for her, hold her close, and be ready when she wakes. I doubt anyone could track us with the fire she caused, but even if they could, it's worth the risk for her to deal with this a bit."

Tyla nodded and moved her arm so that our hands clasped, while we both leaned against the redhead, who was going through trauma that I wished I could fix for her.

But I couldn't. Tyla and I could only support her on the journey through it.

A few minutes went by before Tas jumped in our arms, her eyes opening wide, and she let a small scream.

"Father!" she said.

"Shhhh, Tas," I said when she struggled from our grip. "You're safe, we have you."

Tears came out, and she started crying uncontrollably. "He killed him! I... I saw him die."

Tyla and I both snuggled closer to the woman, both putting our head to the side of hers.

"I am so sorry, Tas," Tyla said, her own tears breaking through as she joined her crying friend.

"I..." I began, not sure what I wanted to say. "I honestly don't know what to say... but I am here for you."

Part of me felt guilty at not being fast enough, but saying that aloud would not help Tas right now, so I kept it inside. If I thought she blamed me for her father's death, which I may deserve, then I would accept that.

Instead of laying blame, she turned to her side facing me, moving down so she could plant her face in my shirt, using it to wipe her eyes as she continued to cry. Grabbing the fabric with both hands balled up in a fist as she did so.

I could feel the wetness sink through instantly, and it brought me memories of the time that Tyla did the same just a few short weeks ago.

It was then that I realized my feelings for Tas were the same as my feelings for Tyla, and the trajectory of our relationship was heading on a similar path. I honestly was not sure if I could or should stop it.

I was not even sure if this was another mental push from Vex.

Tyla scrunched up and spooned the back of Tas, putting her chin on the top of Tas's head and looking up at me with knowing eyes.

She felt it too.

We sat like that for a long time as Tas continued to cry, and Tyla and I just let her. I was not sure exactly how much time passed, but eventually, the crying died down to the occasional sob.

Even when the sobs finally ended, no one moved. We each just appreciated the comfort of each other while we came to grips with what had happened the night before.

"Thank ya," Tas said, finally lifting her head, putting her hand to the side of my face and kissing me on the mouth.

Shocked at the sudden movement, I could only react by returning the kiss. My passion for the woman almost overriding my sense of propriety.

But she broke it off before it got too heated, then smiled at me with a small smile, looking beautiful even with her red-rimmed and puffy eyes. She then turned over to Tyla and gave her the same kiss on the mouth as she had given to me. Again, it was just a simple kiss, no passion involved, but it lingered like that of lovers comforting each other, not friends.

With the kiss finished, she got back into her spot, nestled against my now wet chest. It did not seem to bother her as she wrapped her leg around me and Tyla moved her body to fill the void, bringing the blankets over us as we sat like that for the rest of the morning.

"I really do not want to do this," I said to the group, both women looking up at me expectedly. "But I really have to pee."

Both smirked a little, and a giggle even escaped Tasnia's lips.

We pulled ourselves from the pile, and I walked out of the tree and found a bush to claim as my own.

When I returned, Tyla and Tas had set out some of the preserved food we had packed. They had placed some inside a bowl for me while they left the protection of the travelers' tree to take care of their own morning ablutions.

"The sun has hit its zenith," I said around bites of food when they returned. "We need to get moving soon."

"Do we continue on to Riven Hold?" Tyla asked.

"Yes," I said with a nod. "But we only stop by the backup rendezvous we discussed with Stern, leave a message for him to meet us somewhere else if he is not there, and get out as quickly as possible. I do not want to get trapped again."

"Yes, Master."

"Tas, I… I hope you are not angry at me," I said, feeling it was time I broached the topic.

"Why would ya think I was angry at ya?" she asked.

"I… am not sure that you are, to be honest. Just feeling a little guilty and angry at myself for not getting your dad out alive. I would honestly not blame you if you were, but I wanted to know. I think that… if we are going to be around each other for a long time." I paused, trying to get the words I wanted to say right. "We should work on being open with our thoughts and feelings… and I wanted to share them with you to start that off on the right foot." I looked down at the ground, chewing the jerky as I considered the words I just said.

She scooted over to me so that she was in front of me. "I don't, Derk. I blame the one that killed him. But, since you just mentioned being honest with your feelings, I will tell you the truth as well. For a while this morning, I thought about that. How, if you did not come into our lives, he would be alive right now. For a brief second, I was angry at you in my grief."

She paused for a second, changing her gaze from me and then to Tyla. "But I… quickly concluded that I also care for both of you and want you in my life as well. So, I refocused that anger on the one that did it. I want to kill that Demigod right now more than anything else, but I don't want to lose either of you to do it. I… already lost too much."

I reached over and grabbed Tyla in a hug, Tyla joining us a moment later. No one cried this time, but there was a definitive sadness in the group still.

"Will you let me join ya?" Tas asked in a whisper. "I see how ya and Tyla are together, and I find… I want that as well."

A war waged inside of me. The battle of wants and desires waged against my sense of what was right and wrong. I was unsure which would win.

"Say yes, Derrick… please," Tyla said from the other side of Tas's head.

"I… I want to. Part of me is still against it, though. Give me some time to come to grips with it?"

They both agreed and tightened their hug.

After a few minutes, we finally got our bags packed and our stuff ready to travel.

"I now realize that a bow would have been preferable to the crossbow for a few reasons," I said as I carried the rabbit into the small rock overhang that we had decided would be our camp for the night.

We had built the tent we brought with us under it for protection from the winds that had picked up since this morning, a sign of severe weather approaching as the seasons shifted.

"What happened?" Tyla asked as she prepared the fire, and since it was dark enough now that we did not have to worry about the smoke signaling our position to any trackers. We had only gotten a few miles in that afternoon, and I did not feel completely safe.

"I missed the rabbit with the crossbow, and it's a pain to reload when running. So, I had to use my power to run it down and tackle it and twist its neck to kill it."

"At least ya got it."

"How are you doing?" I asked the redhead.

"I... still hurt inside, but I feel better with you two around."

"Anything you need, just ask," I said, casually placing the rabbit on a flat stone someone had cleaned, glancing over at the girls in time to see them share a glance with each other. That hidden language all women could share, apparently throughout time and place regardless of the planet they were on, all with a simple expression on their face, but I did not comment on it. I was pretty sure I had made my decision, and they would just have to accept it when I told them.

"I skinned and dressed it, just need to put a stick in it and put it over the fire when it's ready. Should be plenty for us tonight."

"Tas said she would cook for us. She used to do it all the time at the Inn, and she brought spices."

"That's great, thank you."

Tas turned red in the cheeks. "I hope you like it. I was not as good as the regular cook, but when she had her last child last year, I had to take over for a while."

"I am sure it will be fine," I said, going over to the edge of the clearing to wash my hands. "Let's see if I can make this work today."

I closed my eyes and focused on my power, specifically the blue element that Tyla was giving me. I reached out with the energy inside me and pictured the atoms of hydrogen and oxygen in the atmosphere. Using the power given to me, I... commanded them to come together in the palm of my right hand and shift into the substance I desired.

Sound of water hitting the soil made me open my eyes as I saw a small stream of water coming out of my hand like a faucet. Excitement at the success ran through my body, and I could not help but raise my hand in the air in a fist to celebrate.

It was a stupid move really, especially since water was coming out of it.

I soaked myself all over my right side before I could gather the will to stop the water. You had to consider both the start and stop when summoning water.

Unfortunately, this meant I had to endure the ridicule as both women fell over laughing at what I had just done.

"Of course, I did that," I said, then gazed over at the two giggling girls. "That shall be your night's entertainment, my ladies. I hope you enjoyed the show."

I took a small bow, which made them giggle even more.

I focused again and got the water started without making idiotic celebration moves, and filled up a bowl we were using to wash hands. We even had soap that smelled a little better than what we had before.

Finished, I went over to the bag and fished out a fresh shirt and pants. At least I had taken my armor off. It had some damage from the fight, but it was still serviceable.

I placed my wet clothes on top of the tent, hopeful they would dry overnight. Then I put on new clothes before I sat down. The rabbit was now cooking over the coals and Tas was heating a pot of water with her power next to it.

"I added some spices to it. It's not much, sorry."

"If it will keep us from digging into our prepared food, it will be perfectly fine. I'm just worried just in case we get to Riven Hold, and it's a disaster."

"There are a few other towns, but they will probably be sacked before Riven Hold," Tyla said.

When the food was complete, we ate in comfortable silence for a while. Cooked rabbit and a broth with some vegetable in it to go with it. Simple but filling.

"It tasted great, Tas, thank you," I said.

"Yer welcome."

"Going to be a little chilly tonight and may storm a bit," I said, noticing the rapid drop in temperature.

Clouds had also moved in.

"It's the storm. It means winter is going to be moving in early this year. Glad we got the winter gear," Tas said.

"Me too," I said. "We should plan on moving early tomorrow so we can get some more distance. According to the map, we can move south, west of the main road, all the way down through the woods and... hopefully, miss any trouble that might look for us. Should only add a day extra to the journey if we move fast."

The ladies agreed with me, and we cleaned up the campsite.

We put out the fire with dirt I had collected earlier. Putting all our stuff in the bags and then placing them along the sides of the single tent we had.

It was a little snug, but we would make do.

"I'll change first," I said as I made my way into the tent and removed the clothes I would not be sleeping in, planning on just wearing pants to bed. The bed rolls, which each were just two thick blankets folded in half, could be used individually or together. I unrolled them and placed each right next to each other with me on the side, Tyla in the middle, and Tas on the other side.

When I laid down on my spot, the other two walked in from their run into the woods.

"No master, you are in the middle."

I glanced up at her. "Pretty sure you just called me master, then told me what to do."

"I did, didn't I?" Tyla smiled.

The only light in the room was two candles in a brace hanger attached to the tent pole I had lit before coming in. They were covered in a glass container like a hurricane lamp, providing plenty of light to see by.

"Fine, you win." I shuffled over and moved into the middle as the girls undressed for bed.

Based on the redness in Tas's cheeks, I had a feeling I knew what was going to happen next. So, I braced my will power for shenanigans and considered the words I would use when I stopped them.

But even as they undressed to simple underwear and breast bindings, they did nothing but get into bed with me. Though they each cuddled up against me and settled, not doing anything remotely provocative.

That got me to relax from my earlier alarmed state, and I started to relax.

"Do you want me to blow out the candle? Both are a little bright for me," Tyla said.

"Sur—-" I said but was interrupted.

"I'll get it," Tas said and lifted just enough to reach for the lamp.

However, as she reached, her breast bindings, somehow already loosened, came undone and fell away from her chest, exposing her perky and luscious breast. My mind stopped functioning as I stared at them just above me.

Tasnia blew out one of the candles and suddenly the tent was darker but still enough to see by. Tas slowly lowered herself, not bothering to recover her exposed cleavage, and simply leaned back into my side.

My manhood was suddenly rock hard, and it shattered all the control I thought I had built up into a million pieces.

I took deep, slow breaths, trying to get control when more movement got my attention. Tyla reached up to me and kissed me on the lips. "Good night, Master."

She moved out of the way to be replaced by Tasnia.

"Good night, Derk," she said then kissed me on the lips in the same manner.

Her boobs pressed against my chest as she leaned into me. I could feel the hardness in her nipples, and it sent my brain scrambling even more.

"Uh... good night," I said when she released me and they both resumed their positions, cuddling into me on my sides.

"Good night, Tas," Tyla said, smiling at her friend from across my chest.

"Good night, Tyla," Tasnia replied, and they got up once again to press their faces together to kiss.

However, this was not the same kiss they gave me. They lingered... and soon their tongues reached into each other's mouths to vie for dominance.

My manhood, already fully erect, simply strained in my pants, begging for me to free it as the two beautiful women began making out right in front of my face.

I could honestly only stare for a few minutes, not wanting to ruin the sight in front of me. My decision from earlier gone and my will power destroyed, my inner caveman danced a jig at my surrender.

I could only watch the show.

They stopped their kiss and smiled at each other before turning their predatory gaze upon me with knowing looks from both.

"If this is what you really want," I croaked, not sure if it was a good idea but going with it, anyway.

The only thing making the last vestiges of my conscience feel better was Tas could always refuse the offer, or I could release her later.

But even that thought flew out of my brain as both attacked at once.

CHAPTER 27

— • —

THEN THERE WERE THREE

I'll be honest, I had traveled the world — before it was destroyed, that is — and met many people. I saw some crazy things and did things most guys in the military would do at a young age.

A threesome was never on that list of accomplishments.

So, the horny young man still occupying a part of my brain got to check that box right the fuck off with glee.

The girls kissed me at the same time, our tongues mingling in a rhythm I did not know how we learned so rapidly.

A flash of light happened in the tent, making us pause momentarily as we looked to see its cause. A few seconds later, we heard thunder, and we relaxed, smiling at each other with a brief pause.

I resisted the urge to ruin it, asking one more time if Tasnia was sure she wanted to do it. Her eyes, as I gazed into them, were sure at this moment, which was enough for me now. As I realized I wanted her with us as much as I wanted Tyla.

Was that being selfish? It's possible. But the care and love I saw glancing back at me told me it wasn't.

"Storms coming in," I said, stating the obvious.

"It is," Tas said before she closed her eyes and resumed her kiss with me.

Tyla joined, and again we were kissing each other.

The kiss between the three of us was slow and passionate. Not rushed with need or lust. Our tongues snaking out to meet each other's, shifting back and forth between us.

Hands caressed my body, rubbing up my abs and chest, which had developed well over the few short weeks I had been in the new world.

Then I realized that I could not return those caresses as I had a body of a young, beautiful woman on each of my arms, pinning me down.

There are worse problems to have in this world.

Tyla lifted away from the kiss, letting Tas have my mouth to herself as she sunk lower down my body. I felt her hands grab the belt on my pants and slowly untie the leather binding.

Another flash went through the tent, followed by a boom, much closer to us. I could hear the wind in the distance, but our tent seemed protected from the worst of it. Then the first drops of rain sounded from outside. The smell of ozone and rain permeated the tent and mixed with the smell of arousal and sex we had created.

None of that distracted us.

Tyla released my manhood and pulled my pants and underwear down around my legs. I lifted each leg to help her pull them off me.

Now fully in the nude, I continued my passionate kissing with Tas, my eyes closed, as Tyla moved away from me. I could feel her moving on the ground next to me before she returned, tapping Tas on the shoulder and taking her place, putting her now familiar mouth to mine as we also shared a kiss.

Tyla, now fully nude, mounted on top of me and broke the kiss to sit straight up, her womanhood rubbing against my exposed cock but not putting it into her channel. Slowly moving her hips back and forth over me while Tas joined us by removing the last of her clothes.

When Tas finished removing her own panties, she sat down, staring as Tyla edged me for a while, her hand sneaking down to her crotch. Her bush was trimmed but not shaven, and it was colored the same shade of red as her hair. She fully exposed herself to me as I glanced back and forth between her and Tyla.

"I am getting him ready for you," Tyla said with a smile at Tas.

"Um... what should I do?" Tas asked nervously.

"What would make you happy?" I asked.

"I... don't know. I like the idea of being where Derk is right now, but I also want to give as much as I get."

Tyla smiled. "I have an idea. Why don't you put yourself on his face while I put my mouth on him? Then we can go from there."

"That... sounds like fun." Tas smiled and started getting up. "Is that something you want?"

"Tas, I want you to feel special tonight. Don't worry about my needs. This is about you."

She nodded and moved, albeit with a little uncertainty, and placed herself over my waiting mouth. Looking down at me, she took a hitching breath before placing her entrance on my waiting tongue.

Tasnia also had a flavor to her. While it was not enough to build a scientific consensus, I think the power of the Chosen was the cause. A part of my mind parsed this information, as I tasted hints of clove and chocolate as my taste buds explored her inner depths.

My sight now removed, I could only feel the touch and the warmth of Tyla's familiar mouth enveloping my erection, as she put me inside her mouth and swallowed as far as she could.

"Mmm," I groaned as my tongue never stopped working on Tas, making her squirm on top of me as her breath hitched repeatedly from the new sensations she was experiencing.

Her leg muscles clenched and unclenched around my head. I wrapped my arms around her legs and used my fingers to explore her... other opening.

"Oh," Tas moaned. "Just like that, just like that," she said when I found her sweet spot, running my tongue deep inside her front entrance while pleasuring her rear entrance with my finger.

I never inserted my finger, just rimming her back door in a circular motion.

"Oh, gods!" Tas screamed, timed perfectly with the next round of thunder.

Her body convulsed when the orgasm hit, causing her to lift off me and fall to her side.

Tyla stopped working my cock, moving over to Tas as she recovered from her bliss. "I am guessing you liked that?"

"Yes!" Tas said through her heavy breathing. "Give me... give me a second."

Shivers were still running through her body.

"What did you do?" Tyla asked, glancing up at me.

"Uh, I did that thing with my finger that you like. I think she liked it even more, though."

"Naughty girl," Tyla said, moving over to kiss Tasnia on the mouth. Then she pressed Tasnia's shoulder back and moved her so that she was on her back. Reaching down, she spread the Red-Headed beauty's legs up to me. "Take her, Master. I think she is ready."

Tasnia lifted her head and gazed deep into my eyes. "Please?"

I moved above her and inserted the tip of my manhood to her entrance but not putting it inside, instead glancing one more time at her to make sure it was what she still wanted.

Nodding at me, she reached forward and grabbed my engorged dick, guiding it inside her velvety tunnel slowly.

"Oh gods, it's tight," she said.

"You get used to it," Tyla said with a giggle as she started making out with Tas again.

I took over from Tas and guided my rock-hard member slowly inside her, slowly rocking back and forth, each forward motion going just a little deeper than the previous.

Before long, I was fully inside her, and she wrapped her legs around my back. Tyla stopped kissing her and moved to sit spread eagle behind her new lover and friend, a leg on each side of Tas as she reached down to pleasure herself while she watched us become one.

I gave Tasnia a few more seconds to get used to my girth before I drove into her with force. My motions started off slow and steady before rapidly picking up the pace.

Tasnia used her legs to grip me tighter, hampering my freedom of motion as I bucked back and forth.

"Oh, oh, oh!" she moaned repeatedly as the pleasure invading her body consumed her. Feeling my end was near, I started hammering into her as fast as I could.

"I'm going to cum!" I groaned.

"Accept the offer if you want to," Tyla said into Tasnia's ear.

The girl barely acknowledged the words.

I felt the pressure build and the power inside me pulsed. Before I could do anything else, I was shooting both my seed and power deep inside the sexy and sweaty woman.

"Yes! Yes! Oh fuck, I accept!" she shouted as I spasmed in her.

Her body glowed with my now familiar white light as she came at the same time. It exploded out of the both of us, even making Tyla cum from the residual energy that washed over her.

The darkness assaulted my senses, creeping into my brain and demanding I submit to unconsciousness. I tried to fight, but it proved more than I could handle.

Before even a heartbeat passed, I collapsed forward onto Tasnia and passed out next to her.

CHAPTER 28

---◆---

IMPROVEMENTS

I found myself once again in my... dreamscape? Still not sure what it was, since it seemed to be random in its appearance. Twice, it had appeared to me in a dream, and twice I could enter it while awake.

If I ever spoke to Vex again, I would have to ask for an instruction manual or something. His explanations were absolute shit.

Two spheres were now orbiting me lazily as I gazed around the space created by my mind. Studying it more carefully this time, I noticed I was on a gray concrete looking floor that spanned about twenty feet in diameter around me before it stopped.

At the edge, I noticed a darkness of some type that spread up above me like a dome. But occasionally I could see small lights trying to peek through the blackness, like a star scape that faded in and out. It reminded me of my time back on my old ship in my marine days.

The familiar pang of loss tried to claw its way in from the memory, but I glanced at the two spheres orbiting me and realized that it just did not have the bite that it did even a few weeks ago.

If offered the chance to go back, I could honestly say that I would decline.

I missed Jessica, but the pain was like that of a parent who died twenty years ago. Real, but distant. If I had one regret, it was Adam, my son. I hoped that he — and even his mother — lived a happy life in whatever reality those alien assholes had created for them.

Focusing on the newest sphere in my orbit, I noticed it had a reddish orange hue to it. It also had a link that went down into my chest, intertwining with Tyla's just before it entered me.

I extended my senses to it and felt that it was not sure of itself and its place yet, if I had to place the feeling from the sensation.

But I sensed happiness and belonging with that insecurity, along with all the other emotions I would expect from her.

Anger and sorrow battled with the hope and excitement as well.

The anger and sorrow concerned me only for a moment before I remembered what had happened to her father. Concerned, I pressed a little deeper to see if I could sense her true feelings. Giving me the impression that by accepting her when she asked, and not denying her, it helped relieve some of the pain. The utter feel of belonging to something, and with someone, made her feel better.

She was human in the extreme, with all the complicated feelings that come with that.

That also soothed some of the guilt I felt. I needed to remember that not all people looked at life the same as I did. They just wanted to belong to something, even if they gave up a part of themselves for it.

I moved on and studied the connection where both spheres met in my chest, giving each of them a very subtle shade of lavender along with the normally bright white energy spreading throughout my body.

I noticed that the blue in Tyla's sphere was a deeper shade now, but I was not entirely sure what that meant. Was it a manifestation of her power growing, or from our connection?

Experimenting a bit, I reached forth with my hand and held both spheres, one in each hand. Sensations deeper than before rolled through me. I felt Tyla and Tas sleeping, and I could almost sense their dreams as well.

I wanted to push power into them again to see what would happen, but I did not need a repeat of the last time I tried this. So instead, I tried just a small trickle of energy into each.

I paused quickly after I began, unsure exactly how long it was since I could not tell time in the dreamscape. But I listened intently for any sounds that tried to break through, hearing nothing.

So, I continued my experiment and slowly increased the power in each and watched as their spheres grew brighter, though the color did not change.

I put the two spheres together so that they touched, for it to make it easier to focus, then something odd happened. A slight flash of light burst forth and as I pulled them apart, a new connection formed between the two, each sending a shot of color into the other as though a drop of oil on water.

It was small, almost a thread, no bigger than a hair really, but it was there, and I saw it. Where they met, the same lavender shade formed from it as the energies eventually mixed.

I tried to increase its size by pushing more power into the connection, but before I could get any farther, a sensation of warmth enveloped me near my groin, and it pulled me from the dreamscape before I could figure out what it was.

"Oh, shit," I exclaimed as my body spasmed.

The orgasm consumed me before even opening my eyes, and the sensation sent streaks of light through the darkness.

When the sensation passed, I glanced down at the two girls with their big smiling faces looking back at me.

"Good morning. Who gave me the surprise?" I asked.

"It was a combined effort," Tyla said.

"Since we woke up to a... pleasant surprise ourselves, we thought we would share while ya were asleep."

"Oh, you felt that? I was trying to be gentle."

"You were, Master, it was like a..." Tyla struggled to find the words. "Gentle feeling of pleasure, not the mind-blowing explosion you gave me last time. But I recognized it. Also, something else happened."

"What?" I asked.

Tyla shared a glance with Tas.

"I... am not sure. I suddenly had more power, but I also felt different too," Tyla finished.

"Me too," the redhead added.

"OH, well, the weirdest thing happened..." I said as I explained what had happened.

"Ya mean we might have each other's powers?"

"I honestly don't know what it means. We will just have to test it out and see. Remember, I am in the dark as much as you are about this stuff."

I got up from the tent and took care of the personal business outside, adding to a puddle away from our camp. The rain had passed, but mud and rainwater were everywhere in the dawn's light. Looking north, I could see no sign of the fire like I could yesterday, so hopefully it had been put out by all the rain and our trail was impossible to follow.

Our tent held up well, though it had help from the rock overhang. The trees nearby did not fare quite as well with broken branches and even a couple overturned saplings in evidence.

"Food," Tas said as she handed me a small bowl of leftovers from the night before, along with some preserved fruits on the side. "It's not much."

"Thank you, Tas... How do you feel, by the way?"

"Not much different, honestly. Powerful compared to yesterday, I can feel it deep inside of me and would really like to test out what I can do."

"Not what I meant."

"I know. It's hard to describe. Yesterday, I had a giant hole where my dad used to be, but I also had this desire to be part of what ya and Tyla had. Today?" She thought about it. "I feel I would do anything for ya, and even Tyla. But it does not feel like the compulsion I was expecting so much as... the biggest desire I could want and a feeling of pleasure to see your needs met."

I took a bite of the rabbit. It was cold, but I was hungry.

"I know that doesn't make much sense. I admit, a small part of me was terrified I would want to be yer slave when I woke up, even if I knew you were not that way. But I can feel it here." She tapped her chest. "That ya want me to be happy, not controlled. It's more like my love for you was just amplified, not forced. Like it grew a thousand-fold overnight, and I went from infatuation to the deepest love one can have for another... Does that at all make sense? Or am I just rambling?"

"Rambling a bit." I laughed. "But that's fine. And I can't be sure what is normal. I felt some of what you are going through when I... touched you in my dream-state. I felt the loss you have for your father."

She nodded, and her eyes had a strained expression on them. "That did not change really, but when I... joined with ya, it became less... no, not less. More like a balance of joy to the pain, but not a lessening."

"I think, Master," Tyla said, walking up behind us. "Your bond has matured since you have been here. When we first joined, I felt it as a command to obey, which I did happily at the time, but now it is more like a promise. That you will love me if I am faithful and loving to you. I think you are changing it as we go."

"So, you have a choice rather than a binding?" I asked, hopeful.

Tyla and Tas shared a look.

"It's hard to explain. It's a feeling of warmth that envelopes us, not a chain that binds us. Though it feels like you could do that if you wanted, I do not worry about that happening because of who you are," Tyla said and Tas nodded in agreement.

"Tas, I am going to wait, but I may ask in the future that you allow me to try to release you. Just to be sure it's what you really want and give you the chance to see if this is what you really want."

"If that is yer wish."

"Thank you. I honestly don't know if I made a mistake, but I found I desperately wanted you with us and I couldn't say no last night. I hope you don't hate me for it later."

"I have never felt happier about my direction in life, Derk. Losing Father stings fiercely, but knowing I belong to you... with you... takes the sting out of it some."

I nodded, and we stood there in comfortable silence as we ate our food, each in our own thoughts.

* * *

"That is amazing, Tyla. And no one you have ever heard of has done that before?" I asked, looking at the devastating results of her latest experiment.

"Not by themselves. Combat magic with another person is... complicated. It takes knowing each other extremely well in stressful situations. The instructors at the academy said the most successful were also lovers."

I gazed one more time at the results. "Very impressive Tyla. Well done, indeed. If we get into a fight, it will even the odds with any non-magic users."

"Thank you, master!" she said, beaming at my praise.

It had been three days since Tas had joined us, and we had discovered many things about the bond I created between the three of us.

"I still can't externalize anything, still have to be touching it for it to work." I lifted my broadsword in front of me, willing some fire element into it. A soft glow coated the blade, barely noticeable, really. But the heat that generated off it warped the surrounding air. "But this should cause plenty of damage. Should I hit anyone with it, I am going to guess it's about a thousand degrees. But it makes no sense compared to the physics I learned on earth. The metal doesn't even look warm."

"My understanding is that the magic is using the blade or object as a focus. It is not actually in the blade but using it as a conductor and covering its surface, and your will directs it away.

"It also still astounds me how you can imbue the object so soon but cannot cast a bolt of fire or water, master," Tyla said.

"I am not sure I am following the same rule book to be honest," I said.

"That's why they call it magic," Tas added, a small smirk on her face. She lifted her hands and made a small flame dance from her fingers. "My fire is so much stronger, but I can't use the water outside my body yet, not even someone else's body like you and Tyla. It's just enough to heal myself for now."

"I really wish you hadn't tested it like that. But yes, I am glad you can self-heal too," I said.

"I was right there if it did not work, Master."

"You know I hate self-harm, even if it's fixable."

Tas came up to my side and grabbed me in a side hug. "I'm sorry, love. Ya want me to make it better?" Her eyes told me about the secret intent in her words.

I laughed at the nickname she used. At least it wasn't master, though I had tuned it out now mostly when Tyla said it.

"Later. For now, let's get back to training. How much power did that use Tyla?"

"A little more than a normal blast of water. But since our bond with Tas, my power has almost doubled, even when you do not... fill me." She walked up to me and bumped me with her hip on the last one.

"Surrounded by sex kittens," I said, looking up at the sky.

"You say that like you dislike it, Master."

"Point, but I do like to get the job done first. You make that extremely hard."

"Not yet," Tas said, reaching down to my groin to check. "But soon."

I broke away from the women. "Okay, we really need to stop now."

I was trying for serious but couldn't stop my laugh.

"He is very hard now, I can see the bulge in his pants," Tyla said into Tasnia's ear.

"Whispering only works if you keep your voice down," I said, not looking up at the two.

"I know, Master!" I could almost hear the smirk in her voice.

I sighed. "Soon, but please? Serious for now?"

"Yes, love."

"Yes master, I promise."

I took a minute, forcing my libido to calm down before I said anything more. "Alright, let's get you two to practice sparring with your rapiers while I try to sink into that mediation thing. If I can figure out how to keep you two powered up every day, even if it's not during combat, we will give someone a rude surprise with Tyla's new trick and your ability to heal Tas."

They walked off a short distance to give themselves space, unsheathing their swords and saluting at one another.

The slightest orange glow came from Tas's sword, while a bluish one came from Tyla's.

"Be careful!"

"Yes, Master!" they said in unison, both smiling.

"Not you too, Tas?"

Giggling from the fiery red head was my only response. Rolling my eyes, I sat cross-legged on the ground.

"At least she is getting past the loss of her father," I mumbled under my breath.

She had gone through several mood swings the past few days, but each day she smiled more than she cried.

The first night, we had a small ceremony celebrating his life. Tasnia told us stories from her childhood about her father and her mother. Tears flowed, but I would have to say that it made a major difference for her. We even went to bed that night with no... other activities.

But the next day she woke up feeling better, and she made up for the lost time. I briefly wondered if the bond was helping or simply suppressing them.

But I shook my head at those thoughts. We made the choice and had to accept it.

Deciding to focus back on my task at hand, I tried to relax. I had only entered it once since I had made the connection between Tyla and Tas, just briefly enough to put more power into each of them last night.

It had the effect of causing another orgy, but to be honest, that was kind of my intent. I had no shame in admitting that. They had been ganging up on me a lot lately, and it felt good to make them... squirm for a change.

I smiled at the thought as I closed my eyes, the sounds of the girls' swords going through their practice strikes with each other in my ears.

We just changed everything now that they could share elements, even if just a tiny amount of them. Part of me looked forward to our next fight.

CHAPTER 29

RIVEN HOLD

"This does not look good, Master," Tyla said.

"No, it most certainly does not," I agreed.

"What do we do?" Tas asked.

I stared at the city we had spent the last week getting to. It was in turmoil, but we did not know what kind.

The city itself was on the other side of a river from where we stood. To get to it, we needed to cross a bridge. The problem was there was a refugee camp on this side of the river, and it looked like the guards on the bridge were not letting anyone pass.

The city itself did not look promising either. The town outside the walls looked peaceful, but the castle that sat on the small rise had smoke billowing out of it. More so than you would expect from controlled fires, anyway.

"We could avoid the castle. We don't want to risk that anyhow, but we still must get across the river. I know it's a way away, but do you recognize who those guards might be loyal to Tyla?"

"The flag is a Riven Hold flag on the bridge, but I can't tell you about the soldiers. The colors look right."

I bit my lower lip while I thought.

"Any ideas?" I asked my women.

"I can try to play the up-tight Chosen and bully my way past."

"Maybe, I don't like it though. Any other way across the river?"

"Not that I know of. This river splits the great plains and only has three natural crossings. Or at least, that is what I remember of it."

"Tas?"

"No, I never much ventured outside of Hills Crest growing up."

"Alright, Tyla, we don't have enough time to figure out another way. That river is as wide as the Mississippi. Let's try your way."

"Is that another Earth term, love?"

"Huh? Oh yeah, a huge river back on Earth. Sorry."

"It's fine, Master. It helps us understand you when we ask."

"Fair, let's go, Tyla you're the boss, I'll be the bodyguard, Tas you be the servant."

"Why am I the servant?"

"Shit, trapped myself there, didn't I?"

"Yes, love, but it's fine. I'll play the lowly servant, forced to meet the wicked needs of my Chosen and her... well-endowed guard."

"Little thick." I laughed, raising my hand and putting my fingers about an inch apart. "Give me the packs and let's go, you two."

"Master, if you are the guard, you cannot carry all the gear."

"But..."

"I've got it," Tas said.

Tyla strode out of the bushes and onto the nearby road like she owned the place, me following to her left, and Tas to her right. Both of us were just a half step behind the beautiful brunette.

Our clothes were not exactly those of nobility, but hopefully, we could bluff it. Tyla was in her light leather armor, her rapier at her side, having handed her crossbow bow and pack to Tas to carry.

"You okay, Tas?"

"Yes, love. Since we joined, my strength has increased a lot. The added load doesn't bother me."

"Let me know if it does."

She reached over and squeezed my hand. Quickly, but it was there, then we resumed our march towards the refugee camp.

"Look at all these people," Tas said as we entered the camp.

It smelled of people and shit. No sanitation measures could be seen. The dirt road was the only place that was clear of any type of trash or excrement.

"This place is ripe for disease," I said.

"Do you want to help them, master?"

"I really do, but we can't afford the risk yet. We do not know how far away a potential enemy is."

"I agree, love. But it breaks my heart."

"The only saving grace," Tyla said, "is that this side looks peaceful, if not organized. I don't see any suffering other than the conditions."

"They just want to get away," I said. "Desperation has not fully set it yet or it would be worse. If an opportunity arrives, we will help."

The people in their tents, or carts, or even just a blanket strewn on the ground looked at us as we passed. Some held anger in their expressions, others just hopelessness. It was heartbreaking.

We finally got to the bridge where about ten guards were stationed at the entrance. They stood menacingly in front of a small crowd of refugees, begging to be let through. I wanted to stop and listen to the specifics, but that would not fit the noble cover we had.

Tyla stopped and looked back at me. She gave me a wink, then assumed an expectant expression.

"Yes, my lady," I said and moved in front, pulling my sword.

I didn't even have to say anything. The sound of the sword leaving its sheath was enough to get the people in the back of the crowd to turn around and move away, which caused a cascade effect as I marched forward, the girls following in my wake.

The people parted like I was Moses, and we approached the group of guards at the gate. When we passed the mob, I felt a light tug on my elbow and moved to the side. Tyla walked past me, and I resumed my position behind her.

Tyla did not even acknowledge the guards, just walking past them like they did not exist.

"Halt!" a meaty bruiser of a man said. He had a black beard and a plume on his pot helmet, so he was probably in charge. The armor he wore was serviceable but obviously a mass-produced item to fit an army with, not a custom job.

Tyla stopped and glared at the guard, but she did not speak.

"Name and business? We ain't accepting no more refugees."

Rather than respond, Tyla lifted her hand and a bolt of water shot out into the man's face. He fell back and choked in surprise.

Some of the other guards drew their swords, and I hit the quick release on my pack, sending it to the ground and readying my sword for a fight.

"You will not talk to me in such a manner," Tyla said to the now soaking man. "I have business in Riven Hold. What has transpired here?" She lifted her hand and pointed to the smoke coming from the castle.

The guard, for his part, recovered quickly. "My apologizes, ma'am. I did not know who you was. The witc—I mean matriarch's daughter fled several days ago, and things have been in... turmoil around here since. I was told to keep my post and more orders will come soon."

"Fled?" Tyla asked, ignoring the term he almost used.

"I... don't know ma'am. Rumor was she went to the Matriarch of Casting Harbor for help but had not returned. But I didn't see her cross this bridge, so I don't know."

"Very well. Why are these refugees being kept out?"

"Orders ma'am. We was letting them in until a few days ago. I don't know what changed other than to stop."

"I'll find out then. In the meantime, use some of your men to at least set up more sanitary conditions and organize them. Sickness will soon follow, and it could also affect your men. Try to give them supplies if you can spare them."

Tyla started walking the bridge without waiting for a response. Tas and I followed silently after I put my pack back on.

"Yes, ma'am," the guard said to our backs and started organizing men to carry out her orders.

No one challenged us further as we walked away.

"We will need to be quick. I doubt it will be long before someone confronts us, Master."

"To the contact point, then out as quick as we can then," I said as we walked down the bridge to Riven Hold.

Walking down the streets of Riven Hold, you could see the stress in the town's people.

"These markets are usually full, at least the last time I was here several years ago they were," Tyla said, walking next to me.

We had donned our cloaks and put them over our packs like ponchos, changing up our outline to try and shake any followers. We could have taken more precautions, but we prized speed over stealth at this moment.

"Everyone who is out looks nervous," Tas added.

"Let's just keep going. Which way is the Twin Badger Inn?"

"I only know the basic direction, Master. I have never been to the poor area of town before."

"Fair, just point out the turns as best you can. We will ask someone if needed."

We walked out of the market, and things got worse. People were walking fast, looking at everything around them instead of enjoying their day.

"Haven't seen a town guard since the market," Tas said as we crossed into the poorer part of town.

"Only likely to get worse, keep your guard up."

The building went from two story wooden affairs to wattle and daub style shanties with thatch roofs. Almost no one was on the street here that we could see.

A woman's scream came from down an alley. Without thinking, I diverted towards the sound, unable to help myself.

I expected a voice of concern from Tyla or Tas, but they just followed me down the alleyway without missing a beat.

"I don't say it a lot, but I love you both, just want you to know that," I said.

The feeling had overwhelmed me, and I needed to say something.

"We know, Master. We feel it through our bond."

"Yes, love. We know."

A smile broke out on my face.

As we neared a corner, we heard men yelling and a woman crying in fear. I could not make it out until we rounded the corner, and I stopped momentarily to listen.

"She is a witch!" an older man said, white hair on the side of his balding top. I pegged him as an angry old asshole and probably the instigator. The same type of guy that yells 'Get off my lawn!' at the kids.

The crowd roared their approval as a couple of lackeys tied a woman up to an oil-based streetlamp in the middle of the dirt road intersection. Apparently, replicating the Salem witch trials of earth was a thing here.

She was younger... well, about my current age, I guess. Blonde hair with a hint of red in it, but it was hard to tell since she was filthy and in baggy threadbare clothing. She looked like a street rat that was in the wrong place at the wrong time.

"The witches of old have fallen, my friends! We must find them all and burn them before the Demigods arrive or we shall all be doomed!"

I rolled my eyes at this guy's monologue and started walking. I hunched my shoulders and forced my way to the front of the group, pushing and prodding my way through with my two ladies right behind me, their own righteous anger echoing my own through the bond.

The man held a torch above his head, as my eye shifted momentarily. It was then that I noticed they had covered the girl in a substance that looked like oil. I was just going to be an asshole, but this brought the situation up a notch and I changed my plans.

"Now, we watch this witch—-" The old man began before a crack of my elbow silenced him as I passed.

He was probably going to scream about burning her or something. He would never get the chance. I hit him so hard that I thought I killed him.

"Oops," I said, not meaning it.

I turned to the crowd, Tyla and Tas going right behind me to form a triangle around the girl.

"Next mother fucker that tries to burn a girl at the stake will look at this guy and wish they were him." My voice was loud enough for all to hear.

The group went from righteous anger to shock as they saw the old man hit the ground. "Besides, she is not the one you need to worry about."

The crowd looked at me, going from shock back to anger. I noticed that most of them were men.

"You killed him!" - "Who are you?" and other random questions came from the crowd. One of the younger men even stepped forward, a bean pole type kid, "She is going to bring ruin to us!"

Behind me, I could see two different hues of light form, and all the men cowered in fear at the sight. I glanced behind me to see that both Tyla and Tas had their palms out and each hand had magic ready to go. Blue on Tyla's hands, and the reddish orange of Tas.

"Pretty sure these two are the ones you should fear. Anyway, last chance, run or die. Don't particularly care right now."

The crowd started dispersing. I watched as a few even ran. Most gave us some ugly looks as they fled and I didn't care in the slightest, just glaring back at them in return.

I peeked down to make sure the puritan acting asshole was not getting up, noticing the neck angle he had now.

Not getting up. Might have overdone it.

I turned and found Tyla washing the young woman of all the oil with her water, but it was only so effective against the thick substance.

I stepped up to her, and she flinched back a little.

I paused and backed up a bit, putting my hands up in a non-threatening fashion. "Hi, my name is Derrick. No one is going to hurt you. This is Tasnia and Tyla my... friends. Do you have a family we can take you to?"

The girl looked at me, fear and hope warring inside her. She studied Tas and Tyla, then glanced back at me before shaking her head. "Nnn.... No. I... have no one. I was just trying to eat. The..." She looked at the dead body. "He thought I stole from him... I was just hungry." Then she lost her composure and cried. "I'm sorry I did—" Tyla cut her off as she hugged her, shushing her words, and Tas joined a few seconds later.

"Shh," Tyla said. "No one judges you here. We do what we must when the need arises. No one will harm you or allow you to be harmed." Her eyes met mine, and we nodded at each other in meaning.

I closed a bit, getting within arm's reach, but not coming any closer, not wanting to set her off. "It's ok... miss, what's your name?"

She looked up at me, her beautiful blueish green eyes captivated me for a second, seeming to shift between the shades of green and blue as the sun reflected off them. It was mesmerizing, and I had to shake my head and get my thoughts back to the task at hand.

"You can call me Diane," she said, so softly I could barely hear her.

"Do you want to come with us? I can promise your safety and I will not come close to you if that makes you uncomfortable."

She gazed up at me with those eyes again. Her hair now falling over most of her face, ratty and full of dirt that had not been cleaned in some time.

She nodded at me. "I would like to leave now. Will you take me out of the city?"

Tas reached up and pushed the hair back behind her ears. The girl tried to stop her, but it was too late.

We all saw it.

Her ears ended in points; unlike any human we had ever seen.

She started and tried to make a break for it, but I reached forward and stopped her.

When my hand made contact, it was then that her skin flashed a yellow hue in front of my eyes.

They were right, she's a witch, an elvish one at that.

I backed away from her, realizing my mistake. "Sorry, we did not mean to startle you, but..."

"We'll take care of it, love," Tas said, taking my place around the nervous woman in front of me.

"Shhh," Tyla said. "He will not hurt you, and we will protect your secret as well."

Tyla placed the woman's hair around her ears again.

The woman, shaking from the fear of the last few moments, managed to nod. "Th... thank you."

"Let's go," I said, looking around to make sure no one had seen us. The crowd was fully gone. "We go to the Inn, see if Stern is there, and we get out of here as quickly as possible."

I turned to Diane once more. "You can stay with us, or you can leave as soon as we leave the city. You can have as many supplies as we can spare if you choose to go."

Not waiting for a response, I started walking the direction we thought the inn was in, glancing around for further threats.

I checked behind us and saw that Diane was wedged between Tyla and Tas. They each had an arm around the Elf as though they were almost carrying her.

A few minutes later, we hit a smaller market. This one was obviously where the poor shopped. It had market stalls just like the main, but only half the amount and the structures worn and broken in places. The tarps that covered each were ripped in various places.

"Excuse me, ma'am," I said to a woman in one of the few open stalls.

The older woman stared at me, her gray hair covering her face, before standing up and walking over. "What do you want? You don't look like you should be in this part of town."

"I was hoping," I said, pulling out a small copper and placing it on the table next to the nearly rotten fruits she sold. "That you might tell me where the Twin Badger Inn was?"

She pocketed the coin in a flash, then pointed down the street towards the far end of the market. "First on the right past the building on the corner there."

She turned and went back to the stool she was sitting on.

"Thank you," I said.

She did not reply, and we walked towards our destination, rounding the corner the woman had pointed to and the dilapidated houses that it represented.

We came to another building, all made of wood. It reminded me of an old western saloon more than the Witch's Haunt back in Hills Crest. It was in disrepair now, but it might have been nice at one point.

We walked through the doors and the girls went to an empty table in the corner while I went up to the bar.

The bartender nodded at me, a tall man with a black beard that was showing streaks of gray. "What can I get ya?" the man asked.

"Something to drink, and some information, please," I said, putting the last large copper we had on the table.

"We have ale, dark or light. Not much else. The information depends on what you ask."

"Was supposed to meet an associate of ours. Name was Henri Puchot," I said, giving the code name we had agreed upon.

"Yeah, a man like that said he might get visitors. He has a room upstairs. I'll send the runner."

"Thanks. Uh, just a few light ales and a tea, if you have any."

I left the coin on the table and joined the ladies while the bartender went into the back. He came out again a few minutes later and set the light ales on the table. No tea was in evidence.

Without saying a word, he went back to his bar, and we waited.

The ale was horrible, and I was fairly sure it was half water.

"How is she doing?" I asked Tas.

"I am doing... fine. Thank you for intervening before they...," Diane said.

"Let's not think about that too deeply right now," I said. "Do you want to tell us how you are here? I have not met any of your... kind before."

"Master, maybe now is not—"

"It's fine," the Elven woman said. "I don't mind. I was just shocked before how quickly things transpired."

I sat in silence as she gathered her thoughts, noticing that Tyla and Tas sat on each side of her with their arms on her shoulders in support.

"I... don't normally stay in the city, too dangerous because of my... difference. I was just getting some food, the woods here are so barren of food to eat. But I should have known better, the city has been getting... less safe lately, but I was hungry."

"I still don't understand why you are here," I said.

"I do not really remember much about how I got here. My family came here when I was incredibly young. We were fleeing something, I think it was the Demigods, but I do not remember for sure. My family left me here... and I have been surviving on my own since."

"Left you here?" I asked.

She looked down at the table, not answering.

Relenting, I changed topics. "Is Diane really your name?"

Her face crinkled as she thought about it. "I... don't remember my real name. I picked this one after listening to some humans. It... got me by."

I sensed a much deeper story here, but did not want to pry just yet, she had been through enough. "You don't have to say anymore. Have you eaten?"

She shook her head, and I walked over to the bartender. "You have any food?"

"Bread, couple of days old. Pot of stew on."

"Four please," I said, giving him a small copper. The man nodded and made another trip to the kitchen, bringing out the food a few minutes later.

While it was not the best thing in the world, Diane ate with abandon at the meager offerings. Each of us ate some while we waited, my girls and I trading looks in silence.

After a while, a man came down the stairs from the rooms upstairs. He had chocolate colored skin and a military bearing to him with close cropped curly hair and nice, if plain, woven clothing. A short sword was strapped to his waist. I did not recognize him, but he walked towards us with a neutral expression on his face.

"Derk?" he asked.

I stood, clearing my great sword so that the table did not block it, just in case. "I am, and you are?"

He looked me up and down, gauging me as he decided on his next words. "Cecil is my name. I am Lea's husband."

"Where is Stern?" I asked.

"He... we are not sure. He broke out Lea and some women with the help of a few of the guards that were not turned yet and met up with the rest of us. Before we could escape the city, the guards loyal to... him found us. We ran while he led them away. He never met us like he promised. All we knew was to meet you here and the name to check in under."

I nodded. "Where is everyone else?"

"Not here, we... did not want to take the chance. If you can help us like Stern said you could... Well, let's just say you are going to have to earn that trust from me, but Lea trusted her cousin enough to convince me to give you a chance."

"Fair, how many of you?"

"Just a couple dozen, outside the city, mostly." He stopped and peered back at the bartender before closing in on me to whisper. "He broke out about seven other chosen with my wife, and a few of their lovers and husbands met up with us when we ran."

"Okay," I said. "You want to trust me enough to take us to them?"

"Do I? No. But I promised Lea."

"Fair enough. Let the girls finish eating and we can get out of here. You need to go get your stuff?"

He nodded. "Yeah, be back in a few minutes."

He eyed each of us before he left and went back upstairs.

"Thoughts?" I asked.

Tyla answered, "I should test him, Master."

"Good idea, before we leave the city, we will find a place where no one can see. Don't want to do it here. I don't trust the barman," I said in a whisper.

She nodded, and we waited for Cecil to return.

CHAPTER 30

—— ※ ——

INTERLUDE - ANGER

"Yes, Overseer," Seir said into the black mirror.

He was in his personal study that he had built into the old castle of Nitre, his own god's sanctum sealed against all outside spies, even those who were not of this world. This allowed him to bend the rules and talk to his benefactor.

"I have done what I can in the counsel," the voice representing the Overseer said.

While he was one of the most powerful people in the Roxannez Empire, Seir hated working for anyone. He had spent his entire life, before the Great Ascension, climbing to the top of Roxannez society.

Then he had been stuck as a servant to the Overseer ever since, until he had a chance to come to Timeria and make his own destiny.

"The Controller thwarts me," Overseer continued. "He has just enough votes to stop any further changes to four-five-two and I cannot get the data that you seek. The Demigod you met is unknown to me. Assume he is working against your interest, probably for the Controller himself."

"Yes, Overseer. I will take matters into my own hands, then."

"Be cautious, Takus pushes his elves in your direction. We cannot lose the game, too much rides on it."

"Why can you not simply remove the Controller?"

"That is above your station. Your job is to control the humans for me."

"Yes, Overseer," Seir said, doing his best at keeping his anger in check.

"Go now, prepare yourself for an attack from the north. Worry less about the Controller's pet to the south. Send some of your lieutenants to deal with him, he cannot possibly be that powerful yet."

"By your command."

"Go now," the Overseer said, and the connection stopped.

Seir's knuckles were white as he resisted the anger inside. He hated being treated like a servant.

Seir stomped out of his study, the seals breaking as the door opened. His women were where he left them, in their subservient positions next to his throne. None of his personal spies had returned, but they each had their mission. Their abilities to please him were secondary to their tasks.

Besides, his favorites were always close.

He sat on his throne and tried to relax.

"What news, Husband?" Josephina asked.

"None. The Overseer had no information of use to me," Seir said as he slammed his fist on the chair.

The impact made the arm crack.

Josephina snapped her fingers. Patricia, Miranda, and Einestra got up from their positions at his side to present themselves to their master. Each of them was naked.

Seir viewed the three ladies, thinking for a bit before shaking his head. "Not now, resume your positions."

Each bowed their heads and returned to their places, kneeling near his throne. Seir thought of what he wanted to do to relieve his anger.

"Guard!" he yelled.

The door opened and a muscular guard poked his head through. "Yes, my King?"

"Send in the prisoner and General Taimana to me at once."

The guard bowed. "Yes, my Liege."

"Patricia, stand in front of me," Seir said.

She did as commanded, standing directly in front of him and facing away. Seir appreciated her ass just for a moment, then reached forward and grabbed the small handle she presented him. A small ring just big enough for his finger. He pulled her over to where he wanted her, directly in front of his right arm, and kept his grip. Her new position now gave him a clean line of sight directly in front.

A knock, and then the door opened, the guard announcing the General with his prisoner.

A tall black man led the procession, escorted by two guards that held a prisoner between them, dragging him under his armpits.

The hood prevented Seir's ability to see the man's face, but he wore tattered clothing and was covered in bodily fluids and residue. His arms were locked behind a wooden pole, and his feet were clasped in chains.

The smell of decay and death permeated the air, originating from the prisoner.

They paraded in front of Seir, putting the captive in a kneeling position only six feet in front of Seir's throne. General Taimana stood ramrod straight right behind the filthy man. His nose was covered by a handkerchief to keep some of the smell at bay.

"General, report."

"We assaulted the fort, my King. The garrison did not fight against our attack; they had offered to surrender multiple times before this and hoped we would take mercy. We rounded them up in the center after a thorough search. Only about half of the original army had survived to this point."

"What killed them?" Seir smiled, already knowing the answer.

His purpose was torment, not actual information.

"Some of them died from disease and starvation. The rest were... devoured by their comrades, according to reports from the survivors, my liege."

The prisoner dropped his head, the sounds of sobbing coming from under the hood. Through the baggy clothing, Seir could see the emaciated condition of the man's body.

"And then?" Seir asked, enjoying himself immensely.

"We dispatched them as you ordered. All except the prisoner here."

"How many total?"

"We killed over two thousand men, a few women, none of them Chosen. The prisoners said the empowered all killed themselves."

Seir pulled on Patricia's ring and guided her into his lap. Seated, she leaned back onto his chest with her head on his shoulder. He used his hand to spread her legs wide.

"Would you like me to pleasure you now, my lord?" she asked.

"In a moment. Remove the prisoner's hood."

The guards removed the hood from the prisoner's head, his eyes blinking rapidly at the sudden light. No one made a sound as he adjusted, though Seir caressed up the legs of Patricia, slowly making his way to her nether regions while the prisoner adjusted to the light.

The man's face was gaunt, his cheeks hollow, and his eyes red with tear streaks marked in dirt on his face.

Broken.

"Micheal!" Seir said as if they were old friends. "So good of you to visit us."

Patricia sat on Seir's lap as he smiled at the imprisoned man. His hand reached up in between her legs, moving back and forth slowly, making her moan softly. Her eyes were closed, her legs wide, as she exposed the entire view of her dripping entrance to the doomed man in front of them.

"I wanted you to see that your wife is now mine, giving herself freely to my every wish and desire."

Micheal winced and tried to look away, but the guards moved his head back to the direction of Seir and Patricia. When he tried to close his eyes, the other guard pulled them open.

"How does that make you feel, Micheal?"

The man moaned in despair rather than give an answer before his sobbing renewed.

"Patricia, what would you do if I offered you this man's life and allowed you to leave?"

Micheal's eyes refocused on hers, as a small glimmer of hope tried to break through, but Patricia did not even look in his direction. "I would not, my king. You are my lord and master now."

Micheal's face went slack, and the sobbing resumed. The guards finally released their hold on him.

"Would you kill him for me?"

"Yes, my King."

"Do it. Drown him alive."

Micheal lifted his face, deciding to meet his fate. The sobbing ended with a brave look of acceptance taking over. Patricia's hand lifted but hesitated just for a second. Almost unnoticeable by anyone else in the room, save one. She glanced at her former lover as he saw the tiniest glimmer of moisture in her left eye, barely there for a heartbeat before she blinked it away.

She willed water from her hand into a sphere, sending it forward quickly. The globe encased Michael's head and cut him off from the air around him. She formed a fist with her hand and the water went into his nose and mouth, pushing into his lungs and filling them to the brim.

Micheal did not resist, struggle, or cry out. He instead kept his eyes locked tight on Patricia as he fell over. Even with death coming and the panic from the lack of oxygen, he smirked at the small resistance he saw from her. He knew a small part of her was still there.

His last thought was his hope that she could forgive herself one day. Then he died.

"That was rather fast of you."

"You did not command me to make him suffer, my King," she said.

"Remove this trash," Seir said to the guards. "Anything else, general?"

"Your orders for the army, my King?"

Seir considered this for a moment, continuing his gentle caressing of Patricia, her moans soon returning.

"Take your army to the south, secure Riven Hold, and garrison your troops there for the winter. I will focus on the northern army for a while. I learned the elves may cause some trouble there. If I do not hear from Albris again in the next week, I will send you several of my lieutenants for missions of their own soon. Give them what they need to carry out their mission. That is all."

"Yes, my King," Taimana said with his hand over his chest in salute. He then turned and walked out the door, followed by the guards who carried the dead body.

"Now my dear Patricia, you may please your King."

Patricia got up from Seir and reached down, pulling out his fully erect manhood. "How would you like me to entertain you, my Liege?"

Seir smiled, reaching forward and turning her around, pulling at the device inserted in her ass. "This hole today."

He pulled it out with a pop, followed by a squeal from Patricia.

"Anything you desire," Patricia said as she climbed up on him and prepared herself.

Seir exhaled as he enjoyed the sensation of entering her, feeling much better after relieving the stress caused by the Overseer.

CHAPTER 31

— • —

SURPRISES

"Diane," I whispered. "Are you Chosen?"

I glanced over at the woman, still between my two ladies, as we walked down the dirt road towards the edge of town.

"No." She shook her head.

Tyla looked over at me and raised an eyebrow. I nodded at her and caught the comprehension that dawned on Tasnia as well when I confirmed the unasked question. Now both my girls knew what I had discovered.

I was not sure she was telling the truth, though. Her posture was too hunched over to look for any of the telltale signs I would normally use to judge a person's veracity.

So, I cheated.

"Are you sure?" I asked again when Tyla placed her hand on the girl's exposed arm. The young woman looked up, confusion in her eyes.

"I... don't think so, but I... stay away from the testers."

I glanced at Tyla, who nodded. She was telling the truth.

I made sure Cecil was still far enough behind us to not hear. "What if I said that you were?"

The girl just shrugged her shoulders. "Does it matter?"

I was confused for a second. This girl was mysterious, and her attitudes and story just did not add up to me. I was honestly not sure what to make of her.

"No, I guess it doesn't," I finally said. "But we should probably train you. Tyla tells me that... accidents can happen if you don't control your powers. Do you know how old you are?"

She shook her head. "No, I lost... I don't remember much before I came here."

Another oddity. It could be Memory loss.

"Fair." I gave a look to the girls. "You guys want to fall behind and talk to her? She might be more comfortable around you."

They nodded, understanding what I wanted them to do. I slowed and let Cecil catch up to me.

"What was that about?" he asked.

"You passed Tyla's test, but I think we are both in agreement that we have not earned each other's complete trust. Would you agree?"

"I served Matriarch Blackrun for many years, respecting her family and her daughter. I trust you a little based on apprentice Russel's word... for now, but this world is falling apart, and I have some doubts."

"Fair, which is why I keep some things private as well. We will either earn each other's trust or not. Until then, let's just act openly, at least. I am telling you I do not trust you with everything. What that was is covered under those auspices."

He nodded. "Wise. Will you tell me why Stern trusted you? That man's trust was notoriously hard to earn."

"It's... complicated, but maybe, in time."

Cecil nodded again as we walked, the dark-skinned man was slightly shorter than me but muscled well. I looked down at my own arms and noticed that they had become much more toned and meatier since I had arrived. Still needed to do some weight training, but the tone was a good start for me.

We approached the end of the town proper, and on the road in front of us, the grassy hills opened up before the next mountain range beyond.

I turned to Cecil. "Where are the others?"

"At the foot of those mountains. We set up a camp away from the roads, and I have made a few supply runs."

"Did you have a plan, or was meeting up with us a plan?"

He sighed before answering. "There is some... contention amongst us. Some say run south towards the barbarian lands, the others heard rumor of a great gathering of the races that fled the Demigods in the Eastern Reaches."

"Eastern Reaches?" Something sounded... familiar about it.

"It is a land beyond the great desert, which is just beyond the mountains you see in front of us. Most only reach it by sea, usually during a small period in the spring. The desert has a great number of beasts and other perils. Beyond that, I do not know. There is a path supposedly."

I rubbed the stubble on my face while I thought. I had a feeling I was supposed to go that direction.

Fucking Vex.

He was right, though. I kept getting forced into doing what he wanted. Not because I wanted to but because he knew I could not sit idly by when I saw injustice.

I needed to fix that, get an edge somehow, but I could not figure out what to do.

"What way do you think we should go?" I asked.

"I say south, the barbarians might kill us if we go down there. If we go east, the deserts probably will. It is... unforgiving."

"Simple. I like it. Something to think about. We can talk it out when we meet up with everyone."

I glanced around as we approached the last row of houses. No one was outside, and it seemed even more quiet than I expected from a city in turmoil. Suddenly, the hair on the back of my neck started to stick up. "Be ready for something," I said to Cecil.

To his credit, he did not naysay me. Instead, he casually loosened his sword and went on the hypervigilance lookout that is common for anyone trained to expect trouble.

I looked back and got Tyla's attention. Giving her the hand signal I had taught her to be alert. Her eyes widened briefly, and she leaned over Diane's head to whisper something to Tas.

"Down!" Cecil yelled and dropped to the ground.

I looked back just in time to see a big rock hurtling towards my head.

I stalled time and ducked under the rock the size of a bowling ball, and it sailed past me into a house on the other side with a great crash.

I pulled my sword as Cecil got back onto his feet. I faced the spot that the rock came from and gently grabbed Cecil on the shoulder to angle him to my rear. Tyla and Tas ran over and put Diane in between the four of us as we waited for the threat to appear.

We all released our packs on the ground.

"Stay down here for now, then keep up with us if we run," Tyla said to Diane who only nodded. Fear was clear in her eyes.

"Be prepared to run, but I don't know where they are all at. Could be in the buildings," I said.

A giant figure casually walked around the corner, smiling as he faced me. "Thought you lost me?" Albris asked with his two women following him around the corner.

It was then that other men started coming out of the buildings and homes near us. We were surrounded. Most of them were shirtless, which I found odd. All of them were the large and athletic types, looking more like gym rats than soldiers.

But they each had a weapon in their hand, and that was enough.

I glanced around for the ranged threats but did not see any. Did this guy not think about this? I really hoped he was that stupid.

I finally gave Albris my attention. "Honestly? Yeah, I kind of hoped for that. You want to monologue again or something, or should we just fight?"

The joke went over his head, he just looked confused for a second before speaking. "Seir has ordered me to kill you. He knows the girl is ruined now, but my master said you must die."

"Thanks for... telling me?" I said, almost a question.

Was it a Roxxanez thing to act like a super-villain from earth movies? I wasn't sure. Instead of talking further, I just said one word. "Tyla."

Her hands lifted, and out flew hardened projectiles at the soldiers she faced.

Water turned to ice from Tasnia's borrowed power.

Formed and sharpened to points as ice spikes ripped forth from her hands.

Each one at speeds faster than arrows.

Men died. Quickly.

I slowed time and ran directly at Abris, my sword lifting and glowing red with fire energy. Abris smiled and lifted his war hammer to ready it for me.

"Cecil, protect Diane!" I yelled, hoping I did not sound like a man high on helium as my sword came down full swing into the metal part of Albris' hammer.

A loud bang sounded throughout the area, followed by a blast of sparks as our magics fought for dominance.

My arms rang from the blow, but I smiled. I was much better off than last time we had met because we were evenly matched in powers. A part of me was looking forward to the challenge.

A blast of fire from behind me made me look in that direction as I rolled under another swing from Albris. I saw Tasnia shooting jets of fire against the water shield of one of Albris' slaves.

I wanted to save the women if I could, but I was not sure how to do that without putting us in danger.

I got up from my roll and faced off against a large man coming to help his master. It was then that I noticed a different symbol on these guys' heads than Sier's. This one of simple lines that looked like a stick figure human without the head.

As I was seeing this, I chopped horizontally at the man, removing his head with my full powered swing, and spun to face Albris.

"NOOOOOO!" he yelled, his face going red.

My surprise at his reaction was short-lived as he began swinging wildly at me without thought or planning. His attacks were even more frenzied than before, as I found myself back peddling from his repeated blows.

I could not focus on anything but my survival as I dodged the endless strikes. I tried to elude most of them, but he was coming at me full speed, his face red and his breathing heavy as he swung.

When he stumbled just for a second, I took my chance. I rolled underneath, again using my smaller height and less muscled frame to outmaneuver him. His hammer shifted to meet me as I stuck the great sword into his ankle and pulled it out on a second roll to get some distance.

"Argghh!" he yelled.

Whether out of pain, anger, or both, I could not tell.

I got up and ran forward. Away from the angry giant to gain more space.

Evaluating the condition of my compatriots and noticing the bodies from Tyla's ice storm lay strewn about everywhere.

Cecil was standing over a scared Diane, protecting her from harm and engaging one of Albris' men that had gone after them.

Tyla was engaged in a sword fight with the fire witch. Her skills that she had gained in recent weeks were on display as she matched her move for move.

Tas was toe to toe with the water witch, and she had the fight well in hand from my observation, but nothing was guaranteed.

The fight was almost even now, but I hated fair fights. I needed something to cheat.

I turned back to my primary threat, just in time to see him winding up to throw his hammer at me.

The biggest problem with the full wind up is that it takes a long time to do, at least when counting the heartbeats during a fight. You prefer smooth and fast over power and rage. Albris was consumed by his rage, and when combined with his preference for power and strength? He had just made a mistake. A fatal one.

I flung the dagger that I had palmed when getting up from the ground, putting as much strength as I could into the quarter throw.

That turned out to be plenty when you added in whatever this time dilation thing does to your muscles.

The knife hit Albris in his shoulder and arm just as he released the sword. At first, I was angry at my miss, as I had been aiming for his throat, but then Murphy's law took over.

Murphy is a god even the Roxannez shouldn't fuck with, as the hit from the dagger knocked Albris aim off just enough to foul his aim.

The hammer went trailing off from his hand into the house behind me. Missing me by several feet.

But not until after it pinged off his fire witch's head, who was engaged with Tyla, never seeing the hit that sent her to the ground.

Albris reached for the knife in his shoulder just as I made a running jump, swinging my sword over my head, movie style. Even if it was stupid to forget my training like that, I felt great satisfaction as the sword penetrated the man's head with a crunch.

The sword struck deep.

Albris died.

The water witch collapsed with him.

The few remaining men, now freed of their bondage, dropped their weapons and ran for it.

Just like that, the fight was over, and we stood battered and wheezing, but still whole. Well, mostly whole.

Then something happened. Albris' body was consumed in a flash of light. The illumination formed a ball in the air and hovered over his body for a few seconds. I stared at it, not sure what it was or what to expect.

Then it rushed into me. I had no chance to avoid it or escape. Pain resonated throughout my entire being.

I collapsed, but for once did not lose consciousness as I sat there and stared at the sky.

Tyla and Tasnia rushed over to my side, followed by Diane who still looked shell-shocked from the fight.

"Master? Are you okay?"

"Love?" Tas asked at the same time.

Concern was clearly written on both their faces.

I closed my eyes for a brief second, trying to figure out what the hell had just happened.

Satisfied that I was alive but discovering something strange inside me, I decided to deal with it later. "Yeah, think so. Something weird happened. Everyone, okay?"

"What... What are you?" Cecil asked, approaching slowly.

"Uh, it's kind of complicated, I'll explain it later. Let's get out of here before more trouble finds us."

I wanted to loot the dead, but I couldn't take the chance that more trouble would find us.

CHAPTER 32

EPILOGUE

The controller closed his interface and signaled his trusted aid. Having finished watching as Derk and his compatriots ran off into the distance towards the mountains.

"They passed the first hurdle. Many more remain," he said to himself.

With a swipe of his arm, he returned to his gazebo on the southern continent. He sat in his chair, relaxing in the warm ocean breeze that came up from the ocean.

Closing his eyes for a moment, he enjoyed the sound of the wildlife that permeated the place, the salty air that teased his nose, and the feel of the slight reverberation under his chair as the wave crested and crashed on the shore.

In the distance, he heard the screech of his pet as it patrolled his lands. It kept out all but those he considered worthy of entering his personal domain.

Opening his eyes, he smiled as he saw Shyse gliding over the wave tops. As it passed, the golden dragon did a barrel roll as it breathed out fire from its nose, his way of saying hello to his master.

The controller smiled at Shyse. "Hello, old friend."

The great dragon screeched in response, diving into the water for but a moment before it shot out of the waves like an energy beam. The controller could see the water cascade off the beautiful golden horns and its leathery wings.

He smiled.

A chime in his head told him he had a visitor, and he accepted the request. Vex appeared next to him in the gazebo a moment later. "You summoned me, Controller?"

The controller smirked at his subordinate... his friend. He waved into existence a chair just like his. "Please join me, it has begun. I have done all that I can to tilt the odds in our favor. The board is set, and your piece controls our fate on four-five-two. I hope your confidence in him is justified."

Shyse gave a final screech before flying off into the distance at speeds that created a loud boom in the air. Either hunting for more food or sensing an intruder, the Controller didn't know nor care which. Very few beings in existence could best his creation.

"I have faith that he will follow the path we want. His success is up to him. I know he is... tenacious when it comes to his goals, however."

"The Overseer knows that I have been taking action. It will not be long before he figures out what my end goal is. Expect him to be aggressive in his response."

"Can he alter the current rules?"

"No, I have seen to that. But neither of us can act directly anymore. We can insert new pawns, but that is it."

"Should I bring in the other pieces?" Vex asked.

"No, we need to save them for other worlds. We must stay prepared if they expand the games yet again. If Derrick fails, then we can bring in another, but we must bide our resources for now. The other factions watch us, and we need them to stay neutral... for now."

"Even if we win, and the mob calls for his removal, will the Overseer step away from power?"

"Probably not, that is why we have the insurance policy."

Vex nodded. "I must go check on them soon. What of Driea?"

"That world is safe for now, I think. But I have a feeling several factions are moving there as well. It is much more dangerous for our kind to descend into that world. I believe the council will only send the convicted and use it as a gambling arena for the masses to become distracted, but it is too soon to tell."

"Again, they ruin the guidance set down by our ancestors!" Vex smashed his fist into his palm.

"Peace, Vex. You are amongst the like-minded here. This is what happens when a society begins its collapse, we have seen it in countless histories of the races before us and we never listened. Instead, we keep saying that we will be different."

"We are no different, just the latest version of the fool."

"I am afraid you are correct, my friend. But we will do what we can. I just hope that your plan works on Timeria. For if we lose the mob to the Overseer, we are surely doomed."

Both settled into a silence as they looked upon the crashing waves and contemplated the controller's words.

Afterword

Thanks for reading!

Update for 15 April 2022: Book 2 is out! I hope you check it out. Expect book 3 in August/September, presale is for 15 October to give myself some wiggleroom.

If you enjoyed this book, and I hoped you did, please leave a rating and review on Amazon or Goodreads—Independent authors live and die by them and every time you leave a review, an author gets to eat. This is mostly a joke, but it's also somewhat true for a lot of us. Reviews help! Thanks so much for taking a minute of your time. If you just want to leave a star rating without text, just scroll to the end of your reading device, wait for the amazon app to ask for a rating, hit the stars and close the app. Super easy.

I am a brand new writer, only having published my first book in November 2020. I am not as refined as the other big names of who I have beta read and proofread for several, but I love doing this and am striving to get better everyday. Hopefully you like it!

To follow me on FB go here https://www.facebook.com/Patrick.Underwood.Writes

All my other work and social media stuff can be found at this microsite that links to my everything (including how to get on my newsletter) at https://linktr.ee/Patrick_Underwood

About The Author

I'm a fantasy author with a twist!

So what can I share? Well, I have the perfect wife, three amazing kids, two dogs, two cats (one in particular that likes to sit on my keyboard while I write), and all the fun and daily stress that comes with that.

If you liked this one and want more background in the universe and how it got to that point, you may also enjoy:

Unchosen Fate: The Sacrifice of Pawns

So, the book and blurb below is the first story I helped write with Jonathon C. James. We are both new authors, and this was our very first book. We have worked together for a long time now in our day jobs, then we kind of took the plunge. This is the background to this book and our combined universe based on a sci-fi genre novel. This book is totally clean (non-explicit) and non-harem, but if you want to know the history of this universe (like more about Vex and the Controller and even Derk has a small part in it), this is the book for you! It might answer any references you were curious about from the beginning of this one, like who the hell just took out the planet! Vex and the Controller feature heavily in it and you can read more about the "preserve" which will feature heavily in Jonathon's books in the future.

It has its flaws, especially since we had no idea what we were doing at the time, but we loved writing it. We hope to clean it up and add to it, maybe even put out a book 2 as well in the future. In a nutshell, this sets up the stage for my Pawns series, the one I plan after it (I so can't wait to announce this one, hopefully coming in 2023 after I finish Pawns), and the one Jonathon is writing which is Roman legion style fantasy.

Here is the Blurb

Three global alliances. A high stakes cold war. The fate of humanity in the balance.

At the dawn of the twenty-second century, humanity has finally a chieved a permanent foothold in space.

James Smith, a newly minted lieutenant commander in the Western Alliance Navy, is about to embark on a next generation cruiser, purpose-built to counter the expanding threat from Eastern Bloc forces.

As he enters this new assignment, he finds out that the ship is under t hreat. Not from enemy railguns or lasers, but from cloak and dagger w ithin.

But spies and sabotage are not the only threat lurking in the dark of night.

While we play our childish games, humanities rise has also caught the attention of the race known as the Roxannez, their advanced power and intellect unrivalled by anything we have ever imagined.

So far beyond us, some would call them gods.

And they have an interest in James.

The fate of the human race, our very survival, hangs in the balance of what happens next.

-Feel free to check it out below and see if it interests you. We kept the price as low as possible while still keeping it on KU. Hope you enjoy!

https://www.amazon.com/dp/B09J5DVZXN

Join the Community!

Find thousands of your fellow harem fantasy fans at any of the following social media communities:

Facebook Groups:

Harem Lit | Dukes of Harem | HaremLit Readers | Temple of the Storm

Harem Gamelit

Reddit Subs:

r/haremfantasynovels | r/Haremlit

Discord:

HaremLit Discord

MY SOCIALS

Get my socials here by scanning this QR Code

Patrick Underwood

COPYRIGHT

Made in the USA
Monee, IL
12 January 2024

51672112R00150